DESTINATION CAIRO

Alice and Mary's great race.

By Guy Shackle

 New Generation Publishing

For Marsha and Nicholas

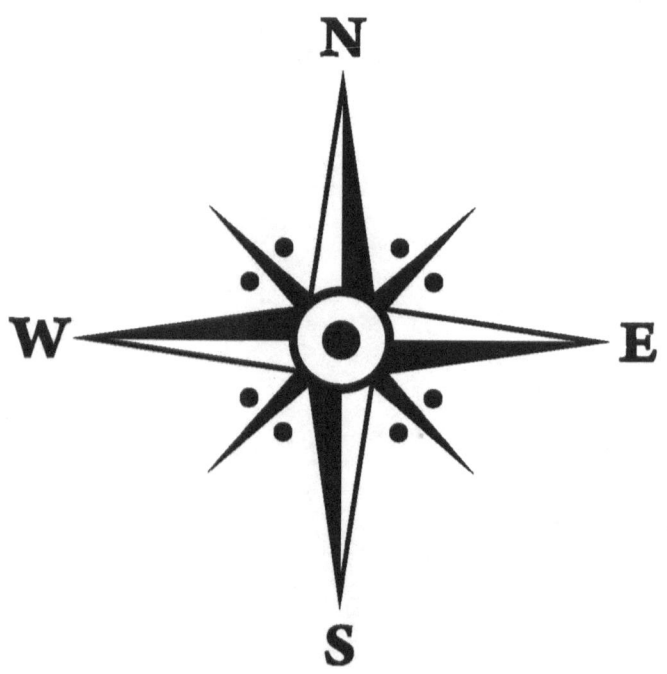

Chapter One

Miss Alice was restless. And Miss Mary was restless. And neither had any idea why. They just could not put their finger on it. Being twins, they invariably knew what the other was thinking. They could easily finish each other's sentences if they felt like interrupting, which was not often. It was as if they were one person with two of everything. But despite their closeness they were not identical to look at. They were both tall and thin with long legs but Miss Mary, who had arrived in the world five minutes before her sister, was two inches taller at five foot ten. They had quite long, but attractive faces, that went well with their height with Miss Alice having a slightly more prominent nose.

They had just celebrated their seventieth birthdays which should have been a time for calm and gentle reflection. As it had been for the fifty three years they had lived alone at The Rectory. This was a solid red bricked building with a vast ancient wisteria covering most of the front. Inside, it was kept spick and span but somehow had a cobwebby feel. The blinds were drawn for much of the time to protect the furniture from the sun and the large rooms with their high ceilings had a cavernous air.

In all those years the twins had been entirely content with their isolated but pleasant surroundings. They rarely ventured further than their large garden except occasionally to visit the nearest village which was three miles away. It had few inhabitants and these were clustered in their whitewashed dwellings around a pub, a grocery shop and a post office. It was too far for the sisters to have newspapers delivered and they had no television. The increasingly modern world which had now reached the nineteen seventies, had passed them almost completely by.

Their daily routine never altered. They rose sharply at seven o'clock, winter or summer, rain or shine, to take a gulp of fresh air by the window. They then had porridge and toast for breakfast except on Sundays when they treated themselves to a boiled egg. After that, they would listen to a church service on the ancient wireless in the drawing room. To help pass the time, they both dabbled in water colours and read avidly from the rows upon rows of books in the well-stocked library. Their favourites were Victorian melodramas.

The only real contact they had was with Archie Roberts their gardener and odd job man. He was a gaunt figure in his early forties who wore a perpetual air of resignation. With their neat lists in his pocket, he did their shopping twice a week at a distant supermarket before, in the summer, spending long hours cutting their spacious lawns. He had long ago stopped trying to persuade his employers to replace his push mower with a mechanical one. They preferred its quietness and felt the exercise was good for him. As for the rest of the grounds, they liked to do the weeding and planting themselves. They lovingly tended their flower beds which were always neat and tidy. They liked best of all the old fashioned varieties such as wall flowers and begonias which were allowed to grow in profusion.

Archie was so used to their sheltered existence, he almost died of shock when Miss Mary excitedly told him they had discovered the reason for feeling so unsettled. It was Miss Alice who had done so, by opening a long disused drawer while spring cleaning to find a rather creased atlas tucked away in a corner. After blowing off the dust, she realised it was the one their mother had brought to take them on a Grand European Tour to Egypt to celebrate their seventeenth birthdays. The pair had been thrilled at the prospect of their first ever foreign holiday, but two days before they were set to depart, the most dreadful thing had happened. Both were struck down with mumps within an hour of each other. So their mother, after much hand wringing, decided she had to go on her own. Their father, a partner in a solicitor's practice could not leave his work, and would stay behind to look after the girls.

Two tear stained faces had peered from the bedroom window as she climbed into the local taxi from the village and with a final wave departed. The sisters received a couple of post cards while she was on her way, but then heard nothing until a fortnight later, on a day that would be forever etched in their memories. It was a blustery morning with the sun peeping out from between bands of scurrying white clouds. They had seen Tom the cheerful postman striding up the drive and had the door open ready for him. Their father, who had come home for lunch, emerged from his study to take the telegram handed to him.

Frowning at the sight of an unexpected delivery, he tore off the top of the envelope and swiftly ran his eyes over the contents. His face turned to what the twins later described as the colour of putty before with a startled gasp, he collapsed at their feet. They could see him now, lying on his back in the porch staring up at them with sightless eyes. They had frantically called an ambulance and tearfully slapped his wrists but it was too late.

The coroner found the cause of death was a heart attack combined with a blow to the head he had suffered when falling. Miss Mary always remembered being irritated by the sloppy wording of the fateful message which informed them starkly that their mother had run off with a camel driver, the word camel being spelt by the Egyptian operator with a K instead of a C.

It was funny she thought, how one noticed trivial things in the most dreadful circumstances.

The double blow of losing both parents in such a dramatic fashion, shook the sisters to their very souls. The world had suddenly become a most forbidding and hostile place. And so they shut their door firmly and irrevocably against it. Any excitement that could have helped to fill their dull, sheltered lives came to an abrupt end. Their long reclusive existence in a prison of their own making had started.

But now they were looking at the newly discovered atlas with wildly beating hearts. The red line their mother had drawn marking their intended journey, snaking through France, Italy and Greece and on to the Middle East, had faded with age but leapt at them from the page. Suddenly for the first time in many years, they clearly remembered sitting round the kitchen table enthusiastically plotting their route. And how their mother had described what they would do when they got there. They would see mummies thousands of years old wrapped in cloth hundreds of yards long. They would hear the faithful being called to prayer in the mosques. And they would take off their shoes before entering, when visiting one of these ceramic wonders. But best of all, the very best of all, would be their camel ride around one of the fabled pyramids. This, their mother had promised, would be their reward to make up for being dragged into museums but they knew they would love every minute of it whatever they did.

Now the vanished years just seemed to telescope, and the twins felt once again the thrilling surge of anticipation. Something inside was telling them urgently to make the very same journey their mother had made although it would be over fifty years late. Their reawakening as they called it, appeared to invade the atmosphere. The Rectory seemed to shake off its long air of slumber and replace it with an undercurrent of crackling electricity. Archie's response by contrast, was one of utter bemusement. It was as if the old girls had been struck by a bolt of lightning from the heavens. Most people in their situation would have woken to the fact that life had long ago passed them by.

Their mother had set off in the roaring nineteen twenties and the sisters could only wonder at how things had changed along the way since then. At least the pyramids were certain to be still there. But what had become of Mrs Harrison? She had been thirty six when she left so would be eighty seven if she had managed to survive the hot climate. They both agreed the chances of ever finding her alive or dead were remote.

The big question was how were they going to finance such an undertaking? Their father had left them a tidy sum, but they had kept this in the bank rather than taking a chance on more rewarding but risky investments and over the years it had dwindled to almost to nothing. The upkeep of The Rectory, being a large house, was expensive and this too had eaten into their savings so now they had come down to existing on their barely adequate state pensions. They had no idea of the cost of fares on the continent but it was obvious that their use of public transport would have to be severely limited. Yet they did not think it would be too difficult to obtain lifts for they believed that drivers of French and Italian extraction at least, were certain to be gentlemen.

Archie spent most of his time sorrowfully shaking his head at their extraordinary decision but did not try to talk them out of it. He knew it would be a complete waste of breath. They were a pair of stubborn old girls who, once they'd got a bee in their bonnet, stuck with it. The lawn mower was a good example. He'd gone on at them till he was blue in the face to try to get it changed. No, with a heavy heart, he would just have to help them in any way he could.

They were luckily both unquestionably fit for their age helped by their passion for gardening and regular long country walks. First and foremost they would need good footwear and lightweight rucksacks which fitted properly. But what to put into these? The sisters had an ample supply of tweed skirts and twin sets and thick corduroy trousers for outdoor activities in the cold. But such gear would not be suitable for the warm climes that were beckoning them. And although they had sturdy no nonsense shoes, Archie insisted they must wear boots which would give much needed support to the ankles. And for times when the going was easier, a pair of trainers.

His listeners blanched at the very thought of being seen in such things, but he said comfort must always come first. After providing him with their measurements, they sent him off to the nearest town to buy the rucksacks and foot wear. Then they settled down to discuss what to take with them. This should not have been a long discussion for there was little space to fill.

Yet although the sisters were extremely close, they had their own very definite opinions about things. For example, when ordering cheese biscuits Miss Mary had once wanted hard baked while Miss Alice decided upon butter puffs. When the deadlock could not be broken, they reluctantly put both on the shopping list. Then when these arrived, they found they preferred each other's choice. They suspected once again, that this was because they were twins.

In the end, they opted to take one dress, one pair of trousers, a blouse, a jumper, two pairs of socks, a towel and two sets of underwear. As they said, you could never go anywhere without a spare pair of knickers. All these were to be as lightweight as possible and they would also pack a small first aid kit. Even with well-fitting boots they knew there was a great danger that they would suffer from blisters. Archie approved of their choices but insisted they took thin waterproof capes rather than carrying umbrellas, even though these were often used in hot places to keep off the sun. One item they both independently decided to take, but were too embarrassed to mention, was a loo roll. Miss Alice secretly wondered how her bottom would react to so many strange locations having been used to the same lavatory seat for over fifty years. She decided not to dwell on the thought.

Once the haversacks arrived, they were put to immediate use. The sisters filled them with stones from the rockery and set out on regular walks to get used to the weight. They became a familiar sight to their few neighbours as the strode past their gates on their rounds. The onlookers could only smile and shrug their shoulders. Miss Alice and Miss Mary were considered by all and sundry to be definitely very odd. But the old biddies as the milkman called them, didn't mind. Their boots were getting worn in and their shoulders toughened up.

The sisters set their departure date for April the first. They felt this could not have been more perfect for they knew they were being such fools. Archie thoroughly agreed with them without actually saying so. Two days before their departure they decided it would be sensible to have a dress rehearsal. They would walk the three miles to the village post office and back to collect their travelling money wearing their full rucksacks. Archie watched them go, bright eyed and bursting with enthusiasm. Yet their appearance could not have been in starker contrast when they returned a little under four hours later.

Alerted by their plaintive cries, he met them at the gate choking back tears. Miss Alice, the most coherent, explained they had sat on a roadside bench to count their money and had left it lying between them in their wallet with their passports. A youth running by had leant down and snatched it up. By the time they had got over their shock, he was out of sight.

Archie could not contain his amazement. "What on earth did you take your passports for?"

"Well, it was a dress rehearsal," replied Miss Mary lamely as he gently ushered the distressed pair into the kitchen. What was needed he realised, was something to buck the poor dears up. He knew the only alcohol in the house was cooking sherry. He had helped himself to it when working in the cold and had been grateful they had not noticed the drop in the level. Reaching into the well-stocked cupboard above the sink, he produced the bottle and poured each a glassful. And as the situation obviously demanded, had a large one himself.

Archie then declared the police must be informed immediately and picking up the phone, called the local station. He listened as first one twin and then the other tried and failed to give an adequate description of the culprit who, it seemed, was unlikely to be caught. Although Archie's face was grave, he was far from, unhappy with the situation. By the time the sisters had applied for new passports as they vowed they were going to do, their silly idea would have left their heads.

Chapter 2

Little did Miss Alice and Miss Mary know the cause of all their troubles was barely two miles away and that evening was feeling as discomforted as they were. Eighteen year-old Shane was sitting crouched on the edge of his bed in his cramped upstairs room. Before him, hands placed firmly on her hips, stood his mother. Mrs Clarrie Porter was a thick set, florid woman who reddened easily when angry and was on the point of going purple. She held in her hand two passports which she had discovered in an inside pocket of his jacket when putting his clothes away. And she did not for one moment believe his story that he had found them lying abandoned in the road. She had at once recognised the names of their owners which caused her great anguish and led to her immediately confronting her son.

Suspecting they had been with other contents, she demanded to know what else he had taken. And she warned darkly she would stand there in front of him until he told the truth. His strenuous denials gradually gave way in the face of her persistent questioning and he admitted there had also been quite a lot of cash. Recoiling from the outstretched hand requesting its return, he explained the money had already been spent. He and his friends had gone to the nearby town that afternoon and bought themselves brand new leather jackets.

Mrs Potts felt a wave of shame sweep through her. Controlling her temper with difficulty, she revealed he had committed a mean trick against two of the most kind and generous elderly ladies. Did he not know the sisters were regular benefactors of the village? It was they who had helped to buy the playground he had once spent many hours in as a little boy. And who had also paid for the goal posts for the football team he loved to play centre half for.

She broke off to stare despairingly at the passports. It was obvious that the Misses Harrisons had been on the point of going abroad. But it was well known they were no longer wealthy and so the loss of the money might even prevent their journey. She looked her chastened son squarely in the eye. "We cannot afford to repay that amount all at once. You will take their passports back first thing in the morning and apologise profusely. And then tell them you will return a certain amount each week out of your wages." Extending a forefinger, she poked him on the shoulder. "And after that do you know what to do next?" Shane ran a hand through his tousled hair and nodded ruefully. He knew only too well what was coming. "That's right," declared his mother with great emphasis. "You will offer your services to help those poor unfortunates in any way you can to make up for your dreadful act. And," she added equally forcibly, "you will not take no for an answer."

Chapter 3

The sisters were just finishing breakfast the following morning when there came a knock on the front door. It was so timid, neither would have heard it if they had been speaking. After a moment it came again, slightly louder. The twins looked at each other wondering who on earth it could be. They very rarely had visitors and certainly not at such an early hour. Miss Mary, wiping her hands on her apron, padded into the hall and after a moment's hesitation, opened it. Shane stood before her, his head slightly bowed.

Having been inspected by his mother before leaving on his mission, he wore his only suit, a crisp white shirt and tie and his hair was neatly parted. Without saying a word, he thrust the two passports towards her. She stared at them eyes wide in amazement, barely taking in what was happening. Slowly she became aware that her visitor was trying to explain something in a small, contrite voice. Not knowing what to say, she waved him inside and he followed her into the kitchen where Miss Alice let out a cry at the sight over what her sister was carrying. Miss Mary pointed to a chair and Shane after a moment's hesitation, sat down gratefully. He was feeling a little weak at the knees but the meeting was turning out to be less intimidating than he had feared. The sisters, who were paying rapt attention to what he was saying, had kind if troubled faces.

On the way to see them, he had dreamed up and dismissed, several differing versions of why he acted as he did. But with Mrs Porter's words firmly implanted in his brain, he found himself telling the exact truth including his mother's lecture and her demand that he somehow redeem himself.

After hearing him out the twins, after a short discussion, decided to accept his apology and to take no further action. They had their passports back and the promised reimbursement of their lost money which they felt confident would be honoured. And having heard of their plans, he was adamant that he would escort them as far as Dover. And it had to be tomorrow because it was his only day off from his job at the garage for the next fortnight. Otherwise, he urged, he could not go home because his mother was likely to kill him. The sisters looking at his earnest expression, were happy to accept his offer. They could use the money left behind for bills which would be replaced by Shane's repayments. It would get them quite a distance until Archie began wiring their pension instalments as previously agreed. And it would be nicer going in Shane's car to the ferry at Dover rather than the bus as they had planned He would reappear, he promised, at nine o'clock the following morning.

That evening they took a final stroll around the grounds savouring the much loved sights before staying up late over cups of cocoa in the kitchen. They knew an early night would be sensible to conserve energy, but realised sleep would be difficult to achieve and so it proved. Anxious visions crowded into their brains as the full impact of what they intended to do hit home. Without a foreign language and with no knowledge of the outside world, they were facing a journey of over a thousand miles.

Yet at breakfast they were pictures of calm resolve as they buttered their toast and stirred their coffee with steady hands. Their rucksacks stood neatly side by side in the hall together with the packed lunches they had made themselves. They had telephoned Archie to give him the good news about their passports and to explain their eminent departure. He had once more wished them good luck with a sigh and promised to come later to lock up. They were sorry they would not see him but were glad not to be leaving under his sardonic gaze.

Just before the appointed hour, a deep throated roar came from the direction of the road. It steadily grew louder and louder before ending abruptly outside their gate. Six youthful riders dismounted from their gleaming Harley-Davidsons and parked them in a row. They were beautifully kept and the early rays of the sun bounced off their highly polished surfaces. The leader gave his wing mirror a rub with his gloved fist and set off up the drive to the house. He was dressed from head to toe in black leather. A red scarf round his neck fluttered a little in the breeze. The deafening noise had brought the sisters hurrying to the hall window and they gazed anxiously out of it.

"It looks like a motorcycle gang," said Miss Alice uncertainly. "They must know we're going away and want to burgle the house."

As she spoke, there came a sharp rat-a-tat tat on the front door. The pair stood rooted to the spot glancing in dismay at each other. It was repeated even more loudly. At last finding her nerve, Miss Alice opened it an inch or two. Then in the calmest voice she could muster she called out. "We're not alone. Our friend Shane is coming to see us in a minute."

"I am Shane," said the newcomer, removing his helmet and ruffling his hair. "I've arrived as promised to give you a lift."

"Good Lord," exclaimed Miss Alice looking over his shoulder at the motorcycles. "We couldn't possibly travel on one of those. We imagined you would be taking us by car."

"It's very kind of you and we do appreciate it," added Miss Mary, "but we really will be going by bus."

"Buses cost money and my mum said you don't have much."

"We have enough. We really could not face those

machines at our age. They are much too dangerous. We could fall off."

It was then that their young escort redeemed himself without realising he was doing it. "If you want to get to Cairo," he warned, "things you think are impossible will just have to be done."

Nobody had put what their journey would mean quite so succinctly before. His words struck home forcibly and the sisters looked at each other in consternation. It was something they had never considered deeply enough in all the excitement of getting ready. They had never been really tested by a serious upheaval while living their sheltered lives. And any small problem they'd had, Archie was always there to help if needed. They sensed Shane's eyes on them as he awaited their reply. The thought of being carried on a motorcycle was terrifying but they knew there could only be one answer. If they opted out and went by bus, they would try to opt out of other things and then their resolve to carry on would vanish.

It was Miss Mary who reluctantly put their thoughts into words. "Thank you Shane, we accept your offer. But please do not go too fast. We have never been on one of those things before." Realising there was no point in delaying any longer, the two frightened passengers, with a distinctly uneasy feeling in their stomachs, picked up their rucksacks and followed Shane into the road.

Two spare helmets were produced and Shane, with a business like air, made sure they fitted properly and that their rucksacks were securely fastened before leading the pair to their machines. He introduced his friends who responded with cheerful greetings which contrasted greatly with the feelings of their passengers. Miss Mary was to ride behind Ricky Thompson and Miss Alice, behind his brother Carl. She could never have imagined the first man she would put her arms around at the age of seventy, would be a leather jacketed teenager. In her youthful dreams it had always been film stars like Clark Gable or Leslie Howard. Oh, how she'd cried when she heard during the war he'd been killed in an aeroplane crash!

Having seen the sisters seated to his satisfaction, Shane climbed aboard his own machine and at his signal, all the engines roared into life. As their convoy picked up speed, Miss Alice and Miss Mary had the sensation they really were birds fleeing the nest even if it was rather late. Their surroundings began to flash by, but they saw nothing of them as they hung on tightly with their eyes shut. Gradually however, they became accustomed to the rhythm and were able to relax a little although the uneasy feeling in the pit of their stomachs never left them for a moment.

Their way wound through the greenery of the Kent countryside and was almost deserted. Shane constantly glanced behind him to check everybody was in line and keeping the correct distance. He had stressed that if either of the sisters showed the slightest discomfort, Carl and Ricky should immediately pull over onto the hard shoulder. Yet they were coping better than they had expected under what was proving to be a considerable strain. So the twins were surprised when their speed dramatically slackened and they found themselves coming to a halt in a lay-by containing several lorries. Surely, they wondered, they could not be at the port in Dover yet? Dismounting stiffly and fumbling with the straps of their helmets to free their heads for a moment, they saw the flashing lights of a police car.

Shane had said what he meant when he'd promised to keep within the speed limit. But as he ruefully admitted to the two officers who emerged from the vehicle, Harley-Davidsons had a habit of going faster all by themselves. Unlike his interrogators, he had not realised how fast this was. If the twins, waiting several yards away, had been within earshot, they would have heard him plaintively explaining that he was not joyriding. No, nothing could have been further from the truth. He was running an errand for his mother. He was taking two of her best friends, Miss Mary Harrison and Miss Alice Harrison, to Dover where they would catch a ferry to France.

One of the officers, with sergeant's stripes on his sleeve, decided to verify this tale for himself and walked over to Miss Mary who was standing nearest to him. "Excuse me madam," he said eyeing her closely, "are you happy in this company? You look a little flustered."

After a moment's hesitation, surprised to find herself irritated by the question, she replied more firmly than she intended. "I am perfectly all right thank you and so is my sister."

"I would have thought another form of transport would have been preferable," persisted the officer. "There are plenty of buses and trains along your route."

"We were made a very kind offer and it would have been impolite to refuse," declared Miss Alice who had come up to join her twin.

The sergeant gave them a lingering stare before shaking his head. "Well I have to say it's a free country." He turned to Shane. "You were clocked doing over eighty on a two mile stretch. I'll be issuing a warning this time but I shall be watching you carefully the rest of the way."

With that, he climbed back into his patrol car where his companion was already waiting behind the wheel. "I'll tell you one thing sarge," said the driver as he eased into the road. "I've seen a few biker grannies in my time but certainly none quite like those two."

Shane watched them go with relief while at the same time hoping the sisters had not overheard the speed they had been going. They gave no indication that they had, or any inclination to find out. They were too busy being amazed with themselves over the way they had reacted to the officer's questioning. He had after all been concerned with their welfare, yet their attitude had been almost hostile. What on earth had started to come over them? The party set off again, this time keeping strictly to the speed limit. They did not notice any further police presence but the warning had been enough.

Arriving safely at the port's entrance with their mission accomplished, the cavalcade turned around their motorcycles and with cries of 'Good luck!' disappeared. All that is, except Shane. He declared that to please his mother, he would escort the sisters to Calais. He would still be in time for work if he returned on the same ferry. He stressed it was also to please himself. He could not shake off his shame at stealing their passports. It was one thing to rob strangers but quite another when you got to know them and they forgave you.

Miss Alice and Miss Mary said they would be perfectly all right on their own but their protests lacked conviction. They were secretly glad they would have a friendly face accompanying them for a while longer. But despite his presence and the growing queue of fellow passengers around them, they could not help feeling quite alone.

The clouds, which had been gathering over their heads during the last part of their ride, began to darken and a rising wind was whipping up waves out to sea. It was going to be a choppy crossing. Shane set about commandeering comfortable seats for the twins in the lounge as the rain began splattering against the windows. He looked with concern at his charges who were busy settling themselves and appeared oblivious to the approaching storm.

They were feeling hungry and regretted giving their packed lunches to their young escorts. Their appetites, which had disappeared while on the back of a motor cycle, had returned with a vengeance. As the ferry cast off, they decided to have something cooked to eat. Shane warned that this might not be a good idea. The boat would roll once they were out of the harbour and they were not used to travelling by sea. A few dry biscuits might be a more sensible solution until they arrived at Calais.

Miss Alice and Miss Mary however were determined to have a proper meal. Especially as they had had only a slice of toast for breakfast. Shane reluctantly followed them into the restaurant where, after closely inspecting the menu, they ordered a mixed grill. He asked for the same but with only one sausage and no bacon. He had a strong feeling they would not be finishing theirs and he would have to take over. Waste not, want not, as his mother was always telling him.

With the wind battering at the windows, many passengers appeared, like Shane, to be thinking more of eating dry biscuits. That is if they were going to have anything at all. Nearly every table was empty and the meals were not long in coming. Under the watchful eye of their youthful escort, the sisters tucked paper napkins under their chins and picked up their knives and forks.

The boat was now clear of land and the uneven motion of the deck was becoming more pronounced as they tackled what was before them with relish. It seemed they had been born with sea legs. They knew they would learn a lot about themselves on leaving the safety of The Rectory and luckily this appeared to be one of their strengths. Watching his companions wolfing down mouthful after mouthful, Shane realised he was not hungry at all. In fact it was turning out that a fry up was the last thing he wanted. The baked beans for some reason, kept staring him in the eye and the eggs had a shiny, malevolent look. He felt increasingly queasy but managed to keep his stomach under control until Miss Mary asked him to pass the Ketchup. They had never had it at home, and she wanted to taste what it was like.

His response was to leap from his chair, and hurry towards the door under their startled, but sympathetic, gaze. Fearing the sisters were the ones likely to be ill, he had earlier noted where the nearest lavatories were in relation to the restaurant and this knowledge proved to be a godsend. Later, in desperate need of fresh air, he made his way to the top deck where he sat with his back against a comfortingly solid funnel. Although he could not see them, the choppy green waves below perfectly matched the colour of his cheeks. Down in the restaurant the sisters, realising he would not be coming back, divided his sausage. They too had been brought up to waste not, want not.

The restaurant now had only one other diner who was sitting at a nearby table. And he watched them with growing fascination as he tackled his more digestible cottage pie. Bert Knowles was a thick set man of about sixty with a shock of brown hair. He had made hundreds of crossings with his lorry and had earned his sea legs long ago.

The ferry to him was like a village. And during his time he thought he'd seen every type of traveller. The young, the old, the rich, the poor, the happy, the sad, the drunk and the sea sick. Yet there was something different about these two women and he felt drawn towards them. The rucksacks by their chairs and their sturdy walking boots suggested backpackers but they looked far too old for that. And he could tell by their accents they were what he would call posh. And those types climbed into their Mercedes and BMWs at the end of the voyage to sail effortlessly past his lorry. They were obviously not going to do that. And then there was their destination. From snatches of their conversation they appeared to be heading for the Middle East. Those with their kind of background on this route usually ended up no further than the South of France.

The sisters, oblivious of being under such scrutiny, were discussing between mouthfuls how to proceed after they reached Calais. Shane had promised to organise a lift for them from among their fellow passengers but was now in no state to carry out his task.

Their eavesdropper, who was listening ever more intently, laid down his knife and fork and carefully wiped his mouth with a crumpled red handkerchief. "Pardon me for interrupting," he began, "but may I speak to you ladies for a moment?"

The twins, who had just finished eating, pulled off their paper napkins and looked blankly at their solitary companion whom they had barely noticed. Taking their startled silence for assent, he continued. "I could not help overhearing you are looking for a lift and maybe I can be of assistance. I am driving as far as Le Mans and there is room in my cab." Seeing his listeners were hesitating to reply he introduced himself, emphasising he was a bona fide driver who worked for a reputable firm.

The sisters slowly began to realise that here was someone who could be the answer to their prayers. Their mother had always warned them about getting into vehicles with strange men, but that was a long time ago and their circumstances had changed. Before they set out, Archie had also warned it was illegal to hitch a ride in lorries but mention of this concern was met with a dismissive wave of the hand. Everybody broke the rules, said Mr Knowles. But if he didn't mind them saying so, it was usually for much younger women. They would not be able to board immediately the ship docked because he had to go through the customs checks alone. That was, he added, looking at them thoughtfully, if they wanted a lift for they had not yet said they did. Miss Mary, knowing what her sister was thinking, replied straight away for them both. "You are most kind and we would like to accept your offer."

"Good," Mr Knowles replied. "Now listen carefully while I give you instructions. As pedestrians, you will be allowed off first. You must walk along the main route out of the port and wait at the first lay-by. I should be along within half an hour." Selecting a pen from a row of three protruding from his top pocket, he wrote down his vehicle's colour and registration number on one of the paper napkins. Handing it over, he warned them to keep their eyes peeled. If he passed them he would not be able to turn back.

With the French coast nearing, the sisters hurriedly went in search of Shane. The storm had abated a little giving hope of a calmer return crossing. They found his subdued figure slumped on a chair in the lounge where they had first been sitting. At the sight of them he started to rise, remembering he had yet to carry out his mission. They were quick to reassure him they had organised a lift themselves and that he need not worry.

Yet he demanded as forcibly as he could, to know all about the driver. It was always a risky business putting yourself in the hands of complete strangers. The sisters were becoming uncomfortably aware of this and realised they would have to do it time and again if they were to continue in their bid to reach Cairo. Having convinced Shane they would be quite safe, and with the ferry docking, it was time to say goodbye. They had become quite fond of their young friend who, it had to be said, had more than made up for his crime. After an emotional farewell, he watched them make their way down the gangplank wishing fervently that he too was stepping onto dry land.

Chapter 4

The sisters stood for a minute among the teeming crowd, trying to get their bearings. Although they had not been affected by the crossing, their feet felt strange now the ground beneath them was no longer moving. Having worked out their route, they set off knowing they had no time to waste. It was Miss Alice who noticed first that they were on the wrong side of the road. Archie had warned them that motorists drove on the right on the continent but in the excitement of their arrival, it had not sunk in. Stepping instinctively off the kerb, they were greeted by a blast of horns and hurriedly retreated. Panic stricken, they looked desperately for a place to cross. Lorries from the ferry were passing and several seemed to match the colour of Bert Knowles' vehicle. Finally they spotted a gap in the traffic and taking their lives in their hands, scurried to the far pavement, their rucksacks bouncing on their backs.

Without waiting to catch their breath, they marched on craning their necks to look at each lorry as it roared past. Within two hundred yards they came upon a lay-by and could only hope it was the right one. Mr Knowles had said he was near the back of the queue but as time went by without any sight of him, the sisters became increasingly fretful. They'd never believed people saying every second was like an hour when you were waiting for something. Now they knew it to be perfectly true. Their eyes were strained from trying to check every number plate, but it was extremely difficult with the vehicles going quite fast and closely following one another.

Just as they were resigning themselves to being abandoned, a strident blast from a horn reached their ears. A red and green lorry with its right indicator flashing was pulling up in front of them. It was an enormous forty four tonner with six axles. The sisters looked up to see a familiar face smiling at them through the vast windscreen. It was a long, awkward, climb to reach the cab but finally they were safely installed. Waves of relief swept through them as they poured out their thanks. To be left stranded in their first hour on foreign soil would have been a nightmare. Having checked his passengers were comfortable, Bert Knowles edged his way out into the flow of traffic. They were on their way.

Their benefactor proved to be a constant talker. He told them all about his wife Maureen who was back home in Reading, his two married daughters, Shirley and Sandra, and his Labrador dog Sam. The twins were happy to let his words swirl around their heads and nod occasionally in reply.

The outskirts of Calais had been left well behind when Miss Alice began to shift uncomfortably. She would very much like, she told herself, to spend a penny. If only she had gone before they left the ferry. She always made sure she did before going out at The Rectory. Oh if only she was there now! She pictured her spotless lavatory with its white walls and cactus plant in its cream bowl by the window. She always visited the loo that was downstairs while her sister used the one in the first floor bathroom. Soon she would have to pluck up courage to ask their driver to stop and reddened with embarrassment at the prospect.

Then, miraculously, as if he was reading her thoughts, Bert Knowles brought the vehicle abruptly to a halt. Yet a glance out of the window showed it could not have been at a worse place. The countryside was flat and wide open without a bush or tree in sight. It was then she heard voices as he wound down his window. Looking out again, she saw a barricade of farm carts strung across the road barring their way.

Bert Knowles had picked up a little French during his travels and the man he was in earnest conversation with, appeared to have a similar grasp of English. He was a tall, muscular figure with a mop of black hair that tumbled down over his forehead. He seemed to be the leader of a motley group of a dozen men dressed uniformly in corduroy trousers held up by thick leather belts who stood in a solid rank behind him. After a few minutes the Englishman, his fingers tapping restlessly on the steering wheel, turned to the sisters. "The French farmers are out on strike," he said. "They're blocking all the roads. Nobody is allowed to pass - especially foreign lorries. As far as I can gather, it is to do with them not getting the right price for their lamb."

"But you're not carrying anything to do with that sort of business are you?" declared Miss Mary.

"No, I'm taking a load of kitchenware there and will be bringing back wallpaper. But it doesn't make any difference. It is a ban on all traffic."

Her face was etched with dismay. "Well, how long will we be stuck here?"

"It could be anything from hours to days. It was the first question I asked, but Andre as he calls himself, has no idea. It is all controlled from Paris."

"Can't they make an exception?" broke in Miss Alice who was becoming increasingly agitated. Fate was so cruel. Through the windscreen a few hundred yards on the other side of the barrier she could see a small belt of welcoming trees which would provide ideal cover in her predicament. When she asked plaintively if they could go just that far, Bert Knowles shook his head sadly and decisively. He had been held up by such disputes before. You could talk until you were blue in the face but a striker would never budge. She realised if she did not act quickly, there would be an accident in the cab. "I'm so sorry," she blurted out, "but it is imperative that I go to the lavatory."

In all his years on the road the recipient of this news had never been confronted by such a delicate situation. Leaning out of the window, he conferred anxiously with Anton whose reply was reassuring. The lady should not be embarrassed. His compatriots were entirely men of honour. They would, as one man, turn their backs while she went to the toilet. Miss Alice was not one to go to the toilet She went to the lavatory, but decided this was not the moment to mention it. She remembered her mother's warning from long ago. Never, ever, for one minute, trust a Frenchman she had declared with great emphasis. The twins had wondered if this warning had arisen from personal experience for as a young girl, she had been a student in Paris.

No, Miss Alice decided, she could not perform this duty of nature in the vicinity of so many strange men no matter what direction they were facing. Somehow she must get the lorry to move past the barricade and on to those oh so welcome trees.

It was then she remembered Amelia Alsop-Higgins who was in her class at school. Nature had called upon her during a lacrosse game against one of their most bitter rivals. The teacher who was refereeing, would not allow her to leave the field as the team were trailing 1-0 and pressing hard for an equaliser. So she had gone to the centre circle and, removing her knickers with a flourish, squatted down. Miss Alice could still hear the astounded gasps of parents and girls strung along the touchlines. Before anything could happen, the match was stopped and the sufferer hurriedly ushered to the safety of the cloakroom. Amelia escaped punishment because the dramatic and unexpected hold up unsettled their opponents who went on to lose 3-1.

There was only one thing for it, thought Miss Alice,

she would have to use shock tactics too. Luckily she was wearing her dress and not her trousers. She would climb out of the lorry and go and bend down in front of the barricade. Her sister meanwhile would take a photograph of her with their little box camera. They would announce they were sending it to an English newspaper to show how such uncivilised and selfish Frenchmen treated a lady by refusing to let her cover her modesty in more helpful surroundings which were just a few hundred yards distant. The only newspaper they had any knowledge of was The Times which was unlikely to use it, but the strikers wouldn't know that.

After a hastily whispered conversation with her sister, who looked aghast but nodded her head, Bert Knowles was informed. He, with the air of someone who could not take in what was happening, passed the message to Anton, who in similar disbelief, proceeded to scratch the back of his neck. Miss Alice got out of the vehicle under the studied gaze of the assembled strikers to be followed by her sister.

With a show of calmness she did not feel, she walked to the barrier and selecting the cart right in the middle, hitched her dress slightly and bent her knees. Miss Mary stationed herself a few feet in front of her and began adjusting the lens. At this, any man in danger of being caught in the picture smartly dispersed. Then came a startled cry from their leader who, vigorously waving his arms, issued a volley of commands.

The response was immediate with two of the carts being manhandled hurriedly to the side of the road. The sisters turned to see their driver beckoning to them urgently through the windscreen. They hurriedly scrambled aboard once more as the engine was brought roaring back into life. Then they were through the gap, passing an array of open mouths and astounded faces as they hurtled towards the distant trees. Miss Alice, who never took her hand off the door handle during the short journey, was climbing out again before the vehicle barely had time to stop.

From that moment on they made excellent progress. The conditions were good and the traffic light. Yet Miss Alice was oblivious of her surroundings as she tried to discover what was happening to her. Where was the meek and mild woman she had always considered herself to be while living at The Rectory? Where had the nerve she had suddenly acquired to do such as thing come from? Yet she had to admit Amelia would have been extremely proud of her.

These rather uncomfortable thoughts were constantly being interrupted by the loud chuckling of Bert Knowles who could not stop marvelling at the sheer audacity of his passengers. "Talk about one good turn deserving another," he said, shooting an admiring glance in their direction. "If I hadn't given you a lift, I could have been stuck at that barrier for days or even weeks. They'll never believe it when I tell them down at the pub. Especially when I tell them you're pensioners." He threw them another look. "You wouldn't mind if I did that would you?"

The sisters still flushed with their success, said no, they wouldn't mind one little bit.

Mr Knowles pulled gratefully into his depot on the outskirts of Le Mans in the late afternoon. Miss Mary and Miss Alice climbed out stiffly and waited in the shadow of the lorry while he supervised the unloading and tried to find them accommodation for the night. He would be starting his return journey as soon as his new cargo was safely aboard. None of the workers could help, but by chance one of them was talking to a smallholder who had arrived with a first batch of spring lamb for sale.

Hearing of their plight, he volunteered to put the pair up at his home which was a further twenty kilometres in the right direction. He spoke a smattering of English and said his wife, who admired Britain, would be pleased to have visitors. She always said nobody ever came to see her. The sisters bade a heartfelt goodbye to their faithful driver who shook their hands warmly and wished them the very best of luck.

Chapter 5

The twins had been delighted to be offered a bed, but followed their latest saviour round the corner to his truck with a growing feeling of anxiety. He was short, swarthy and stank dreadfully of garlic. And his battered mud caked vehicle matched him perfectly. But, as Bert Knowles had said, never turn down rides going in the right direction. They would not be always easy to get.

The pair's schoolgirl French allied to their host's little knowledge of their language had opened up a tenuous line of communication. Yet Marcel, as he had introduced himself, waved them silently into the back. It was open and the droppings littering the floor, showed it had recently contained sheep. The sisters, crouching among the mess as they jolted their way into the open countryside, were already missing the comfortable cab of their lorry. Dwellings slipped away and twenty minutes later, as dusk was falling, they found themselves bumping along an isolated lane. It ended in a clearing of scattered buildings surrounded by a thick belt of trees. The whole place had a dilapidated air. The main house which appeared dark and deserted, overlooked a couple of rickety sheds and a long, low barn.

Waiting in the yard was a fair haired youth in dungarees that had long seen better days. He wore an agitated expression and held in his hand a creased white envelope. As Marcel alighted, the young man strode forward biting his lip and thrust it towards him. Taking it with a look of bemused surprise, the farmer ripped it open and extracting a single sheet of paper read its contents. There followed a torrent of words between the two with the boy resorting to helpless shrugs of his shoulders. The twins having removed themselves from the truck, could only look on in consternation.

The reader of the note had become purple in the face and was aiming imaginary blows in the air as if at an assailant. His companion, having retreated to a safe distance, watched with an anguished expression. Gradually Marcel brought himself under control and with a start remembered he had guests. He regarded the pair who were standing motionless by his vehicle, with a baleful glare. They had an uneasy feeling they were not wanted, but were unaware that this was about to change.

He appeared to come to a decision and straightening the piece of paper he had crunched in his fist, handed it to them. It contained a single sentence but with their limited knowledge of French, they could not make head or tail of it. Seeing their confusion, he jabbed his finger at the words and cried "Monique my wife - she has gone!" Without another word he picked up their rucksacks and set off for the house. Not knowing what else they could do they followed on his heels. They did not have enough French to offer any commiserations and sensed in this situation, the less they made of their presence the better.

He led them to a room at the back where two small cots, each with a blanket, stood among unopened boxes of seed and fertiliser. As they surveyed their cluttered surroundings they heard the door being closed behind them. They looked at each other in growing alarm. Were they being locked in? Miss Mary waited for the footsteps outside to die away before gingerly turning the handle. No they were not. In their relief they began to realise how hungry they were. It was getting late and they had had nothing to eat since their meal on the ferry.

Cautiously they began to explore their surroundings. At the end of a passage on their left they found a large, airy kitchen. The solid, well scrubbed wooden table in the centre was empty. A battered refrigerator hummed noisily in the corner but they felt too intimidated to open it. Looking through the window, they could see Marcel in the gathering dusk talking earnestly to the youth whom they took to be his farm hand. He was pointing at the house and they realised they must be the object under discussion. They felt they should immediately go out and confront him as to what was going on, yet neither could summon up the courage or the energy that would be required. The day's already dramatic events had taken their toll and they felt desperately tired and deflated.

Not knowing what else to do, they returned to their room hoping after a rest to be able to confront their host when they heard him come in. But the house remained cloaked in silence. Eventually they fell into a fitful sleep broken occasionally by the hoots of owls flittering to and fro between the nearby trees.

It was after eight o'clock by the time they awoke the following morning to discover a chill in the air under a grey sky. After hurriedly dressing they entered the kitchen to again find it empty. As were all the other rooms they cautiously ventured into. Going outside they discovered an equally deserted yard. Marcel and his young helper were nowhere to be seen.

The twins decided to make their feelings clear about wanting to leave in no uncertain fashion. Collecting their belongings they proceeded to go and sit in the front of the truck that stood where it had been parked the previous evening. They would stay exactly where they were until their so called host drove them back into town. Yet as the morning began to slip away leaving them in splendid isolation, they started to feel foolish. At one stage the youth had passed by carrying a spade over his shoulder apparently off to some unseen job. He had given them a fleeting grin but by the time they thought of winding down the window to call to him he was gone. The only other movement they had seen in a deserted landscape, was of a rabbit which bobbed into view before disappearing into a nearby thicket.

They began to shift restlessly in their seats. What if Marcel was content to leave them sitting there all day? They had seen the devastating effect his wife's departure had had upon him. Maybe it had upset his mind and he was no longer rational? They had of course to admit their own stance was hardly sensible, but they just could not bring themselves to give up and go in search of him.

It almost was noon when they heard the front door of the house creak open and saw the farmer appear in the doorway. They had not noticed him enter but realised there must also be a way in round the back. His face expressionless, he beckoned to them silently with an outstretched arm. Miss Mary in turn, stuck hers out of the window and summoned him forcefully in their direction. If he wanted a battle of wills, so be it. They could not bear to wait at his farm a moment longer.

His response was to vanish into the interior and re-emerge a few moments later holding a large plate aloft. The message was obvious and the sisters looked at each other in dismay as they suddenly realised how extremely hungry they were. They had not eaten for over twenty four hours. Anger mixed with a desperate desire for food rose in Miss Mary's breast. This was nothing more than pure blackmail to remove them from the truck. As their mother had said, never, ever trust a Frenchman. She was determined to stay where she was, but her resolve was immediately undone by Miss Alice who proceeded to get out of the other side with some alacrity. With a stifled sigh her sister reluctantly found herself following and the pair, staring straight ahead, retraced their steps to the kitchen. The first thing they were going to do was to give their host, who was doing untold damage to Gaullic hospitality, a piece of their mind.

Yet as they crossed the threshold, a most delicious aroma entered their nostrils. On the table clouds of steam were rising from three large helpings of thick vegetable strew accompanied by two long loaves of crusty bread. There had been no sign of Marcel having been out shopping so everything must have been in the fridge. If only they had had the courage to open it earlier their stomachs would not have let them down at such a crucial time. Thoughts of having what would certainly have been a heated discussion with the farmer, vanished at the sight of such a feast. They picked up their spoons in a most unladylike fashion and set about devouring everything that lay before them.

The sisters could not help their spirits rising with each succeeding mouthful. Miss Mary, pulling off another generous hunk of bread, remembered what Lord Byron had said. You could forgive almost anything after a really good dinner. She was sure this would equally apply to a lunch, but realised that they had no alternative but to be hard hearted in this case. They really had to get away as soon as the meal was over although it would only be fair to offer to wash up first.

Yet when the conversation resumed with every plate wiped clean, their efforts to bring up the subject of their departure were doomed from the start. Marcel proved to be obsessed with his wife and would entertain no other discussion than that of her betrayal. The sisters sensed they would be wasting their time making any further pleas until they had let him pour his heart out.

Hiding their overwhelming desire to be gone, they forced themselves to become sympathetic listeners with an interest in his plight. There were many painful pauses as they consulted their little pocket dictionary to interpret his increasingly emotional phrases. But as far as they understood it, Roger, a butcher in a nearby village, was the one who had enticed his Monique away. He had been Marcel's best friend, helping around the farm and providing the choicest cuts of meat. The memory of this was making Marcel tremble with rage. Oh how he had thanked him for looking after his stomach. Yet it had not been Marcel's stomach but Marcel's Monique that he had been looking after. His wife of forty years. He clapped a hand to his head. He had been so trusting! The day the pair had gone out hunting for mushrooms and had not come home with any. What had they been doing? Mon dieu! Now he knew. Oh yes, he continued clenching his fists, Roger had been so helpful. Go and plough your field he had said. I will help Monique collect the hay bale from the barn. The speaker, conjuring up the most distressing visions, was momentarily lost for words.

Miss Mary, despite her growing impatience, felt a genuine sense of compassion for the farmer so obviously suffering opposite her. Stretching out a hand she touched his arm. "Please do not torture yourself," she said as reassuringly as she could with the help of her much thumbed dictionary. "Those meetings might have been entirely innocent. You do not yet know why Monique left." He shook his head at this but her consoling words did seem to have some effect. What appeared to be a slight brightening of his mood gave the sisters much needed encouragement so they were utterly unprepared for the bombshell that followed.

Marcel had become calmer and his chest was no longer heaving as he put his hands together and looked at the sisters carefully over his fingertips. Yes, he had lost his wife but an ever wonderful Providence had smiled upon him. It had delivered not one, but two ladies of great value to take her place by his side. He welcomed them with the utmost joy in his heart.

It took Miss Mary and Miss Alice some minutes to get the gist of what he was saying but there was no mistaking the earnestness of his tone or the newly acquired look in his eye. After a moment of startled silence, they rose in horrified unison from their chairs to denounce such a monstrous suggestion with all the force they could muster. The response was a flash of anger from a darkened brow as the farmer in turn rose from his seat and without another word or glance in their direction stalked from the room. The twins fought back an almost uncontrollable urge to chase after him but they realised any further confrontation would be pointless until they had all calmed down. Above anything else, they must not take leave of their senses. They would avoid any mention whatsoever of his extraordinary proposal while they quietly plotted to escape from their predicament.

The sisters resolved that before dawn tomorrow they would set out on foot back to Le Mans. There could be no other way out of the serious situation they were finding themselves in. They had expected to have to do a lot of walking on their journey and there could not be a better time to start.

That evening, after a supper of cold mutton eaten in almost total silence, they expressed their desire for an early night and retiring to their room, packed as quietly as possible everything apart from the clothes they were wearing which they would sleep in. It was when Miss Alice was making a final check to make sure nothing had been forgotten, that they realised their passports were missing. They could have cried in their helpless rage and frustration. What was it had Archie said? Keep these most important documents upon your person at all times. He had even made them repeat this dictum to him out loud. Well, it was too late now.

They wondered when Marcel had taken them for there could be no other explanation for their disappearance. He always seemed to be one step ahead. And they knew without doubt they would be very well hidden and make any search fruitless. They were disconcertingly also aware that this showed the farmer's desire to keep them was no idle threat. They decided after much painful thought, that there was only one thing for it. They would have to set out without them. When they reached Le Mans they would go straight to the police station and report the matter. The gendarmerie would surely be forced to take immediate action. You could not go around kidnapping civilised English gentlewomen with impunity in modern day France.

Having decided what they were going to do, Miss Mary straightened her shoulders and began to feel better. But poor Miss Alice, putting her hands to her face, burst into tears. Uncontrollable sobs wracked her body as the full horror of their plight came over her. "I'm so sorry," she said taking a hastily produced handkerchief from her concerned sister. "I've never done that before."

"We've never been in this situation before," came the sympathetic reply. "But we have no option but to pull ourselves together or we'll never get out of here."

"I know," replied Miss Alice in a firmer voice as she fought to control her sniffles. "I promise you it won't happen again."

At the first hint of daylight, the sisters arose and picking up their belongings as quietly as they could, tiptoed from the house. Marcel's bedroom door was closed and there had been no attempt to lock the front one. Their meek behaviour at supper the previous evening when they appeared to accept their fate, must have lulled him into a false sense of security. Miss Mary smiled grimly to herself as she cast a final look round at what to all intents and purposes had been their prison cell.

The air was decidedly chilly as they crossed the yard but that would help them move all the more quickly. They wanted to put as much distance between themselves and the house by the time the farmer woke up. They had belatedly realised it was a Sunday when he could be expected to rise a little later. They felt an urge to break into a run when they reached the lane but knew they would conserve their energy better by keeping to a steady pace. Heads thrust forward, they strode on grateful for the foresight which had enabled them to build up their strength by practice walks on the roads around The Rectory.

A thick belt of trees stood close to the track just before it reached the main road and a flock of birds rose squawking from it as they drew level. The sisters soon found it was not their presence which had disturbed them. A squat figure emerged from the shadows to stand menacingly in their path. Silhouetted against the growing light, Marcel wore a belted leather coat to ward off the early morning chill and carried a hunting rifle that the sisters had last seen hanging on the wall above the mantelpiece in the kitchen. Without a word he aimed the barrel towards the sky as if shooting at the departing flock, but then slowly brought it down inch by inch until it was pointing directly at them.

It was what the pair were later to call one of their Rectory Moments. When they would have given anything in the world to be back safely at home among their treasured belongings.

Later they were to ask themselves a thousand times whether Marcel would have fired his gun if they had kept walking. But they did not. He continued to remain standing there silently but the darkening scowl on his unshaven features made his feelings abundantly clear. And given his emotional state, the sisters realised it was a risk not worth taking even if they had been brave enough to attempt it. Turning round slowly so as not to startle him, they began to retrace their steps with feet that now felt leaden and reluctant to move. Not once did they look over their shoulders but they could feel the farmer's malevolent presence as he followed a few yards behind them. They were being herded like farm animals and felt just as helpless.

They were beginning for the first time to understand just how serious the situation was they were finding themselves in. Their captor, for that was the only way to describe him, really meant business. They were on an isolated farm with nobody else about apart from the youth who would obviously do nothing to help them.

That evening they sat on the edge of their beds and discussed every possible option of escape. In the end they came to the conclusion that the most difficult one was the only realistic solution. They would have to persuade Marcel to go and see Monique. After forty years together there must be some sort of bond between them. Maybe she had acted on the spur of the moment and regretted it. Unless he went, he might never find out. Their only chance was to try to bring them together again.

They decided to act the following night after supper. That was the time when the normally taciturn figure was at his most mellow. By then he would have had one or two jugs of the potent local wine and be lighting up one of his strong smelling cheroots. The sisters knew everything would depend on their own performance. They must hide their growing frustration and anger and be wise and encouraging. It would be a hard act to carry out for they knew nothing of relationships between men and women. But much of it was plain commonsense which those who were emotionally involved, often could not recognise.

For the first time they each had a glass of wine themselves with their meal. They hoped it would settle their nerves and make them more articulate. Progress was not easy to begin with after they had finally put down their knives and forks. At the first mention of Monique, Marcel held up his hands and said, "Bah!" He did not want to hear that name ever again. But underneath it was obvious that he did. So slowly and surely with much use again being made of the dictionary, the subject took hold.

The farmer began to sweat and repeatedly mopped his brow with a large coloured handkerchief. It was plain that he had tried to push Monique to the back of his mind but she would not stay there. The sisters, being only too well aware they had no experience as marriage counsellors, made every effort to tread warily. They had to steer him in the right direction knowing that if they put a foot wrong, he was likely to storm out of the door. 'Are you a man or a mouse?' was one question that had been hovering on their lips but they discarded it. From what they could gather, Roger was a large and intimidating figure and that could well be the reason that was holding Marcel back.

Under their relentless barrage, the farmer finally admitted it made sense to seek out his wife if only to confirm her desire to leave him. Many women had acted in haste in deserting their husbands and then found it difficult to return. She might only be trying to teach him a lesson although Marcel with furrowed brow and much concentration, could not think of why she would. He was certain he had been a perfect husband. It was at last resolved that no further time should be wasted. They would set out after breakfast the following morning. The sisters could only hope their host would not change his mind after the effects of drink had worn off.

They need not have worried. When they emerged from their room shortly after eight o'clock, he was already busy in the kitchen. They felt like rubbing their eyes as they stared in wonder at the unfamiliar figure before them. Gone was the uneven stubble of several days, the dirty corduroy trousers and the sweat stained denim shirt along with the heavy lace up boots. Instead, Marcel was attired in a dark worsted suit with matching black shoes, a white shirt and carefully knotted tie. He gave them a rather sheepish look as if inviting inspection. They responded with a series of admiring glances and impressive nods of approval. They felt as if the balance of power was shifting in their direction. He had insisted they go with him and they sensed it was rather more for their support than to keep an eye on them. They were reluctant to witness what could well be a distressing scene, but realised it would give them an opportunity to get away from Marcel if they needed to. He could hardly try to keep hold of them in a village street.

As they went to leave the kitchen, the farmer reached up for the rifle that was once more hanging above the fireplace. At this, the sisters took advantage of their new found resolution and quickly put their foot down. Despite his protestations that he would only use it in self defence, they declared it was far too dangerous a thing to have with him if tempers could be lost. They would not be party to one of those all too common French crimes of passion. Reluctantly, as if leaving a treasured friend behind, he followed them empty handed out into the yard.

Forsaking the truck for this delicate mission, they

set off in their host's rusty Renault which, like everything else at the farm, had seen better days. The sisters were greatly relieved that Marcel had agreed to leave his weapon although he plainly felt at a loss without it. His hands gripped the steering wheel with a vice like intensity and his breathing came in irregular bursts. He was impervious to their presence, muttering to himself as if preparing for what he was going to say. They were grateful for this lack of attention although the tense atmosphere was taking its toll of their nerves. The butcher sounded as if he could be fierce and they felt sure they would be branded as interfering troublemakers when it became clear they had encouraged the meeting.

The half hour journey ended with the nervous participants entering a quiet side road at the entrance of the village. They pulled up outside a solid two storey stone house with faded blue shutters that overlooked an overgrown front garden. The three peered out of the vehicle at the building which appeared to be deserted. Marcel switched off the engine and sat there as if not knowing what to do.

The twins were about to urge him to get out and see if anybody was there when the front door suddenly opened. The onlookers froze as Roger wearing a threadbare T shirt stood framed in the opening. The twins could see he did indeed have the physique of someone used to wielding a meat cleaver. His muscles bulged menacingly beneath his tightly stretched garment. Marcel who was diminutive by comparison, uttered what sounded like a growl but made no effort to move. The butcher without hesitation strode down the path through the already open gate and tapped commandingly on the driver's side window. The farmer, as if his actions were not his own, slowly wound it down. Roger thrust his head through with one swift movement and immediately burst forth with a torrent of exclamations. His listener with an increasingly incredulous look, launched into one of his own, waving his hands back and forth expressively in the confined space.

The sisters, completely ignored, could only hold their breath and watch in fascination as the crescendo of words reached a climax. It was then the butcher noticed their presence and with raised eyebrows looked inquiringly at Marcel who indicated the reason for them being there.

Reddening with embarrassment at this unexpected audience, Roger explained to the foreign onlookers what was happening. "Excuse me mesdames." he said stretching his neck in their direction. "My English is poor, but I tell my friend there has been a terrible, terrible mistake. He ask why did I take his wife away. I did not take his wife away. She took herself away." He threw a glance at the aggrieved husband who was tapping his fingers restlessly on the steering wheel. "It was a big shock for me, Roger, to find her here. Yes, there were moments of madness at the farm but it was Marcel's fault. He leaves Monique and I alone with bottles of his wonderful wine on the table and goes off ploughing." He shrugged his massive shoulders. "You know how it is. It is spring. The birds were singing the sun was shining."

The sisters with their sheltered background most certainly did not know how it was, but listened in utter fascination. The speaker's voice took on a note of disbelief. "He wants to know if Monique is happy. He does not ask if I am happy. Monique, she does not stop talking. Marcel says he knows this. He says your ears are never rested. Do this, do that, come here, go there." He emitted a large sigh. "It is true, so very true. All the time it is impossible to speak for yourself. I ask Marcel 'what took you so long to come?' Monique wants to go home. I want Monique to go home." Straightening up, he turned and waved urgently towards the house. Monique, who had apparently been watching unseen from within, appeared in the doorway carrying a suitcase that had obviously been packed in advance.

The sisters, peering through the car window, felt a surge of matronly pride. So they had been right after all. The grass is not always greener on the other side. The errant wife must have been anxiously waiting to come home. Roger, keeping his gaze averted, stowed her luggage in the boot and opened the front passenger door. Monique eased herself in and gave Marcel a nervous smile.

She was a small, round woman with close cropped grey hair and a pair of dark penetrating eyes. These she turned with astonishment upon the twins as she became aware of their presence behind her. This brought forth an outburst of words between her and Marcel while Roger again explained to the listeners as best he could what was taking place. Monique was demanding to know why he had brought in two women on the very day she had left him. How could he do this if he loved her? On the very day! Marcel was explaining that they only wanted a night's lodging and the timing was pure coincidence. He had no idea she had gone until he had arrived with them. It was they who had urged him to come and reclaim her. Now they were together again their guests would leave immediately.

This welcome news caused a flood of relief to sweep through the sisters. At least they could say they had earned their release. Monique was not above throwing them an occasional suspicious glance but in the end appeared satisfied with the explanation. As Roger pointed out to them in barely a whisper, she'd warned him she could always tell if a man was lying.

The journey home was conducted mainly in silence. The reunited couple exchanged a few short sentences at first but seemed reluctant to talk in the sisters' presence. They for their part, could think of nothing to say. Now the tension had gone, they felt exhausted even though they had done nothing but sit in the car. Secure in the knowledge that they would soon be on their way again, they watched the passing countryside through contented eyes. Monique meanwhile had begun to rest her head on her husband's shoulder as if she had never been away.

That night, the returned wife, who was a cheerful, constantly humming presence in the kitchen, produced a beef stew awash with dumplings and numerous vegetables. The sisters, who had found their passports laid out on their beds soon after they arrived, tucked in with relish. Revelling in the dramatically changed atmosphere, they were finding it hard to believe the previous two days had existed. Everything seemed surreal. The beaming presence of Marcel, who in his relief, had apparently quickly forgiven his wife, was a complete contrast to the scowling figure who had threatened them with a gun. They felt like the guests they had hoped to be on what turned out to be that first nerve-racking evening. If only they had come a day earlier before Monique had decided to run off! They were learning the valuable lesson that timing is everything in life.

Chapter 6

Marcel had offered to take them back to Le Mans early in the morning and they had accepted with alacrity. So after a hurried breakfast the next day, they found themselves setting out in the Renault armed with a substantial packed lunch provided by his wife. They had explained to the farmer they would like to be dropped at the coach station. They had decided to spend a little of their precious funds on public transport on the next stage of their journey to make up for lost time. He made it clear he understood but merely smiled and mysteriously shook his head. He glanced repeatedly at his watch as if fearing they would be late in arriving at their destination.

They drove through the more industrialised part of the town before entering the large yard of what appeared to be some sort of depot. Three heavy trucks were waiting in line with their engines running and a man standing by the open door of the first, beckoned to them urgently. Marcel almost pushed the sisters out of the car before taking each by an elbow and hurrying them over. Clutching their rucksacks, they found themselves being given a leg up into the cab. The driver climbed in the other side and with a grinding of gears, set off. The twins just had time to return Marcel's farewell wave before they were out in the road. Their companion, his flat cap shiny with age pulled low over his eyes, looked straight ahead and showed no inclination to talk.

It began to dawn on his passengers they had joined some sort of workforce which was why it was important they had to leave when the shift started. Feeling too intimidated to talk, they sat in silence as the little convoy made its way through the crowded streets to the outskirts of the town. After half an hour, it pulled up onto the verge of a straight stretch of highway and the sisters, after being motioned to get out, climbed down stiffly. All around them equipment was being unloaded; wheelbarrows, drills, shovels, picks and cones. The pair looked at the muscular crew in their singlets with incomprehension. Surely they were not expected to swing a pick?

It was then the last item from the third lorry came off the ramp. Temporary traffic lights. It took the twins less than a minute to grasp their significance. Traffic lights meant stopped vehicles and stopped vehicles made it easier to ask for a lift. They stood looking on with admiration as these were put in position and their cables unwound. Good old Marcel! At supper the previous evening they had explained the difficulty of hitching a ride when discussing their future plans. Later they had heard him on the telephone. He could only have been ringing his friends in the road works department. That certainly helped to make up for the distressing time they had been through.

Their companion from the cab who seemed to be the foreman, pointed out to them where they should stand. Having been briefed by the farmer, he would know they were heading south and this reassured them they were in the right position. None of the crew appeared to know one word of English and made no effort to talk to their strange guests. Yet the atmosphere was friendly and the sisters gratefully accepted a cup of coffee when the men stopped for their first break.

It had not been a fruitful spell for the twins. Traffic was sparse and most of it gave the impression of being local. It began to grow busier towards noon but again nothing seemed to be suitable. They knew they could not afford to be too choosy, but already their experiences on the road had made them wary of fresh encounters.

They left the kerbside for their lunch of cold sausage and bread rolls in a sombre mood wondering what would happen if they were still stranded there by the time the work force came to leave. They had just brushed away the crumbs and returned to their position when a coach coming from the right direction, appeared in the distance. It slowly drew up in front of them as the light fortuitously turned red. It bore an English number plate with the sign LUXURY TOURS - OXFORD emblazoned in large letters on its side.

Now the sisters put into action the plan they had devised. Miss Alice stood in front of the coach frantically waving at the driver while Miss Mary hammered on the side door. A row of startled elderly faces began to peer down at her. There was an agonising wait before it finally opened. A young woman in a smart green and black uniform stood on the top step. Miss Mary looked up as she was joined by her sister. "I don't suppose you would be kind enough to give us a lift?" she said in a hopeful voice. She went on to explain their plight and after a moment's hesitation, the intrigued courier invited them on board.

They appeared to her to be a bizarre pair but looked respectable enough, and after all, there were two spare seats. They just had time to have a last look at their previous companions who appeared too busy to notice their departure. As the vehicle moved off, Miss Mary gave a fuller version of their quest, saying their limited funds meant they had to travel as cheaply as they possibly could. Petra James, as their youthful benefactor introduced herself, listened with a bemused air while behind the sisters, necks were being craned and an excited buzz was beginning to break out.

The courier revealed their fellow passengers belonged to the Church of the Sacred Heart in Oxford and were on their way to Lourdes hoping for a miracle to improve their health at the famous shrine. To quell speculation, she switched on her microphone to explain that the sisters had thumbed a lift on their way to Cairo the capital of Egypt. This was greeted by gasps of astonishment from the audience who all lived in sheltered accommodation and most could only get around with the help of walking sticks or a friendly arm.

The fifty six seater coach was almost full and looking at the sea of faces being whisked to their destination in air conditioned luxury, made the sisters realise exactly what they were taking on. Yet they appeared to be a good ten years younger than their fellow travellers and were obviously a lot fitter.

After a while, Miss Mary became aware of a pair of inquiring eyes being fixed steadily upon her. A woman with perfectly permed grey hair sitting two rows behind, leaned forward and asked which Catholic church she belonged to.

"We don't belong to any." she replied. "We do not follow your faith. My sister Alice and I are Protestants." The recipient of this news shot her a rather suspicious glance and did not continue the conversation. Instead she leaned over to the woman of equally coiffured appearance beside her and whispered urgently into her ear. Her companion in turn treated the sisters to a look of disfavour before talking in low tones to a third woman in the seat behind her. Whatever was said, had the same effect on this person too for she proceeded to peer at the newcomers with an expression of clear distaste. The effect of this evident hostility was not lost on either of the twins who began to feel most uncomfortable. Surely in this day and age they wondered, being of a different religion should not cause such animosity? Not in a civilised society like theirs which everybody aboard the coach certainly belonged to.

Feeling it might be better if they got off, they broached their fears to the courier who after an initial look of surprise, went to speak to the first woman. The sisters could not hear what was being said, but after a minute Petra James returned fighting desperately to keep a straight face. With a determined effort she finally gained control of herself and took a seat next to them as their leaned forward to hear what she had to say. "They think you're prostitutes," she managed to get out before being convulsed by another wave of laughter. Wiping away her tears with a little cream handkerchief which she had tugged from her breast pocket, she explained that the woman was hard of hearing and had mistaken the word 'Protestant.' The sisters, after a moment of stunned silence, reacted with astonished disbelief. "What an extraordinary thing to think," exclaimed Miss Alice. "We know absolutely nothing of that sort of occupation but are obviously too old for it."

The courier could not hide her amusement. "I have to say you are considerably younger than my charges and you do look it. To them you are still full of the zest for life. And after all," she added, "you are heading for Cairo which as everyone knows, is a famous den of iniquity."

The twins, completely at a loss for anything more to say, could only look at each other open mouthed. Their companion continued to regard them with a quizzical expression. "I would be lying if I said I was upset that this has happened," she said. "I can only thank you for a magnificent story." Seeing Miss Mary's rather disconsolate look, she put a hand reassuringly on her knee. "Don't worry. No harm has been done and it must be nice to think other people consider you are attractive." She stood up and reached for her microphone. "The rumour will have reached the back of the coach by now. I must clear the air before it gets out of hand."

"What are you going to tell them?" asked Miss Alice nervously twisting her fingers.

"Only that you are highly respectable hitch hikers and most certainly no ladies of the night." Carefully clearing her throat, Petra James did an admirable job keeping her voice even but the announcement was greeted with an outburst of animated merriment. Everybody wanted to have another peek at the two interlopers, even though they were not what they had seemed, and necks craned again. But this at least broke the ice and the woman who had started it all, struggled to her feet and scarlet with embarrassment, came forward to apologise. The twins replied that it was perfectly all right. As the courier had said, no harm had been done. It was just one of those silly things.

Amid the excitement, a man sitting near the back suggested there should be a whip round for the pair. It would provide what appeared to be much needed money for the next stage of their journey. The sisters' protests were drowned out by a chorus of approval followed by a flurry of arthritic fingers fumbling about in hastily produced purses. Most of these emerged clutching a five or ten franc note which Petra James collected before adding a couple of her own. It represented a valuable sum for the sisters who realising they could hardly refuse, made every effort to show their gratitude.

Three hours later, when the coach was about to take them too far to the south west, they alighted to a show of waving hands and cries of 'Good luck!' Despite having made excellent progress and receiving an unexpected but most welcome addition to their funds, they were in a reflective mood as they stood at the edge of the village where they had been dropped. Having seen the frail condition of the majority of their fellow passengers they were only too well aware of what lay in store for every human being who lived to an advanced age. And it was one they would be approaching all too soon themselves. There was a frighteningly long way still to go and they had no idea whether their health would hold out.

It was Miss Alice who saw it first as they walked down the steep main street with its uneven pavements and narrow crowded buildings. It took up most of the shop window with the rays of the late afternoon sun picking out its sleek bright yellow lines through the dust covered glass. The handlebars and wheels were chrome and the pannier baskets strapped to its sides were of a fetching contrast in black. The price tag for the tandem hanging from the front seat by a piece of string showed a sum just short of the windfall they had received on the coach. After staring at it for several minutes, they agreed fate had provided them with an opportunity that was just too good to miss. They each had their own bicycles at home but could not imagine there would be any difficulty in sharing one. There was plenty of flat country ahead and if they kept off the more major roads as much as possible, they should be in little danger from traffic. It would just be a simple case of synchronizing their pedalling and they would take it in turns to sit at the front or the back.

With their minds made up, it was only a matter of counting out the money and handing it over. If he felt any surprise at the rather incongruous appearance of its new owners the shopkeeper, a rotund figure who kept his trousers up with a pair of frayed red braces, did not show it. Humming busily under his breath, he carefully removed their purchase off its wooden platform and wheeled it out into the street. Before that, he had taken the two water bottles from their handlebar brackets and filled them from his chilled supply in the fridge. It was a kind gesture given with foresight which the sisters were to much appreciate later on. Having transferred the majority of their possessions from their rucksacks to the panniers, they set off with only the slightest wobble which quickly disappeared as they gained momentum. There was, as Miss Mary sitting in the front shouted over her shoulder, absolutely nothing to it.

Negotiating a sharp turn at the far end of the village, they found themselves pedalling along a straight road in flat, open countryside. Conditions could hardly have been better for helping them to get used to their new form of transport. With the cool of the early evening beginning to take over from the heat of the day, they had stowed their hats in their luggage to let the wind blow through their hair. It was an exhilarating experience and for a while it seemed a more satisfying way to travel than in an air conditioned coach. They were gratified to be moving smoothly along propelled entirely by their own efforts. But as the sun sank lower, the breeze grew stronger and despite their exertions, they started to notice a growing drop in the temperature. And as they breasted a slight rise, a wave of tiredness suddenly came upon them.

It was time to find somewhere to stop and rest for the night. Darkness was swiftly approaching, but on neither side of the road could they see the slightest sign of anything that might provide adequate shelter. Making a mental note that they must start such an important task earlier in future, they rode resolutely on into the thickening gloom. Finally when they could barely see more than a few yards in front of them, they came upon a small shed on a patch of long grass a few yards back from the road. It proved thankfully to be unlocked and empty with a disused air and they hoped they would be able to get some sleep there without being disturbed. Pushing the tandem inside, they settled down on a pile of dusty sacks and proceeded to share out a packet of oatmeal biscuits and the last of the apples that Monique had given them. They could hardly believe it was only twelve hours since they had left the farm so much had happened in between. They started to discuss the events of the day but it was not long before their eyes refused to stay open and they quickly fell into a deep and dreamless sleep.

The twins awoke shortly after daybreak to find they were so stiff it was virtually impossible to move. It seemed as if every muscle in their legs had seized up. They were making the disconcerting discovery that those used for cycling were different from the ones used for walking. They wondered if they would ever be able to bend them again. It took a great deal of patient and painful rubbing before they were able to stand up and move about. But once they had forced themselves to continue their journey, the blood began to flow once more.

Before setting out from The Rectory, the sisters had hoped they would be blessed with fine weather but were finding their prayers were being answered a little too successfully. April was proving to be a dryer month than usual and with mainly clear skies, the temperature was rising to uncomfortable heights for the perspiring cyclists. Despite regular stops to ease the strain of constant pedalling, and the judicious use of their water bottles, it became evident they would have to escape the full heat of the day.

It was then that Miss Alice remembered one of their more illustrious ancestors, Major General Charles Henry Harrison. This Victorian hero of the British Raj had ensured his troops stayed fresh by starting their marches at the crack of dawn and then calling a halt when the scorching rays of the Indian sun became unbearably hot. The sisters could see the obvious sense in this solution and decided without further ado to follow his example. They would get on their way as soon as it began to get light and then take a break round about noon. Then with provisions brought from local markets, they would have lunch in the shade followed by a siesta before embarking on another shorter ride in the late afternoon. Adapting to this routine, they continued to meander their way at a slow but regular pace across the south of France.

Yet their excitement of first seeing the tandem in the shop window and the exhilaration of their early rides was fast beginning to pall. Though their muscles had become reasonably well accustomed to their new form of exercise, it was still proving to be hard work. Each hill however slight, always seemed to be steeper than the previous one and, on some difficult stretches, they found themselves doing more pushing than pedalling. They started to pick out distant objects they had to reach before earning the reward of a much needed break, but this could be demoralising when, particulary in flat country, these never seemed to come any nearer.

The sisters faithfully adhered to what they were to call their Henry Harrison Habit until the fateful day when there was a sudden change in the weather. Scudding white clouds propelled along by a stiffish breeze, kept the sun to fleeting appearances while the air had a sharp and fresh tang to it after overnight rain. And to add to this happy situation, most of the way as they set off proved to be mainly downhill. Freewheeling with the wind at their backs, they were soon making excellent progress. So much so, they decided after the briefest of lunches of bread and cheese to forfeit their rest and to keep going into the afternoon. They could see no reason to waste time when they still had plenty of energy left.

Yet by three o'clock the weather had started to change again. The breeze died and the clouds disappeared leaving the sun's rays to unerringly pick them out from a clear sky. And as if on cue, the road began inexorably to wind its way upwards.

The twins, struggling to pedal at the necessary speed to keep up a steady momentum, were perspiring freely and reaching more and more often for the water bottles. In the cooler conditions of the morning they had neglected to top these up and they soon became empty leaving the pair with a raging thirst.

It was then that Miss Mary, again in the front, caught sight of a one storied stone house with a rust coloured tiled roof and nicely matching red window shutters. The sisters had taken one of the minor highways shown on their increasingly tattered map and it appeared to be the only one in the vicinity. It stood a little back from a cross roads and was flanked on two sides by neat rows of poplar trees offering inviting patches of shade. The sparse front lawn, which had yet to be turned brown by the sun, was dotted with lavender bushes while one or two stunted fruit trees stood forlornly along the far fence. There was no sign of life but the front door stood open which the twins felt must indicate the presence of an occupier. Surely, they reasoned, whoever it was would be kind enough to give them a drink and replenish their supply?

Miss Mary dismounting with relief, collected the bottles from their brackets and leaving her sister to guard their possessions, set off up the stony drive. Reaching the door, she proceeded to tap on it first gently but when this elicited no response, with increasing force. The result was the same. Every effort was greeted with silence. Feeling bolder measures were required, she stepped gingerly over the threshold and called out, inquiring if anybody was there.

This time she thought she heard a noise. It sounded like a kind of a shuffle followed by a dull thud. She wondered if her mind was playing her tricks but then it came again only more distinctly. As her eyes became accustomed to the semi darkness of the hall, she noticed a small door of what she took to be a cupboard set in the wall directly opposite her. As she stepped closer, the sound of the thudding became louder and more urgent as if something was pushing against it from the inside.

There was a key in the lock and without stopping to think, she leaned forward and turned it. The door swung open to reveal a trussed and gagged figure wriggling among a collection of brooms and mops. With nothing now to lean against, what proved to be a small, dark haired man dressed in a blue track suit fell out at her feet. His handsome brown eyes looked up at her in desperation above a luxuriant black moustache. He was trying to say something through the handkerchief that had been stuffed into his mouth. She bent down and carefully pulled it out to be greeted with a babble of unintelligible French. Then it stopped abruptly as the speaker began to take in her appearance. "Ah madam, of course you are English," he said, switching languages with perfect ease. "I heard you calling for attention. Please untie me quickly we have not a single moment to lose."

Bursting with questions, but sensing this was not the time to start asking them, Miss Mary obediently began to fumble with the knots yet almost immediately realised they were too tight for her aging fingers. The captive, overcome with frustration and impatience, found it hard to keep still. "There will be a knife in the kitchen," he blurted out hoarsely. "But please hurry."

As she rummaged frantically through a drawer she could hear him calling "Hurry! Hurry!" ever more sharply. She returned with a long blade bearing a serrated edge and with several quick cuts severed the cords on his wrists. He flexed his hands painfully. "Now the legs if you please madam," he urged. "Now the legs." She did as she was told and then helped the victim stiffly to his feet. He put a finger to his lips as if for silence and cocking his head listened intently.

Miss Mary frowned. "What is it?"

He flashed her an apprehensive glance. "He will be back at any second."

"Who will be back?"

"The burglar who savagely attacked me. He is a very dangerous man." He gently fingered an ugly looking bruise on his head. "He hit me from behind with a large frying pan."

Miss Mary looked round anxiously but the house seemed empty.

"He will not leave without those," said her companion, pointing to a bundle with one of his now freed hands. She noticed for the first time a canvass bag with several gleaming silver candlesticks protruding from it.

"He is even now loading my valuable paintings into his car which is parked round the back," went on the victim. "Then he will return. The telephone line has been cut so I must hurry to my neighbour across the field to call the police. He must not be allowed to escape." He turned his luminous eyes upon her, brimming with affection and gratitude. "Pierre is most obliged to you madam," he whispered. She felt his moustache brush against her cheek with the slightest of tickles as he planted his lips firmly upon hers. A tingling sensation like a warm electric current shot through her but it was mingled with a wave of shocked indignation at his astonishing behaviour. What a liberty he had taken. They were complete strangers! But before she could protest, he had ducked away and was gone.

Miss Mary, whose eyes had been tightly closed, opened them just in time to see him disappearing out of the door. For some reason, her legs were suddenly feeling weak and she leant against the wall as she ran an exploratory finger over her lips on which his electrifying presence still lingered. It was all so confusing. Never, ever, in all her seventy years had she experienced such a feeling of extraordinary giddiness.

She was brought to her senses by the sound of footsteps coming from the rear of the house. It could only be the burglar returning intent on collecting the rest of his booty! The one thought on her mind was that he must not get Pierre's possessions. Heart pounding, her eyes alighted on the frying pan which lay by the cupboard door where it had been cast aside. Picking it up, she noticed it smelt of fried onions which had been left too long and had burnt. There was also a spicy aroma which she did not recognise having only cooked solid English fare at The Rectory.

Pressing herself as closely as she could against the wall by the kitchen door, she held the frying pan with both hands over her head. It was heavier than she expected and made her arms tremble violently. She feared she would not be able to maintain that position for long when she caught a fleeting glimpse of a broad, muscular man in a red shirt approaching. As he drew level, she brought her weapon down with what little strength she had left onto the top of his head. The effect was immediate with the intruder collapsing with a startled cry like a sack of potatoes at her feet. This was followed by a series of groans as, after a stunned pause, he gingerly began to feel his scalp from which was oozing a trickle of blood. "Bloody hell," he finally gasped in a broad south London accent. "What happened?"

Miss Mary let the frying pan slip to the floor in surprise. "You're English," she exclaimed.

"Of course I'm English."

"Then what are you doing burgling homes in France?"

"I'm not a burglar. My name is Terry Potts and I own this house."

"No you can't be. You are a burglar."

He glanced up at her for the first time. "Look, I know who I am but who in the world are you?"

Miss Mary introduced herself in faltering tones and explained why she was there and what had happened. He began to shake his head in amazement but the pain quickly stopped him. "It beggars belief," he managed to get out. "You come here asking for water, free a famous local criminal, and then viciously attack the innocent householder. And to think I left London to avoid the violence."

Miss Mary could not bring herself to admit she was wrong. "You are lying," she retorted. "I can tell by the tone of your voice you are."

"It was me who tied up the burglar," came the resigned response. "I had to go across fields to a neighbour to phone the police. He had cut the line."

Miss Mary began to feel faint. "But Pierre definitely seemed like the owner to me. When I untied him he immediately hurried off to phone the police himself."

"So that's what he told you is it? He is better known round here as Le Grand Bandit. He wasn't running to call the police but to make good his escape. They are already on their way but I fear they will be too late to recapture him."

"How do you know his name?"

"Everybody does. He is one of the most elusive

criminals in the south of France. He usually operates in resorts like Cannes and Nice where the pickings are richer. But their owners are becoming ever more security conscious which is making life difficult for burglars."

"But what is he doing so far out in the countryside?"

"I put my candlesticks up for auction but then decided to withdraw them. Thieves like Le Grand Bandit attend these sales and if they fancy something, find the address of wherever they end up. He must have thought this was an easy job because the house is out of the way and empty. I came home and surprised him."

"But what about the paintings?"

"There aren't any. Just the candlesticks. He said that to explain my absence."

"But why did you put a handkerchief over his mouth? To stop him calling an accomplice?"

Her victim shook his head. "He always works alone. No, it was to stop him talking."

Miss Mary looked confused as the speaker, dabbing his wound, continued. "Le Grand Bandit has a silver tongue and can speak several languages. He has talked his way out of many situations. I did not want to take the risk of him making a fool out of me."

"Yes," she replied nodding her head with great feeling. "I do know exactly what you mean."

They were interrupted by the impatient figure of Miss Alice suddenly appearing in the doorway. She had become increasingly restless on being left outside in the sun and could no longer contain her thirst. What was the delay? she demanded to know. The owner had passed her at the gate a few minutes ago and had said they could have as much water as they wanted.

"No, this is the owner," Miss Mary responded lamely, pointing to her unfortunate victim who was still languishing at her feet. "And this is my sister Alice," she added, giving him a wan smile.

"What is he doing down there?" asked the curious new arrival. "Has he had an accident?"

"Your sister laid me out with a frying pan," came the weak reply from the floor. "She thought I was the burglar while you met the real one outside while he was making his escape."

Miss Alice's eye widened with astonishment as the unintentional wreaker of such havoc somewhat hesitantly explained her embarrassing mistake. And it was one she discovered that had turned out to be costly as well. As he was being helped gently to his feet by the pair, Terry Potts revealed there had been a reward of several hundred francs on Le Grand Bandit's head.

Before Miss Mary could make a heartfelt apology, a large rather plump man in a tight fitting dark suit came bursting in clutching a camera. He had a florid complexion that was matched by a scarlet handkerchief sprouting from his top pocket. Removing this, he mopped his brow after what had been a most hurried journey. "Inspector Jacques," he declared in eager and authoritative tones as he looked swiftly around the hallway in search of his prisoner.

The home owner, now steadier on his feet, moved forward and pointed dramatically to the empty cupboard and the coils of cut rope that lay in front of it. Words were not needed. The inspector took out a gleaming silver whistle and blew several short, sharp bursts. The sisters, watching through the open doorway, could see uniformed officers emerging from a van and spreading out rapidly across the countryside.

Terry Potts, feeling a desperate need to rest his legs, ushered everybody into the small but neatly furnished sitting room. The twins perched nervously on the edge of the sofa while the men sat in armchairs facing each other in earnest discussion. The two women had no idea what was being said, but the inspector uttered several loud exclamations of annoyance, twice slapping his knee, as well as casting disapproving glances in their direction.

Finally Terry Potts turned to them with a serious expression to explain what had been taking place. "The inspector is far from happy," he said stating what to the sisters was patently obvious. "He had been greatly looking forward to being photographed with Le Grand Bandit. It would have been a great shot for the family album as well as for the newspapers and the Police Gazette. However his real anger concerns the burglar being allowed to escape. I have managed to convince him it was a genuine mistake on your part, and that in no way could you be considered his accomplices."

Miss Mary could not help herself from heaving a deep sigh of relief. "So we can get on our way immediately then?"

The speaker shook his head. "I'm afraid not. It's not as easy as that. This is a major incident and there will have to be a proper investigation."

"But the inspector has been given the whole story and accepts that we are innocent," said Miss Alice.

"There is a process that has to be gone through. You will both have to give lengthy and detailed statements at the police station and this will take time. The inspector must cover his back and facts can look different when put down on paper whatever the motive. The plain truth is you coolly freed a much sought after criminal and then mounted a vicious attack on me which greatly helped him to make good his escape. And in doing so I might add, robbed me of a substantial reward."

Miss Mary, now fighting back tears, could only blush and look down at the carpet which she noted, had a rather unusual oriental pattern.

"The whole thing is likely to take at least a couple of days," Terry Potts continued. "And as you have no fixed address and are just passing through, there is the question of the police making sure you remain available." As if reading their thoughts, he pointed out that regretfully they could not stay in the house because they would be in the way of the forensic team who would be going through it with a fine toothed comb. There were also no hotels they could stay at within a suitable distance which only left one other alternative. He paused and glanced at the inspector as if seeking support. The officer, looking towards the twins with a serious expression, gave a decisive nod. "The only place left," said Terry Potts keeping his voice even. "Is the nearby woman's prison."

Miss Mary and Miss Alice opened their mouths but were so shocked, they appeared to be utterly incapable of saying anything. Taking advantage of their silence, he revealed it was situated right next to the police station which meant their statements could be made more quickly to help send them on their way. They would be housed in a twin bedded cell separate from the other prisoners and there would be no need to lock the door.

Miss Mary, gripping the arm of the sofa as if in a bid to remain upright, finally managed to produce a firm but quavering reply. It was most kind, but they could not possibly entertain the idea of being associated with a prison existence. Even for just a few hours. Miss Alice, nodding her head vigorously in agreement, said they would quite honestly rather sleep in the street. The whole thing was absolutely preposterous. The house holder waited patiently for their indignation to subside, before quietly pointing out that they had no option and should look at the advantages. Instead of living rough as they had been, they would have clean sheets, hot showers and cooked food at the jail and all at the taxpayers expense. They were not being arrested and would be able to remain in their own clothes. It really was the most sensible solution all round.

An air of inevitability began inexorably to settle over the sisters. They could see the sense of it despite their intense distress at the thought of being incarcerated in such a fashion. With a final apology to Terry Potts and without further protest, they reluctantly made their way out into the road where a second police van was waiting. The one that should have carried the sadly missing Le Grand Bandit safely into much deserved custody.

It had two small heavily meshed windows high up with narrow wooden benches alongside each wall to sit on. The twins positioned themselves opposite each other on the uncomfortably hard surfaces and watched silently as their tandem was manhandled in to stand between them. Oh if only their feet at that moment had been pumping away on those now idle pedals! But they were not. The doors were slammed shut which further darkened an already dim interior.

With a grinding of gears, the vehicle slowly began to move off. The twins, straining their eyes in the gloom, could see the broad back of the driver through another small window lower down. Although Terry Potts had again stressed when saying goodbye that they were not being arrested, they had an inescapable feeling that despite the lack of formalities, that was exactly what had happened.

The thoroughly subdued pair sat lost in their own thoughts as the van gathered speed, bumping over a series of potholes littering the winding country road. But as is often the way with twins, they were thinking along very similar lines. If they had not started their foolish journey, they would be back in the blessed safety of The Rectory where everything was sensibly ordered and there were no horrible surprises round the corner. Miss Mary pictured the neat, carefully tended flower beds and the large rectangular lawn which Archie would be giving a much needed first mow to any time now. The bluebells would be coming out in their thick bunches along the back hedge while the robins would be busily looking for their nesting sites in the dense ivy by the sundial.

Miss Alice who had eaten virtually nothing for lunch, found her mind turning towards the late afternoon teas they always looked forward to and enjoyed in the drawing room. As it was Thursday, it would be her turn to be mother and pour from the chipped, but much loved, blue teapot that had been in the family for generations. They would have two of their delicious home made scones each with either strawberry jam or bramble jelly followed by a generous slice of fruit or sponge cake. And if they felt really naughty, they would finish with two fingers of Kit Kat, their favourite chocolate, which were normally kept for after dinner.

The pair were cruelly jolted out of these enticing reveries by the van coming to a halt in a wide courtyard surrounded by high walls that hid the last rays of the fast disappearing sun. The sisters clambered out stiffly and felt a distinct chill go through them which had little to do with the drop in the evening temperature. They were taken by the driver into a compact, sparsely furnished reception hall where it quickly became obvious they had been expected.

A small, middle aged woman with wisps of grey hair plastered across her forehead, made no attempt to register them or take custody of their rucksacks. Giving the new arrivals barely a glance, she beckoned them to follow her as she stepped into a long narrow corridor that led into the forbidding interior. The twins, gripping their possessions firmly, did as they were told, their feet echoing loudly on the stone floor. So far at least, the inspector had been as good as his word. Reaching the far end their escort, who continued to remain silent, selected a key from a bunch hanging from her belt and opened a stout door in front of her. With a sharp wave of her hand, she ushered the pair inside and without further ado, proceeded to close it with a resounding clang. They waited in dread to hear the sound of the key turning in the lock but to their intense relief it did not come.

They found themselves in a cell that was not much bigger than the van which had transported them there. Lit by a solitary shadeless bulb hanging by a single wire from the ceiling, it had a small barred window high up which provided the only source of natural light. There were twin beds, just as Terry Potts had promised, but these were more like cots and there was no sign of any clean sheets. Instead a grey blanket lay neatly folded on each bare mattress together with a small lumpy pillow. There was a tiny white washbasin in the corner with no soap and against one wall, a rickety looking wooden table that lacked chairs.

The invaluable lesson of forcing yourself to always look on the bright side that every inexperienced traveller in difficulties has to absorb, was beginning to make its presence felt in Miss Alice's brain. "At least we won't be sleeping in a ditch tonight," she said as brightly as she could, gingerly testing the softness of her bed which was stoutly defying the pressure of her fingers.

"Yes," responded Miss Mary, catching the need to keep their spirits up. "It could be a lot worse and we will only be here a short time."

Their brave efforts to lighten each others mood, was

unexpectedly interrupted by their cell door suddenly swinging open. On the threshold stood a tall, angular, youngish man dressed in a dark blue blazer and perfectly creased cream coloured trousers. He regarded the twins quizzically from under bushy eyebrows before stepping forwards to introduce himself as Henri Polter the prison governor. Apart from pausing occasionally to search for the right word, his English was good and his accent reminded Miss Alice of Maurice Chevalier one of her favourite French actors.

He had come to see for himself, he declared, the infamous English women who had daringly freed one of France's most wanted criminals. Seeing the look of instant dismay flitting across Miss Mary's face, he quickly held up his hand as if in apology. He had only been trying to produce a little revelry to put them at their ease, but of course it was a very serious business. He had discussed their situation at length with Inspector Jacques and fully agreed with his solution. It was a most unusual situation, he said, most unusual indeed, but in the circumstances, the right one. He had come to explain to the pair their different status would be respected but they would have to adopt the daily life of the prison during their short stay. Sadly, it was not a hotel and they would find the accommodation left a lot to be desired. Their companions too were hardly desirable, but it was a low category jail and so only harboured the occasional murderer among the petty thieves and drug addicts.

The speaker gave an encouraging smile. They must show fortitude. It would only be for a couple of days and the English were famous for their stiff upper lip. The sisters could have told him theirs had trembled more than once since leaving The Rectory but they managed to produce somewhat watery smiles in return.

No sooner had the governor departed then the door

was opened once more to reveal a heavily set woman with faded blonde hair almost the colour of straw which was pulled back in a bun. She carried a tin plate in each hand upon which were heaped flaky potatoes and a lumpy brown congealed mixture that had a passing resemblance to stew. She proceeded to put these side by side on the table that wobbled alarmingly on impact before delving into the pockets of her crumpled and not too clean apron to produce two pairs of plastic knives and forks. These she handed to the sisters who took them with a stunned acceptance. Even now it had not quite sunk in as to what exactly was happening to them.

The provider of their supper threw a glance in the direction of the doorway where the warder was just visible in the corridor standing idly by the meal trolley. Satisfied she was not under observation, she turned back to give the sisters a searching look before beginning to whisper furiously in French. Neither of her listeners could understand a single word and made this plain with an exaggerated shrug of their shoulders. The trusty gave a stifled exclamation of frustration and started to perform actions with her hands.

She staggered as if lifting something heavy above her head and then brought it crashing down. Looking around, she picked up an imaginary implement and began a sawing movement. Miss Alice watched fascinated, for it reminded her for the first time in many years of the charades she used to take part in when she was a little girl. But the performance made it all too clear to a worried looking Miss Mary as to what the woman was asking. Was it true, she plainly wanted to know, that they had freed Le Grand Bandit? The rumour must have swept round the prison like a tidal wave and was obviously causing great excitement. She averted her eyes and tried to keep up an expression of bewilderment at the antics taking place in front of her.

The last thing she and her sister wanted to do was to draw any kind of attention to themselves for their situation was horrifyingly complicated enough as it was. She was saved by the appearance in the doorway of the warder impatiently summoning the prisoner back to her trolley. The trusty gave them a last, long lingering look before reluctantly departing.

Left alone at last, the incarcerated pair toyed disconsolately with their food. The traumatic events of the day had removed their appetites but they realised that it was of great importance to eat something. In the event, although by now stone cold, their offering tasted better than expected and they managed to force down several mouthfuls. Pushing the left over portion to the side of her plate, Miss Mary settled down to tell her sister of her growing fears. If their fellow inmates, for want of a better word to call them, discovered that they had freed Le Grand Bandit they would never for an instant believe it had been accidental. The sisters would almost certainly be considered by such a fraternity as much admired heroines and so earning an impressive but unwanted reputation as part of the underworld.

Yet they had to acknowledge that everything was going to be out of their hands. They could only wait and see what tomorrow would bring. And with that thought firmly planted in their minds, they decided to get as much rest as they possibly could despite their uncomfortable surroundings. It did not take Miss Alice, long worn out as she was by the day's upheavals, to drift into an almost dreamless sleep.

Yet Miss Mary who was equally tired, could only toss and turn at distressingly frequent intervals on the confines of her narrow bed. Her bid to force sleep to come, was foiled by the vision of a pair of luminous brown eyes that gazed constantly and hungrily at her. And every so often she would feel the slightest tickle on her cheek as if a luxurious moustache was softly brushing against it. And then most disconcerting of all, there were those slightly parted lips that seemed to hover tantalisingly just above hers without ever coming any closer. However hard she tried to banish Le Grand Bandit from her thoughts, he just would not go away.

To make matters worse, she could never bring herself even for a moment to share this burning, shameful secret with her sister. It would never do to admit she had been passionately kissed by a complete stranger, one who was a dangerous criminal to boot. It could only bring disgrace upon their family name. The first grey light of dawn was beginning to seep through the little window high up on the wall when she finally managed to escape his troublesome image and fall gratefully asleep.

Awoken shortly after six, they were each handed a towel that was little larger than a dishcloth and led down a separate corridor to a white tiled communal washroom. They had barely crossed its threshold when they felt every inquisitive eye turned upon them and an expectant buzz rose into the steamy air. Trying to ignore their reception, they went to join the back of a long queue for a row of hand basins but found themselves without ceremony being pushed to the front. If they had harboured any doubts over the reason for this preferential treatment they were soon to be resolved.

"It's what Le Grand Bandit would have wanted," declared a flame haired girl who toothbrush in hand, waved away their protests and happily gave up her place at the front. It was painfully obvious to the sisters that this sensitive subject was not going to go away, but they had decided they would not enter into any discussion involving the escape to avoid exacerbating the situation further. They hoped that a lack of English among their companions would help them with this aim.

The girl who greeted them appeared to have a reasonable grasp of the language but having said her piece, made no move to talk to them further. This reluctance may have had something to do with the fact that most of the onlookers seemed to be in awe of the newcomers which left them tongue tied and unable to ask the questions that were swirling round inside their heads. Or it might have been the presence of a sullen looking warder who stood, feet planted firmly apart, at the end of the room taking in everything with a baleful glare. The sisters hurriedly completed their ablutions still feeling the centre of attention, before to their great relief, she abandoned her position to escort them back to their cell which suddenly felt like a much desired hiding place.

They feared they would have to face a similar ordeal at breakfast in the mess hall but soon a familiar rattle outside their door heralded the arrival of the meal trolley. A different trusty, older with a stooped back and long, dank, brown hair, handed them each a mug of coffee and two rather soggy croissants but made no effort to engage the twins in conversation. Once again they found it difficult to summon up an appetite, but bracing themselves, somewhat mechanically chewed their way through them and afterwards felt the better for it.

Miss Alice being less involved, was to give her statement first. On the dot of nine o'clock she was collected by the same warder and taken across a yard to the police station where she was deposited in a side office. Waiting for her was Inspector Jacques sitting behind his cluttered desk, while at a table by the window, a clerk was laying out a collection of pens beside a large lined notepad. Her interrogator rose and waved her to a vacant chair in front of him before returning to his seat and pressing a bell by his side. This was promptly answered by a slim, pale faced young girl who favoured Miss Alice with an encouraging smile and announced that she would be interpreting. The English woman, she said, was to give a full account of the part she played in what the inspector called the unfortunate incident from the moment she arrived outside the house and taking care not to miss out the slightest detail.

Putting a wisp of stray hair behind her ear, Miss Alice launched into her account. She and her sister had become desperately thirsty and had been forced to stop at the first house they came across to ask for water. This turned out to belong to Mr Potts although they did not know it at the time. That was the only reason why they had stopped. A sudden thought crossed her mind. Had the inspector ever suffered from a raging thirst? The interpreter passed on this information which was greeted with a resigned sigh. Yes he had, but if madam would be so kind, he preferred to be the one who asked the questions.

Miss Alice paused to digest this before continuing. She had remained by the gate to guard their possessions while Mary had gone in search of the owner. While there, she had been too far away to either hear or see anything that may have taken place in the house. She was beginning to become impatient over the time she was having to wait, when a man she took to be the owner came out of the front door. He was of medium build with glossy dark hair and a moustache and wore a blue tracksuit. He seemed to be in a hurry, but stopped to explain that her sister was collecting water and they could have as much as they wanted. He had apologised for not being able to linger longer, revealing that he was already late for an important appointment. He had walked off briskly along the road beside the poplar trees and was lost from view. Shortly afterwards she heard the sound of an engine starting and presumed he had driven away.

Then came a question that Miss Alice had suddenly thought of herself. Did she not think it odd that if he was the householder, why he didn't keep his vehicle outside his home? She did now, she replied, but it had not occurred to her at the time. She had reluctantly to admit that she had not been exactly flustered, but was not quite her normal self at that moment. The man had been utterly charming and his brown eyes had been very penetrating. The inspector nodded ruefully on hearing this information. Yes, Le Grand Bandit had proved to be greatly attractive to women. There had been many victims.

Miss Alice continued that not long after that, she had become tired of waiting and had gone into the house to find her sister standing over Mr Potts who was sitting on the hall floor fingering his head. Soon afterwards the police had arrived. Stating that she had nothing further useful to add, she was told her statement would be typed and she would then sign it along with her sister who would be giving her account next.

Led out, Miss Alice passed Miss Mary in the yard which showed that thankfully the inspector, as he had promised, was not wasting any time. Her sister took the seat she had just left, knowing she was about to face one of the most embarrassing moments of her life. It was one thing to have been made a complete fool of but now she was going to have to relive every agonising minute of it before a room full of other people. Well almost every minute. Even if she was about to be pulled apart by wild horses, she could never bring herself to mention that kiss. It would not be lying she comforted herself. It would just be neglecting to reveal an uninteresting detail that had had no effect whatsoever on the outcome. It was just a released person's simple way of saying 'thank you' for her unwitting act of kindness.

The clerk by the window scribbled away furiously as she recounted her fateful opening of the cupboard and the dramatic events which followed. She described Le Grand Bandit's appearance as coldly and as matter of factly as she could aware that the inspector was watching her closely. When she had finished he took a thoughtful sip from a glass of water in front of him and muttered something to the interpreter. "You did not mention his eyes," she said "Were they turned upon you before or after you untied him?"

"I really didn't notice," she replied, realising with a blush that she had to admit this really was a lie.

"Did you notice their colour?"

"I think they might have been a sort of brown," she said, fearing a intimate examination was coming of what for her was a highly emotional subject. Mercifully however, the inspector seemed satisfied with his intervention and took the matter no further.

It was after one o'clock by the time she had finished her statement and she returned to the cell to find the meal trolley had already called. Miss Alice was picking her way through cold pasta and a rather limp looking salad while Miss Mary's plate awaited her on the nearby rickety table. But any thought of food was swept away by the utterly amazing sight of her sister. Her normally untouched grey hair had been permed into a series of neat waves and had acquired a blue rinse. Her lips, which had only known the occasional lightest of touches of lipstick, were a bright red colour while the nails of her hands and feet had been painted a deeper crimson.

Seeing the look of astonishment on her twin's face, Miss Alice laid down her fork and announced. "I can't try to wipe any of this off or they'll become offended."

"Who will become offended?"

"The girls. They just crowded round insisting that they wanted to do things for me." Miss Alice explained that after she had finished her statement, she had been taken to the communal hall where the prisoners were able to congregate when allowed out of their cells. At first their attitude had been exactly the same as the one they had shown in the wash room, but finally their curiosity had got the better of them. It was the flame haired girl called Wanda who spoke English, who had started asking the questions. As they had agreed, she was very non committal but her interrogator became increasingly persistent and there was no escape this time. In the end it got to the point where she felt she was being rude by repeatedly ignoring her. It was obvious that the prisoners knew they were involved so finally she had said, all right, yes, they did aid and abet Le Grand Bandit's escape but she could not give further details.

At this declaration the atmosphere had become electric and there was a spontaneous outburst of clapping. Everybody had wanted to shake her hand and things then began to get out of control. Edith, a drug addict from Marseilles, announced that Le Grand Bandit's rescuer must look her best for the coming court appearance. She had overruled her protests and set about washing her hair. Not to be outdone, Denise from Toulouse who had murdered her husband, and Pauline, a call girl from Arles, were adamant that they were going to paint her nails. "Wanda had tried to be helpful by saying I would be delighted," added Miss Alice. "When of course I wasn't. But I have to say the foot massage Marie, a pickpocket from Nice, gave me

80

was absolutely wonderful."

Miss Mary slowly eyed her sister up and down once more. "Well the result of their efforts is not quite you, but I can see they meant well and that hurdle is now out of the way."

Miss Alice suddenly sounded serious. "But there is another one."

Her twin frowned. "What do you mean another one?"

"They're planning to stage a major protest over the length of time they are being forced to spend in their cells. They're only allowed out on average three hours a day. There is a lot of unrest, particularly among the younger ones who find it difficult being cooped up for so long."

"What is that to do with us?"

"We have been selected to lead it. It's due to take place tomorrow morning during the recreation period."

"This is nonsense. What did you tell them?"

"I thought it best to say nothing. Hopefully we will be out of here by then."

"There can be no hopefully about it. We will have to be. Our statements should be ready to sign later this afternoon and we must leave immediately afterwards."

Yet it was nearly six o'clock before the summons came for them to return to the office. Trying to control their growing impatience, they duly signed their names and provided the address of The Rectory and its telephone number so they could eventually be reached if Le Grand Bandit was ever brought before a court and they were required as witnesses.

By now a light rain was falling and the overcast sky gave the approaching evening a murky look. Glancing out of the window, the inspector said it made sense for them to spend a second night in their cell which was dry and warm. He had spoken with the governor who had raised no objection and had said they could leave in the morning after having breakfast. The sisters were most profuse with their thanks but made it clear they were determined to leave at once. They had their light waterproof capes and the cooler conditions would be ideal for cycling. Seeing their minds were made up, the inspector, with a shake of his head, offered his hand and wished them well.

Chapter 7

Half an hour later they were on their way, revelling in the fresh air blowing in their faces. The rain had stopped and patches of clear sky were beginning to peep through the shifting clouds. Discarding their capes, they rode on for another forty minutes before a small glade set a few yards back from the road beckoned. They set up their pup tent they had bought with the tandem and delved into their panniers to fish out a tin of cashew nuts, a packet of oatmeal biscuits, and a slab of hard cheese. Leaning back against adjoining tree trunks, their mood was subdued despite their relief at being on their way once more. Now they had time to think of them, the calamitous train of events unleashed by their innocent request for a glass of water, had left the pair thoroughly chastened and deeply embarrassed. The outside world was proving to be even tougher than Archie had ominously warned and they were only surviving because there were some good people in it.

Between mouthfuls of their frugal supper, they marvelled aloud at the patience of poor Mr Potts who even now must be gingerly feeling his scalp and mourning the loss of his reward money. And also the inspector, who had lost the chance of being photographed with what would have been the most prized prisoner of his career. They must both have been driven to the edge of despair by the foolish antics of two interfering old English women who had been treated much more gently and considerately than they deserved.

Would they ever meet these two unfortunate men again they wondered? Only, they realised, if Le Grand Bandit was apprehended and they were required once more to give their version of the events. Miss Mary however was loath to linger on the subject and quickly banished such thoughts from her mind. She did not want those disconcerting luminous brown eyes to disturb her sleep yet again.

They awoke the following morning to discover their legs had become much stiffer than usual. They had felt no ill effects when cycling the night before but their previous two day break showed that at their age how quickly muscles could become out of condition as soon as they had stopped exercising them. It made for a painful start, but once the blood was circulating properly, they were able to maintain something like their normal speed.

Even so, they were grateful to stop for a much earlier lunch than they were accustomed to at a little village café whose solitary table outside on the pavement was unoccupied and could not be resisted under its bright yellow parasol. They lingered for double their normal time over fresh crusty bread and a generous slice of duck pate before relinquishing their comfortable chairs to move across the road to sit beside an ancient horse trough with a pleasantly gurgling fountain.

Dipping their faces into the cool, clean water, they refreshed themselves as much as they could before climbing onto their tandem and setting off again in the late afternoon. Their departure was watched by two curly haired youths who had passed the trough when they had been drying themselves with their handkerchiefs. One had pointed at them and said something which had caused both to burst out laughing. "I suspect he was saying we are two old grey mares," said Miss Alice wistfully adding. "And I suppose that is exactly what we are."

The afternoon stint was meant to be the most prolonged but after barely managing a couple of kilometres along a mainly flat road, they felt their strength beginning to give out. When acquiring their bicycle, they had decided to travel a set distance every day come what may. Yet the often torrid weather and their own unpredictable moods made the conditions of each one different.

There was still a good two hours of daylight left when the sisters came upon an open ended barn standing at the edge of a large field a little way off the road and made an instant and unanimous decision to stop. Maybe it was a late reaction to the drama of their prison stay, but they felt they could not go a step further and could hardly keep their eyes open. Somehow their tired bodies managed to lift the bicycle over a low stone wall and push it out of sight round the back. Too exhausted to eat, they collapsed among neatly stacked bales of hay and almost immediately fell asleep.

Miss Mary was rudely roused from a deep and blessedly dreamless slumber the following morning by a sudden sharp pain in her bottom. Turning on her side, she looked up to see a dark figure standing over her. In her stupor, she at first thought it was Marcel who had come back to haunt them. The middle aged man, who was wearing corduroy trousers and a crumpled blue cardigan, was unshaven and of the same height and build. He carried in his rather grubby hand a long handled pitchfork, which, as she became fully awake, she realised she had been prodded with.

Angrily rubbing the affected part, she thought he could at least have used the other end or, if he was anything of a gentleman, bent down and tapped her on the shoulder. But by the fierce scowl on his face she could see he was not exactly enamoured by their presence and she realised she had better keep her own temper under control.

And as if to prove a point, he proceeded to prod Miss Alice who was lying in a similar position, in the same fashion and none too gently. She sat up with a cry of pain and looked with alarm at their assailant who was now standing over her. Giving his own backside a brief, if vigorous scratch, as if in sympathy, he issued a few curt words. The sisters, getting awkwardly to their feet, had absolutely no idea if these represented a question or a command.

The one thing that was obvious, was they were trespassers on his property and should leave as soon as possible. A brief exchange of glances told them that they were in full agreement over this very sensible decision. With rather strained smiles and nods of apology, they began to back away, moving cautiously in the direction of their tandem. The farmer however appeared to read their minds. Hopping over a bale of hay as if he knew what they were after, he made the most of his short cut to reach it first. They realised he must have spotted it earlier and that its bright yellow colouring had revealed their presence. Outside the barn, they noticed the sun was already high in the sky and that they had fatally overslept long after their normal departure time.

The prodder of their behinds had meanwhile grasped its handlebars and was beginning to push the tandem along a meandering path that led away from the road and their much sought after freedom. With their mode of travel and all their belongings in his possession, they had no alternative but to follow in his footsteps. Although he had discarded his pitchfork, he was still an intimidating presence and neither of them had the energy or the will to stage a confrontation in their present state. They trailed two paces behind him with abject expressions on their faces almost as if they were two disconsolate dogs on a lead.

The path soon joined a rutted track which ran alongside a field where a herd of Charolais cattle munched lazily at the sparse vegetation, their tails occasionally flicking away the flies. It was a perfectly peaceful rural scene but the atmosphere which hung over the three walkers remained tense with not a word being spoken. After what seemed an eternity, a farmhouse appeared through a gateway on their right. It was a solid looking building with large windows and a red roof. The farmer, with what seemed exaggerated care, leant the tandem gently against the wall by the front door and, motioning them to wait where they were, disappeared inside.

Left alone, the twins for one wild moment thought of commandeering their machine and careering off on it back towards the road. But they quickly realised it was a considerable distance away and that they would almost certainly come to grief on the track's uneven surface. They were distracted by voices coming from somewhere in the interior and with Marcel in mind, to their great relief, realised one of them was female. Then came the sound of rapidly approaching footsteps and its owner appeared in view. She was several inches taller than their escort who they took to be her husband, but thinner with brown hair flecked with silver.

"Hello," she said proffering a smile. "I'm sorry you were dragged up here. It's my fault. I'm always telling Henri I never have a chance to speak English."

"But how did he know?" responded Miss Mary with surprise. "We never said a word." The woman laughed. "You didn't have to. Anybody can see who you are."

"We thought he was angry because we were sleeping in your barn," interposed Miss Alice. This was received with another short laugh. "Oh don't mind Henri, he's always cross." Her accent sounded to the sisters as if it was from the north of England and this was verified when she revealed her first boyfriend had been a student from Liverpool. But that was quite enough for the moment, she said. They must be desperate for hot water and soap after sleeping in the open.

Beckoning her guests inside, she took two large towels from a cupboard and pressed one on each before leading them to a bathroom tucked away just off the kitchen. They found it already occupied by a large black and white cat that lay curled up in the hand basin. "Wait a minute while I remove Pascale," the woman commanded. "That's his favourite place to sleep. He's not often disturbed because Henri doesn't wash much." The animal struggled in her arms in an attempt to be put down and on achieving his aim, shot out of the door. His mistress, fixing him with a fond smile, followed saying she going to cook them all breakfast.

The shower, hanging at an awkward angle from the wall, was rudimentary and the water barely lukewarm. But the twins, standing under its steady stream, luxuriated in washing away the dust and dirt of the barn. Spotting a jar of skin cream on the windowsill, they applied it soothingly to their bruises caused by the pitchfork which were beginning to turn an impressive purple.

Then feeling they could face the world again, they re-emerged into the kitchen to be greeted by a most wonderful and unexpected aroma. Marise was deftly ladling out a generous amount of fried potatoes, thick brown sausages and mushrooms onto three large plates with pretty flower patterns. "I always did a fry up for Roger," she explained, looking at their eager faces with a smile. "He came over here one summer to pick grapes but ended up picking a ripe fruit in me instead. He said he liked a proper English breakfast more than anything else in the whole wide world." Her eyes suddenly glistened and her voice became much softer as she looked into the distance. "Well almost anything. We were very passionate. You are when you're eighteen aren't you?"

The sisters, with no similar experience, felt this was hardly the subject to become involved in and slightly blushing, declined to offer a reply. Waved to their seats, they needed no second invitation to take up the offer. The hostess noticed their healthy appetite with warm approval as she delicately cut the end off a sausage and dropped it onto the floor by her chair. "Pascale likes a fry up too," she said as the sound of resonant purring instantly rose from under the table.

It was the only noise that was to break the silence for a considerable time apart from the rhythmic clink of three pairs of busy knives and forks. At last, with every plate empty, Marise rose and brought a steaming pot of fresh coffee from the stove with which she proceeded to fill three sizeable mugs. For the visitors, it was the final act of an absolutely perfect morning and they could not have been more relaxed.

Their hostess however, taking a first tentative sip of hers, came out with the question she had wanted to ask since they first appeared on her doorstep. "I hope you don't mind me saying this," she said. "But how old are you? You seem to be rather elderly for such a long distance cycle ride. I can see how tired it makes you. Are you doing it for charity?"

"No, we're not," replied Miss Alice. "And we're seventy."

"Well, what are you doing it for?"

It was the question the sisters were always fearing and were reluctant to answer because it made them feel foolish. Yet Marise had kindly taken them in and deserved to know the truth. "The reason we are making this journey is to find our long lost mother," replied

Miss Mary.

This brought a puzzled frown from their companion who appeared not to be sure she had heard correctly. "Your mother?"

"Yes, the last time we had any contact with her was over fifty years ago. She went to live in Cairo and we are hoping she will still be there."

"You have an address?"

"No, but that's where she sent her letter giving us the news from."

"If you're seventy, she must be very old. How do you know she is still alive?"

"We don't. But she would be eighty seven now so there is no reason why she should not be."

"But how can you possibly find her? It is an enormous city with a huge population."

Miss Alice felt there was no answer to this while her sister also said nothing and looked uncomfortably out of the window. They sensed their hostess's eyes switching gravely from one of them to the other. "Only you eccentric English would try and do something like this," she said more kindly. An embarrassed silence followed before their questioner, realising she had been too insensitive, added that they were being very brave and she felt a tremendous admiration for them. They must stay the night to give her more chance to speak English and then she would send them on their way in the morning well stocked with provisions.

The sisters protested they had already received overwhelming hospitality and really ought to be on their way as they could not afford to waste any more time. But Marise was adamant. One more day would not make any difference and they would have to pace themselves carefully as they were not getting any younger. And anyway, she desperately needed more of their stimulating conversation as Henri was not exactly sparkling company.

"But we feel he does not want us here," interposed Miss Alice for both she and her sister sensed his brooding presence even though he was spending most of his time outside working on the farm.

"Oh don't worry about Henri," came the reply. "He can't help being morose but underneath he is quite harmless." This remark brought rueful expressions from the twins who remembered all too vividly their rude awakening in the barn but neither felt it was the right time to broach the subject. "He used to be much more cheerful," she went on. "But trying to earn a living for us without any help has really got him down. We are quite isolated and there is nobody around who is available for hire."

Rising to her feet, she ushered them out onto a small stone terrace at the back of the house with breathtaking views across the valley to a range of hills in the distance. Pointing to a weather beaten wooden bench, she said she had things to do but they should sit down and enjoy their surroundings. They did as they were told, and it was not long before they began to doze fitfully in the warmth of the sun. But they were aware of their hostess coming out to look at them from time to time. She would stand there for a minute or two wearing a thoughtful expression before disappearing inside again.

And during a supper of thick slices of ham with new potatoes and a green salad, her absorbed mood made her almost as taciturn as her husband despite her earlier plea for stimulating conversation. Hardly had Henri left at the end of the meal to put his chickens and ducks to bed, than she was reaching into a cupboard on the wall behind her to pull out a large canvass rucksack. The sisters immediately protested she had already been incredibly generous and they could not possibly accept it as their own were perfectly adequate for the few possessions they had to carry.

"Oh no," she replied. "It's for me. I am coming with you." Holding up her hand to stifle any reaction from the startled twins, she declared they had transformed her life. What she at first thought was a harebrained scheme undertaken by two extremely silly old fools she now realised was nothing less than a valiant bid for freedom from a suffocating humdrum existence. There must be people all over the world who were condemned to live out their days in mind numbing routines because they lacked the resolve to do anything about it.

She had been one of these but would not be any longer. No, they were living proof of what you could do if you made the effort and she was going to do it. To be truthful, she had thought of leaving Henri several times but when it actually came down to it, she could not summon up the courage and energy that was required. But her mind was made up, she would be leaving with the sisters in the morning.

"But what will Henri say?" exclaimed Miss Alice, alarmed at the prospect of a dramatic confrontation between the pair for which they would certainly be blamed. "I will leave him a note," she replied. "He will be working on the far side of the farm at that hour so we will be able to reach the road without him seeing us."

"But how will you travel?" asked Miss Mary who, like her sister, was worried about the upheaval they were unwittingly causing.

"I have a small scooter which will be very useful," said their hostess with a note of pride. "It will enable me to go ahead in the last part of the day to find a good place to stop and then I can start getting things ready while you catch up. And of course I will be your interpreter. That will be a big help as you still have a large part of France to travel." She looked unwaveringly into their eyes. "You will find you cannot do without me. You are very good for your age but I am nearly twenty years younger. I will have much more energy. We will be the Three Musketeers." She gave her brightest smile. "Oh it is so exciting!"

The other two so called Musketeers were at a loss as to how to respond to a development they were beginning to find not at all welcome. They were grateful for any support they were offered on their journey but having lived most of their lives solely in each other's company, and knowing each other's little ways, the prospect of having a companion thrust on them was a daunting one. Yet having received so much kindness from Marise and while still being under her roof, they felt it was not the ideal moment to pour cold water on her plans. They could only hope that she would have changed her mind by the morning.

As soon as they decently could, they retired to the spare room they had been given overlooking the yard at the side of the house. They could see through the window Henri on his hands and knees clearing a drain and wondered what his reaction would be if Marise kept her word and secretly left with them in just a few hours. It was all too horribly familiar to what had happened to Marcel but at least this time they could expect to have safely left what was certain to be a harrowing scene. "Honestly, the whole thing is absolutely extraordinary," said Miss Alice watching the industrious figure outside scooping handfuls of leaves from the narrow channel.

"What is extraordinary?" queried her sister who was combing her hair in front of the mirror and thinking sadly that it had become even greyer in the short time since they had left home.

"Whenever and wherever we stop, we seem to cause

absolute chaos," came the reply. "Although I say it myself, we are not riffraff or hooligans. We have been properly brought up like any decent English gentlewomen. We are civilised, have good manners and always try to conduct ourselves with decorum so as not to cause people problems. Yet the exact opposite always seems to happen."

Miss Mary nodded soberly in agreement. "Archie would say we're not used to the outside world, but maybe it is because it is not used to us."

"Well whatever it is, we will have to try to be more careful about the situations we allow ourselves to get into."

They were awoken by a soft tap on their door on the dot of six o'clock and hurriedly dressing, entered the kitchen to be met by a scene of imminent departure. Packed provisions lay in a heap on the table while Marise's luggage, similarly ready, stood waiting by the door. It was painfully obvious to the sisters that their hostess had no intention of changing her mind at the last minute.

They had got their own belongings together the night before and had them in their hands but were promptly ordered to sit down. Henri would not be in for his breakfast before ten o'clock so there was plenty of time for them to have theirs. The sisters meekly did as they were told and found steaming mugs of strong coffee and bread rolls fresh from the oven placed before them.

The three travellers ate in silence for with everything decided, there did not seem anything left to say. When they had finished, Marise piled the dishes neatly in the sink and taking a small white envelope from her jacket pocket, left it propped up on the table by a pepper pot. The twins were dying to know what the contents of the message inside were but neither could summon up the courage to ask. After a cautious look around the yard, Marise collected her scooter from the shed opposite while the sisters reclaimed the tandem which was still leaning against the wall. Then the escaping party, pushing their machines as quietly as possible, made their way down the bumpy track towards the road. The sisters, lacking Marise's steady nerve, cast constant anxious glances behind them but there was no vengeful figure to be seen on the horizon.

Once on the highway, their hostess started her engine and they set the fastest pace they could to put as much distance as possible between themselves and the farm. If Henri kept to his normal routine as his wife was sure he would, they should have at least a three and a half hours start on him. She was also certain he would not set out in pursuit, but if he did, it would be in his ancient white van. Therefore if they saw any vehicle of that description approaching, it was essential to get under cover at the side of the road without delay.

This warning immediately had the sisters looking over their shoulders again but Marise was adamant it was not in her husband's character to be distracted from working at whatever job he was doing. Of course in his own way he loved her, but she was not nearly as necessary to him as his animals. The sisters had no idea what it was like to have a relationship with a man, but Miss Alice could not hide her curiosity and asked how they had met.

"I found it hard to get over Roger and did not go out for a long time," Marise replied, reigning in her machine to keep pace alongside the slower moving tandem. "I lived in the next village which put on a dance for young farmers and Henri came. He was cheerful in those days but I suppose like many of us he gradually became disillusioned with life." She did not elaborate further on this sensitive subject and they rode on in silence for a while each with their own rather sombre thoughts.

They stopped for a lunch of cold sausage and cheese shortly after midday, sitting on a low stone wall shaded from the sun by a belt of overhanging trees. It was now over six hours since they had left the farm and as Marise had predicted, there had been no sign of a pursuing white van. Feeling it was no longer imperative to hurry, they found a piece of flat ground and settled down for a much needed siesta after their early morning exertions. The secondary road they had taken was devoid of traffic and the only sound reaching their ears as they drifted off to sleep was the incessant whirling of countless cicadas.

Waking in mid afternoon, they continued in a much more relaxed and cheerful mood. Marise in particular, became increasingly animated. It seemed at last it had begun to sink in that she was beginning a new and carefree life. Her almost constant chatter required only monosyllable replies which allowed the sisters to concentrate thankfully on their pedalling as a series of small rises beckoned. The third Musketeer, sitting effortlessly on her scooter, declared once again to the heavens she was as free as a bird and how wonderfully kind the sisters had been to release her from her chains.

This was to be a constant refrain until towards evening when the sky began to cloud over. The ever more gloomy atmosphere after the endless bright sunshine, appeared to effect her mood. Her chatter died away and she became preoccupied with something that seemed to be greatly troubling her. She looked to the twins to have entered a world of her own when without warning, she pulled onto a grass verge and held up her hand for them to stop.

Their first thought was she was concerned about how to find the right camp site, but even as it crossed their minds, they saw her turn her machine around. "I am going home," she said simply, but in a tone that showed her mind was made up. "I really can't leave him. We have been together for so long and he relies on me."

Miss Alice and Miss Mary, though at first surprised, could not help exchanging knowing glances. They had half expected this to happen but certainly not so soon. They might be spinsters, but they were beginning to understand the bonds of marriage. It reminded them vividly of Marcel and Monique. It seemed when couples grew old together, they might virtually ignore each other's existence under the same roof, but if one disappeared the other discovered how desperately they needed them. Miss Alice, feeling she and her sister should offer their support and understanding, said brightly. "Henri will be pleased."

Marise frowned. "Henri? I'm not talking about Henri, I'm talking about Pascale. There'll be no one to cut up his chicken or give him crumbled cheese. He'll be left to his own devices and will have to hunt for food in the farm yard or starve."

"But I thought you said Henri was good with animals?"

"He is, but only with ones that earn their keep. To him, Pascale is just a wasteful extra mouth to feed. And if he wants to wash, and pulls him from the basin he won't check first to see if he's got a foot dangling in the plughole." The mere thought of this possible danger to her pet, banished any ideas of wavering that might have surfaced. "No," she said abruptly. "I must set off without delay. I am already far too late to give him his supper."

She unloaded the rest of her share of the provisions and pressed them upon her companions who with a little reorganisation, found enough room to squeeze everything into their panniers. Then in a final act, she reached into the front basket on her scooter to produce a small notepad and pencil, the end of which she proceeded to lick before starting to slowly write in a neat copperplate hand. "Although I am turning back, I can still help you," she said. "This is the address of Sophie Orleans, an old school friend of mine. She lives near a small town right at the foot of the Alps and it will be an ideal base from which you can carry out your preparations to cross them."

Admiring her handiwork, she applied another lick before adding a dot to the end of the last line. "She is a middle aged widow and has a sixteen year-old daughter, Claudia, who is attending a language school and will be keen to practice her English on you. Theirs is a friendly house and you will find yourselves quickly made most welcome. I will contact her as soon as I get back to let her know you are coming." She tore the page carefully from the notepad and folding it in half, handed it to Miss Mary who along with her sister, was most voluble with her thanks.

Marise's scooter had already spluttered into life and raising her voice above the noise of the engine, she gave a final piece of advice. "I almost forgot. Whatever you do, do not raise the subject of her late husband." The twins looked at each other with eyebrows raised, wondering what such a cryptic comment could mean. But it was too late to ask for an explanation, for their erstwhile companion was already disappearing round a bend in the road behind them.

They watched her go with mixed feelings. There was no doubt they were relieved to be on their own again but Marise had proved to be a good friend and they had become quite fond of her. Miss Mary stowed the address securely away with their passports for it could well turn out to be a godsend when they were getting ready to tackle one of the most perilous parts of their journey.

The sisters spent the night in an isolated bus shelter having first discovered to the best of their ability, from the timetable on the wall, that if there had been a service that day it had gone. Lying end to end on the narrow wooden bench with their rucksacks as pillows, they mused in the growing darkness over what the fate of Marise would be on her return home. They tried to picture the scene of her arrival in the middle of the night but found it too disquieting and gradually dropped off to sleep.

Chapter 8

Late spring was turning into early summer as the sisters made their way steadily towards the still invisible mountain range. The weather was slowly becoming hotter which made cycling ever more tiring despite the early starts. The perspiring riders thought longingly of the coastal resorts far away to their right where the traffic was too heavy for them to negotiate.

People of their sort would now be thronging the best hotels in such exotic places as Cannes and Nice. They imagined them sitting at tables spread with spotless white cloths and being served by a host of deferential waiters who would instantly respond to any beck or call. They could almost hear the tickling of the ice cubes being dropped by silver tongs into their frosted glasses as a string orchestra played discretely in the background. These lucky diners would later retire along cushioned corridors to their air conditioned rooms with their freshly laundered duvets neatly turned down at the corner.

Miss Mary and Miss Alice could not resist a collective sigh. And what were they doing? They were sleeping in the dust and dirt of wayside orchards and meadows where it was becoming ever more difficult to force their pup tent pegs into the hard ground. Afraid to spend their dwindling funds on overnight accommodation, they rarely managed to keep themselves properly clean and would catch each other discretely scratching. They were greeted by endless rows of vines stretching away into the distance as they moved further and further south. Sometimes among these a bent figure could be seen checking the progress of the fruit under a ripening sun.

Now and then they came across giant sprinklers at work among fields of thirsty crops, their fine spray rotating steadily in a wide arc refreshing everything within its reach. To the weary riders it was an enchanting sight. As Miss Alice, in her hot and sweaty blouse remarked with feeling, she had never been so envious of a vegetable before. But their spirits would begin to rise whenever they stopped to rest in the shade of welcoming roadside trees. They would lean gratefully against their trunks hungrily devouring juicy fruit and enormous tomatoes which they had bought in the local markets.

It was Miss Alice, taking her turn pedalling in front, who was the first to catch sight of the mountain range. It was just a faint, hazy line in the far distance which for a long time never seemed to come any closer. But gradually it took form until the vast array of rock disappearing ever upwards into the clouds could be clearly seen.

How were they going to cross this extremely formidable barrier? It was a problem that began to exercise their minds more and more. There were of course buses and trains that would carry them easily and comfortably over the top. Yet they had already come a great distance without paying as much as a penny on public transport apart from the ferry where they had had no option. It was now becoming a challenge to continue in this fashion. If nothing else, it would help conserve their meagre funds.

The Alps were beginning to become an overwhelming and intimidating presence by the time they reached the village they were looking for, which stood right in the shadow of the range not far from the town of Brianco. On approaching its outskirts, they halted by a little stone bridge that spanned a narrow, sluggish stream to take stock. Two questions dominated their minds. Had Marise kept her promise to contact Sophie Orleans? And why was it so important not to mention her late husband? And being only human, this was the one topic they knew they would have difficulty avoiding.

Taking advantage of the nearby water, they set about washing off as much grime as they could from their bodies and gave a thorough and somewhat painful combing to their matted hair. They then replaced their blouses, soaked through with perspiration from their constant pedalling, with clean but creased ones from their rucksacks. They were never the sort to underestimate the importance of keeping up appearances and were determined not to arrive at Sophie's gate looking like tramps. Inspecting each other, they had to admit their efforts had been only partly successful but realised nothing more could be done. Remounting, they made their way slowly into the village, closely inspecting the names of each little street as they passed. Despite themselves, they could not stop the tension rising inside them as they wondered what kind of reception they would receive.

The road they wanted soon appeared. It was short with only four stone terrace houses in it and theirs was the last one which boasted a small side garden containing two rather straggly bushes. Miss Mary gave a tentative knock but received no answer. After a few minutes she tried again only to be once more confronted with silence. Was it the right house? She checked the number on the door. Yes it was. Were the owners away? Although the shutters were open it seemed quite deserted. If that was the case, they could have trouble finding somewhere to stay in such a small place.

At that moment a youthful voice called to the sisters who were peering into a front window. "Hello. You must be those two funny women Marise said were coming." A pretty girl wearing a pink dress whose hair was held in a bob by a ribbon of the same colour, appeared at the gate. The twins, overcome with relief that Marise had kept her word, knew it must be Claudia.

They suddenly realised how nice it was to be recognised and greeted in unknown surroundings even in such a fashion. Yet the remark had been artlessly made and without a hint of an insult and they had to admit, contained more than a grain of truth. As they confirmed their identity, the young girl explained her mother had been expecting them. They had just returned from shopping and she would be along in a second. Even as the daughter spoke, a thick set woman with blonde, tousled hair came into view along the pavement armed with a large bag in each hand. These were instantly dropped at the sight of the sisters who found themselves being crushed against an ample bosom in an emotional welcome. A flow of unintelligible French followed which Claudia's more than serviceable English translated into an invitation for them to stay as long as they wanted. It was important they all got to know each other and it would be good for her daughter who was preparing for her exam at the end of the summer.

The twins needed little persuading to take up the kind offer because they felt, in one of the colourful expressions they had learnt from Archie, completely knackered.

Having been ushered inside, the sisters were shown up a flight of creaking stairs to a sparsely furnished room with twin beds that looked as if it had been prepared in readiness for them some time ago. The only decoration was a photograph perched on the edge of the dressing table showing a strong looking, square jawed man with swept back hair who they took to be Anton the grieving widow's husband. Descending to be shown round the rest of the house by Claudia, they became aware that his picture was on display in every room.

"Mama was truly devoted to Papa," explained the girl, casting an eye towards the kitchen from where came the welcome sounds of a meal being prepared. "His loss has hit her very hard."

"How did he die?" asked Miss Alice who could not contain herself but felt she was not breaking any rules by discussing the subject only with the daughter.

"That's the trouble," replied Claudia with a barely audible sigh. "We don't know exactly. He was always going out hunting and one day he just never came back. The countryside round here is wild and the undergrowth very dense. People have disappeared before with their remains sometimes not being found for months or if at all. It was a great shock when he failed to return."

"How long ago did it happen?" interjected Miss Mary who was equally as intrigued as her sister.

"Two years ago, but time is not a healer as far as Mama is concerned. She will never find any peace until she knows his final resting place. She is convinced his body is lying somewhere out there in the woods at the mercy of wild animals. That's why we never raise the subject. She becomes so agitated if we do, that whatever the weather, she'll go out searching again. Of course we've looked everywhere possible countless times and we still haven't given up. No, mama pays old Bernard, a local countryman, a small sum to keep looking. He knows every inch of the countryside and works from a grid, doing a certain area at a time. If anybody can find poor Papa he will."

With their curiosity partially satisfied, the twins found little difficulty in keeping clear of such a sensitive topic. They were kept busy washing and ironing their disconcertingly threadbare garments with

Miss Alice, the more proficient with a needle, attending to the patching.

The pair spent the mornings visiting the village street market with Claudia who knew all the vendors and was adept, despite her youth, at finding the best bargains. The sisters, adamant that they must pay their way, dug even deeper into their dwindling funds relieved that in her company they were not being taken advantage of as tourists often were. They were quickly becoming attached to their hosts who seemed genuinely filled with sympathy for what they were attempting to achieve and were helping them as much as they possibly could.

Sophie, probably because of her own predicament, was greatly interested in how the sisters would find their mother and wanted to know every detail of their plans. Miss Mary, had to admit with a feeling of slight embarrassment, that at this stage they had not actually worked out any details. Those would have to wait until they arrived in Cairo. At the moment they just had a vague notion that once there, they would think of a way of tracking her down. This brought a frown from their hostess as she listened to her daughter's translation. "But it is a vast city," she declared. "And your mother is so old she may no longer be alive."

"Yes we know," agreed Miss Alice. who was getting used to being asked this question. "Marise said the same thing but something inside tells us we just have to keep going."

Sophie nodded soberly. "Yes, you are like me. You cannot give up."

As their departure drew nearer the twins began to face up to the difficult task of deciding how they were going to tackle the Alps. A quick look at their financial situation told them what they already knew. The cost of paying to go by public transport which they did not want to use anyway, would leave them virtually penniless. They had arranged with Archie to wire them additional funds when needed, but they wanted to put off this day for as long as possible. The only answer, they felt, was to try to hitchhike. Claudia agreed to go with them to the main highway to help find a good spot to wait but was secretly dubious about their chances of success. The two women, together with their bulky rucksacks, would take up a lot of room in a normal sized car and it was unlikely that larger commercial vehicles would take the time to pull over. While confident that she could easily obtain a lift herself, she was too polite to point out that their age and appearance were hardly factors to count in their favour.

Having said what they hoped would be a final goodbye to Sophie, the sisters set out with her daughter on a clear, breezy morning with high hopes. They had to walk nearly a kilometre to reach the right road and found it strange to be on their feet rather than pedalling their tandem. Realising it could be of no use for the next stretch of their journey, they had presented it to the Orleans family although they could not help feeling a pang of regret over the parting. It had been an inspired buy and they had looked upon it more as a friend than a machine. Without it, they would not have come nearly so far so quickly or so cheaply, and wondered how they would fare on the other side of the mountains now that it had gone. Due to their rest and the attention they had paid to their clothes, they now looked smarter than at any time since they had left England. They had put on their dresses rather than their more workmanlike trousers which like their boots, were stowed at the bottom of their freshly scrubbed rucksacks.

After a cursory inspection of several likely positions, Claudia called a halt at a small weed covered lay-by situated on a straight stretch where approaching vehicles would be easily visible. Not wanting to give the impression that three people desired a lift, she went and sat on a rock quite a distance away. Left to it, the twins stood as close to the edge of the tarmac as they dared and began waggling their thumbs at the passing drivers. The traffic was heavy and they repeatedly had to change arms which quickly became tired from their constant movements. In times of crisis, the pair had developed the habit of searching for a suitable saying to give them badly needed encouragement. And it was Miss Alice who came up with one first. "If at first you don't succeed," she declared firmly and loudly. "Try, try and try again."

Unfortunately this exhortation made not the slightest difference for the vehicles continued to stream past without any show of slowing down. Claudia, watching from afar, could not resist a rueful shake of the head. It was exactly what she had expected and she could not see the situation changing. Yet with only an hour gone, she felt it was too early for her to interfere and decided to let a further one pass before rejoining them. By that time, her frustrated and disillusioned companions were nearing their wits end. The young girl decided there was only one thing for it, she would have to try to get them a lift herself. The only nearby cover was a rather stunted bush which she ordered the sisters to hide behind. They had to crouch to remain out of sight which they found less of an ordeal than expected because they had constantly had to bend their knees while cycling.

Claudia, who had considered the possibility of this happening before setting out, was wearing a T shirt that looked a good size too small and close fitting jeans which further accentuated her attractive figure. It was, as Miss Alice observed later, as if she had waved a magic wand. No sooner had she taken up her position than a black car pulled up and a curly haired young man leaned over and thrust open the passenger door. The girl beckoned to the twins, but on seeing the pair approach, the driver quickly pulled the door shut and disappeared with a squeal of tyres.

Waving them back to their bush again, Claudia was determined to persevere but a distressing pattern soon made itself clear. Three more vehicles were effortlessly enticed into the lay-by yet on each occasion when the real identity of those who wanted a lift became clear, their hoped for Good Samaritans lost no time in driving off. By mid afternoon the disheartened trio were ready to admit defeat. They conceded that by the law of averages, there must be good hearted motorists somewhere on the crowded highway who would be prepared to stop. But it could even be days before they appeared and the twins did not have that much time to waste.

The walk back to the village was conducted in silence. Uppermost in the sisters' minds was the fact they would now have to part with their precious funds after all to travel over the Alps with a bus ride seeming to be the cheapest option. Arriving home at last, they found Sophie engaged in an engrossing conversation across the kitchen table with a man whom they took to be Bernard the searcher of Anton. Once again, by the look on their hostess's face they knew he must have drawn a blank and that the hunt for her husband would have to go on. Having completed his melancholy message he rose from his chair, arm outstretched, to greet the newcomers. His handshake was firm and his grey eyes steady as he looked at them with an air of appraisal. He was short and stocky with a mane of white hair and a wrinkled, weather beaten face which betrayed his wandering existence. Although approaching eighty, he had looked after himself and appeared to be impressively fit for his age.

"Bernard likes to meet fellow travellers," explained Claudia as he muttered a few words aimed in their direction. "He does have a smattering of English but is too shy at the moment to use it. After Italy changed sides in the war, he used to take British airmen who had been shot down, over the Alps to escape the Germans. It's a great pity you three didn't meet years ago because he might have taken you. Of course you are all too old for such a thing now. He's sorry you had no luck on the highway," she added as he turned to go. "He has no time for car drivers himself."

The sisters spent the rest of the afternoon with the daughter's help, perusing the coach timetables. They decided to catch one leaving early the following afternoon which would allow them time to buy some fresh fruit in the market to take with them on their journey. After a somewhat sleepless night, they were just finishing breakfast when there came a knock on the door and Anton's searcher stood on the threshold. An earnest and somewhat lengthy conversation with Claudia ended with her looking up at the ceiling and rolling her eyes. "Bernard says he's always wanted to make a pilgrimage over his wartime route before he dies," she explained. "But he has never had anybody to take before. If you're keen to go he'll consider it, but whatever happens you must be fit enough." Seeing their astounded look, she added quickly. "Don't worry, I'll tell him you've already decided to take the bus. He doesn't realise it but he'll never be able to manage it himself."

"Well if he's made an offer," Miss Mary responded equally hurriedly. "I think we ought to listen." For some reason she felt her heart beginning to beat more quickly. Miss Alice said nothing but gave her sister's hand an encouraging squeeze in support.

"Yes, I suppose he's made the effort to come and see you," responded the daughter. "In that case, he wants you both to step outside." The twins exchanged perplexed glances wondering why the conversation could not continue where it was, but once in the garden the reason became clear. "Now look at the mountain range," instructed Claudia indicating the endless wall of rock that towered above the village casting a most gigantic shadow in the early morning sun. "By look, I mean stare at it, really stare at it. Bernard wants to know if you really think you can climb what you can see."

The twins did as they were told, thinking it was all a little too theatrical until it began to sink in the old man was making an important point. They had to be completely aware of exactly what was involved and be fully committed for this would test their endurance to the very limit. They forced themselves to concentrate, looking unblinkingly at the solid mass rising up before them without having any thought whether they could successfully climb it or not. Yet both knew instinctively inside they would say that they could although the truth was they wouldn't know until they tried.

Bernard came to stand between them, putting a rather inquiring hand around each of their shoulders. Unused to such familiarity, they found the feeling uncomfortable but restrained themselves from brushing it off for fear of him taking offence. Yet worse was to come for kneeling down, he proceeded with sturdy fingers to feel the strength of their calf muscles. The prodding was careful and methodical and they realised he had earlier been exploring the condition of their backs which would carry the weight of their rucksacks. Miss Alice said afterwards she had felt like a mare at a horse fair and had expected him to look at her teeth next.

His examination complete, he retreated a few yards but continued to observe them in a most thoughtful manner. "Mama's told him all about your gruelling journey," explained Claudia. "He said it sounded impressive but people tended to exaggerate their hardships and he wanted to make sure that your physical condition confirmed your deeds. He believes it does, but there is a couple of more things he wants to ask. He says mountain climbing is completely different from anything else. When you get to the higher reaches, the air is so thin you could be gasping for breath. But the big question is, do you have a head for heights? If his old route is still open, there will be narrow ledges overlooking sheer drops that you will have to walk along."

The sisters knew the honest answer was they did not have a clue. Having spent nearly all their lives in the shelter of The Rectory, they had no idea of what they were capable of until they had set out. They'd only discovered they had sea legs when the ferry had been caught in the storm. The highest they'd been was shaking a duster from the third floor attic window at home, but they felt this was enough and confirmed that they had. Bernard digested this encouraging response, but still did not look completely satisfied.

His biggest fear, the daughter said, was what would happen if one of them collapsed? It would take a long time to effect a rescue and then it might be too late. He did not want one of their deaths on his conscience. Or more likely, two. On their journey so far, there had always been sporadic traffic and the odd inhabited dwelling even in the most sparsely populated areas they had travelled through. Once they were away from the lower reaches of the mountain they would become completely isolated as if they were the only ones in the world. Were they prepared to accept that because it could do strange things to the mind? Miss Alice and Miss Mary had long since decided to reply to everything in the affirmative as they were determined to go. They said it would not worry them at all.

To their somewhat tentative inquiry as to how long their stamina testing trek would take, Bernard refused to speculate. It was a question of keeping up morale, he explained. If they did not set a schedule, they could not fall behind it and so feel depressed over making slow progress. A lot would depend upon the weather for even though it was early summer, it could be vicious and change in the twinkling of an eye to catch them unawares.

Another factor he was keen to emphasise, was how far his memory would serve him as he tried to find a trail he had not used for over thirty years. Parts of the landscape would have changed and the way could be overgrown in many places. He knew every shepherd's hut and hunter's cabin on the lower slopes so they could expect to be under a roof however basic, on most nights. But once they left these behind as they climbed higher, they would have to find what shelter they could.

On the day of their departure, the old man presented each of them with a stout walking stick which he had carefully cut from the surrounding woods himself. Then he checked that the weight of their rucksacks was evenly distributed and that these fitted snugly on their shoulders. The sisters tactfully did not tell him that by now they were well used to the procedure. They were slowly beginning to understand the ways of men. It was a bright and rather chilly morning, ideal for walking. Sophie and her daughter stood at the gate to see them off as the great trek got underway. There was the odd tear in their eyes as they repeatedly cried 'Good luck' and waved their handkerchiefs after the departing figures.

Bernard set off at a pace the sisters at first thought was too slow, but once they adopted his measured stride, they had to agree it was a sensible speed for the arduous journey that lay ahead. And the veteran traveller insisted that they halt for ten minutes to rest every half hour without fail. The twins at times found this frustrating for they felt they could easily have gone on further, but once again came to find his judgement was sound. There were also other enforced stops when Bernard had to cast around to rediscover the track which had disappeared into a mass of tangled undergrowth or come to a dead end before an outcrop of rocks

As they slowly but surely made their way upwards, they began to realise they could never have attempted such a climb on their own. Despite the tremendous effort required in the steepest places to put one foot in front of the other, the sisters found somewhat to their surprise they were actually enjoying themselves and took great satisfaction in the progress they were making. Sometimes a mist or low cloud frustratingly obscured their view when during their break, they looked back down the mountainside.

But on a clear day and from certain vantage points, they could see some of the valley now far below and the cluster of reddish pinpricks that represented the roofs of the houses. Sophie had said that if their climb became too much they would be warmly welcomed back and that it would be downhill all the way. Yet as the objects they could see below continued to become smaller and smaller, they felt that whatever happened in the future it would be easier to keep going up.

Every evening as dusk approached, Bernard would seek out a sheltered spot and gather fuel for a small fire which would help to ward off the effects of the falling temperature. There was little cooking to be done for most of their rations had been chosen for convenience sake to be eaten cold. The sisters were so tired from their exertions that they had usually fallen asleep before the flames had started to die down. Miss Alice would enter a blissfully dreamless existence but Miss Mary began to be plagued again by the luminous brown eyes of Le Grand Bandit and his ticklish moustache and those lips that never, ever, came any closer. He had recently disappeared from her imagination and she wondered if the more rarefied air she was now breathing was the cause of bringing him back. Yet try as she might to get rid of him, he accompanied her for most of the rest of the climb.

The day disaster struck had begun like any other. The twins awoke in the chill of the morning to rub the stiffness from their arms and legs before helping Bernard to make sure that nothing was left behind and that any rubbish they had accumulated was safely buried with the fold away spade he kept lodged between the straps of his pack. Shortly after their first break, which had been most warmly welcomed following a difficult rocky stretch, they set off across a grassy patch of ground that sloped away to the edge of a cliff. It had rained during the night and the surface was wet despite the increasing rays of a pale sun that were breaking through a slowly dispersing bank of cloud.

Miss Alice, who was bringing up the rear, stuck her stick into the greasy turf to gain support but it slipped off an unseen stone and her feet gave way beneath her. Before she could recover, she slithered helplessly downwards away from her companions, who alerted by her cries, could only watch in horror as she vanished from sight. Attempting to rush after her, Miss Mary found herself being held back by the restraining arms of Bernard who then led the way, step by cautious step, towards the point where Miss Alice had disappeared.

Following at his shoulder, Miss Mary gasped in relief as her sister's head came into view no more than ten feet below them but agonisingly out of reach. Her slide had been arrested by a sturdy bush which was growing diagonally out of the rock face. She was sitting astride its narrow trunk with her hands tightly grasping a protruding branch. The drop below her was steep but not precipitous, and was strewn with boulders and razor sharp pieces of flint running for a distance of three hundred yards before flattening out into a scrub filled plateau. But she had no intention of taking in the terrifying view. Her eyes were tightly shut and she was determined to keep them that way. She knew the golden rule. Do not look down. She was trying to think of a suitable prayer to sustain her in her predicament when her sister's voice broke into her thoughts. "Are you all right?"

A wave of anger fuelled by fear, swept through her. "What a stupid question," she shouted back in an almost hysterical tone. "Of course I'm not all right."

"Are you hurt?"

Miss Alice forced herself to remain calm. "I don't think so."

"Can you hang on? Bernard is going to go and find some rope."

"I will try. How long will he be gone?"

Miss Mary put the question to the grave faced figure beside her. He had said the only chance they had of getting her back to the top was with the help of one. He had earlier noted an isolated woodman's hut where there would certainly be a supply, but at his best pace he estimated it would take him a good three hours each way. Without wasting a minute further, he departed leaving Miss Mary to deal with the daunting situation as best she could.

"Bernard will not be any time at all," she called out as gaily as she could although her heart was full of dread. She too, did not like looking down, but proceeded to lie flat on her stomach with her head just over the edge of the cliff. She felt safer that way as she put all her efforts into taking control of the situation. Her main problem was to make sure her sister stayed alert and concentrated as hard as she could on not losing her balance. One second of absent mindedness could send her tumbling down onto the rocky slope below. Even if she was not killed, her injuries were bound to be such that their mission would be brought to a swift end.

Miss Mary remembered for a moment Bernard asking them if they had a head for heights. Well, they had been found out in no uncertain fashion this time. Almost as sick with anxiety as her twin, she furiously wracked her brains for inspiration. What, she wondered, did people do in such desperate situations? One solution quickly came to her. She had read of it in books and seen it in films. She peered over the edge and called. "What about a sing song?"

There was a long pause before an angry reply tinged with an incredulous air of disbelief came back. "Don't be so stupid."

Miss Alice, clinging on for dear life, was having a Rectory Moment, wishing with all her heart that she was safely back in her bedroom at home. Her sister was upset by her retort but realised she had to make allowances for the figure below, half hidden by a thicket of leaves, was badly frightened. It was a shock because their minds were almost always in tune but for some reason, this unique family trait was not working today. But it was no time to be sensitive and whatever happened, she had to keep making suggestions. Her mind went back to the country walks they had taken with their mother when young and it produced another one. Leaning out a little further, she called. "What about playing I Spy?"

This time there was no response. Miss Alice was having difficulty taking in what she had heard. How could you possibly play that game with your eyes shut? And even if she opened them she could not look down. She could only look up and all there was to see there was the sky.

The voice came again. "Did you hear me? What is your answer?"

This time there came a reply. "My answer? If you can't say anything sensible then please keep quiet."

"But we have to talk to stop you dozing off and losing your grip. I'll just say 'Hello' every few minutes."

"That could startle me. I'll be better off if you leave me alone."

And so silence descended over the mountainside with the two sisters, barely ten yards apart, each left with their own terrifying thoughts.

Yet after quite a while, it was Alice who spoke first. "I'm beginning to feel numb."

Miss Mary, whose mind had wandered, peered down from above. "What?"

Another wave of irritation convulsed the sufferer. "I said I'm feeling numb."

"There's no need to shout. Try shifting your position slightly."

"I can't do that. It's too dangerous."

"Well, move one limb at a time."

A rather desperate response rose from below. "All right, I'll try."

Miss Mary watched intently with her heart in her mouth, as she saw her advice taken and the bush start to shake slightly. Then came the welcome news. "I've

117

waved a leg and now I'm waving an arm."

"Good. Is the blood beginning to circulate?"

"It must be. I'm beginning to tingle. I'm now wriggling my toes."

"Well done. Just hang on. Bernard can't be long now."

Yet it was late on what had been a long, agonising afternoon, that he finally reappeared marching resolutely into view with a coil of rope round his shoulder. It was obvious Miss Alice was in no condition to tie it round her waist with a firm enough knot. So with the twins being of an almost identical build, Bernard used Miss Mary as a substitute for his calculations. Expertly fashioning a loop, he placed it over her head and she pulled it down to let it settle round her middle. His experienced eye had not failed him for it proved to be neither too tight nor too loose.

The next step was to lower the noose to Miss Alice which was far from an easy task. The uppermost branches with their dense clusters of leaves barred the way as she tried to grasp it with a hand she had freed in readiness. At the fifth attempt she succeeded and following Bernard's instructions, manoeuvred the rope over her head and into position. There was a frustrating pause while she worked to restore enough circulation in her hands to hold onto it with sufficient strength to be safely hauled up.

Bernard meanwhile had taken the opportunity to make a series of footholds in the treacherous turf and being the anchor, placed Miss Mary immediately in front of him. He tied his end of the rope round his waist and waited for Miss Alice to give a tug to show she was ready. When this finally came, it took the combined strength of himself and Miss Mary to complete the first stage of dragging her clear from the thick and tangled foliage. They then stopped to recover their breath before deciding how to set about the slow and painful process of bringing her back to the top. The distance was mercifully short, but a close inspection of the rock face revealed numerous razor sharp projections which Miss Alice had fortunately avoided on the way down through being mainly airborne.

Safely removed from the bush, she in turn was contemplating how best to tackle what was certain to be a very bumpy ride. With a concerted effort, she twisted onto her side so the smallest part of her body was exposed to the dangerous surface. But after being pulled a few jarring feet, the pain in her hip became so unbearable she had to flip over onto her back again. Progress was incredibly slow as the pullers, heeding her cries at each fresh obstacle, found themselves having to constantly halt their exertions. But at long last her face, streaked with tears of relief, came into view and their outstretched hands pulled her away from the dangerous edge.

Bernard, with great care, lifted her to her feet and she immediately fell into the outstretched arms of her overjoyed sister. Their delighted reunion ended when Miss Alice's legs gave way and she was half carried to a nearby grassy knoll where her injuries where inspected. With the help of her own, and Miss Mary's gently exploring fingers, they discovered that no bones were broken. There were several lacerations among a mass of bruises but none were very deep and would be expected to heal quickly in the clean mountain air. Physically, she had suffered little from her ordeal, yet it was obvious to her companions her mental condition was a cause for concern. She was suffering from shock and would be in no fit state to continue their journey for at least a couple of days.

Scouting around, Bernard discovered a sheltered spot beneath a pair of stunted trees and set up camp as dusk was closing in. Miss Alice, curling up as near as she could to the newly lit fire, fell fast asleep before a supper of cold pork and biscuits could be served and the others decided it was sensible not to wake her. Everything must be done to aid her recovery for precious time was passing and their supply of food was beginning to run low.

Sleep took a long time to come to Miss Mary that night. At last able to think clearly now the crisis was over, she could not believe she had suggested a sing song or playing a trivial game while her sister was precariously stuck on a dangerous cliff face. It was an extraordinary thing to do. She realised just how right Archie had been in saying how ill prepared they were to deal with such situations. It was a lesson she would learn from, and in future, she would think a lot harder before she acted.

It was during this enforced rest that the sisters found themselves drawing closer to their normally taciturn guide. Previously all their efforts had gone into concentrating on their walking rather than in making conversation, and in the evenings they had been too tired to do anything other than sleep.

The next day, with their early morning ritual of preparing to depart in abeyance, they lay sprawled around the fire whose still red embers had been blown into flame by Bernard. His previous shyness overcome, he began to remember more of the English phrases he had picked up from the allied airmen he had escorted during the war. This effort, together with the twins' schoolgirl French and their well thumbed dictionary, brought about a marked improvement in their communication. Progress was often frustratingly slow, but they had plenty of time on their hands and as he gained confidence, Bernard reminisced at length on how, as a youth, he had roamed the vast tracts of countryside that surrounded his village.

While he was on this subject, Miss Mary saw her chance to ask a question that had been on her mind for a long time. Did he think he would ever find a trace of Sophie's husband Anton? At this, Miss Alice, who had been dozing at her sister's side, managed to raise herself on her elbows and look alert. She too was eager to know the answer. The old man glanced briefly at their expectant faces before carefully positioning another log of wood on the fire. He seemed to be turning over in his mind how best to reply and the delay only served to further whet their growing curiosity. Arriving finally at a decision, he came straight to the point. He would tell them the truth, but they had to promise to keep their mouths shut. Anton, he declared almost in a whisper, was alive. The sisters' mouths dropped open in unison at this revelation as they strained their ears to catch every single word.

It proved to be a distressing tale of matrimonial deceit which spinsters though they were, left them absolutely horrified. The fugitive husband, it transpired, had been conducting an affair with Edith, a blonde woman who ran a dress shop in Brianco. When she delivered an ultimatum that he choose between her and his wife, he decided to leave Sophie. Bernard said it made sense from a man's point of view because the mistress was at least fifteen years younger, with an exceptional figure, as well as having a good income.

Miss Mary and Miss Alice shifted restlessly at this remark but felt it was not their place to make any comment. Both were intently thinking the same thing. What was Bernard doing searching for Anton if he knew exactly where he was? And equally as important, why was he taking Sophie's money for doing it?

As if divining their thoughts, the old man gave the fire a poke and asked them a question in return. What would they have done in his place? It had been a devilishly tricky problem knowing what to do and he had thought long and hard before taking the action he did. The plain fact was, that either way, Sophie had lost her husband. Was it better that she should grieve honourably for Anton believing him to be lying somewhere in the arms of nature? Or for her to live in the knowledge that he was barely twenty miles away nestling in those of another woman? If she was not told, she was unlikely to ever discover his deception for Anton had made a concerted effort to change his appearance, dying his hair and shaving off his moustache.

Remembering the photographs of him in Sophie's house, Miss Mary for a split second found herself comparing it unfavourably to Le Grand Bandit's before Bernard continued. He was happy to say the money he had been paid for the searches and had reluctantly accepted, was being kept firmly in the family. He had spent every franc of it drinking with Anton.

Miss Mary closed her eyes in disbelief at this but immediately opened them again as an image of the two men laughing uproariously in a bar floated into view. She felt she should have imagined them conversing earnestly and wondered which of the visions was the truer. She knew enough of the world to realise that taking money under false pretences could be construed as fraud, but Bernard was unrepentant. The purpose for having regular meetings with Anton, he emphasised, was to give him news of his wife and daughter for whom he was still extremely fond.

Reflecting later, both she and her sister admitted they could see the logic in his reasoning but the whole affair made them feel uncomfortable and they wished they had been left in blissful ignorance. The Rectory may have been responsible for giving them what now seemed to be an incredibly humdrum life, but at least it had protected them from men.

If there was one thing the twins had learnt since leaving home it was to be resilient. And Miss Alice was to show this trait in abundance when they set off again on the third morning. She had woken on the day after her rescue describing herself as stiff as an ironing board and forty eight hours later, did not feel there had been much improvement. Yet she could see in the faces of her companions an increasing desire to get moving and so putting on a cheerful front she did not feel, she pronounced herself fit enough to walk.

Under the watchful eye of her sister, she began almost at a hobble, but as had happened so often before, once she got her blood circulating properly, the effort became easier. Even so, the distance they made that day was shorter than usual and the stops more frequent. Yet there were to be no more alarms as they continued steadily upwards and at long last found themselves approaching the border where they would cross over into Italy.

Bernard, who had been so talkative during their enforced break, had resumed his taciturn manner and if anything, was even more reserved in his dealings with the two sisters. He had spent the second day of their rest by making the long journey back to replace the rope and it seemed to have taken a lot out of him. For the first time, they noticed the tiredness in his eyes and a more pronounced slope to his shoulders. They had forgotten he was nearly a decade older than they were and despite his vast experience and remarkable fitness, the Alps were testing his iron resolve to the limit.

On their final night together with a roaring fire going, he attempted to be more cheerful but it did not last long. The three travellers were so exhausted that sleep overtook them with barely a word being spoken.

The light from the dancing flames flickered over their motionless bodies seen only by a passing fox which crept forward unobserved to share some of the warmth.

Miss Mary was the first to wake the following morning and a quick glance at her watch revealed they had slept much longer than usual. Normally she and her sister would be roused by the comings and goings of Bernard as he collected belongings and prepared a frugal breakfast. She could see him across the still smouldering fire, cosily wrapped in his groundsheet under the lee of a jutting rock. She smiled fondly at the shock of white hair sticking out at the top. She had to admit he deserved a rare lie in after all he had done for them.

She dozed off again and woke a little time later to find him still in the same position. A wave of unease crept over her. Crawling stiffly from her sleeping bag and stepping over her still slumbering twin, she approached the old man. Bending down, she touched him lightly on a protruding shoulder but there was no response. A sharper jab with her finger also brought forth no answer.

Kneeling beside him, she peered into his face which was half hidden in the coat which he used for a pillow. It seemed to have an unnaturally pallid colour. With an effort, she pushed him from his side onto his back, instinctively knowing as she did so that he was dead. Feeling as if she was someone else, she pulled away the groundsheet and taking his wrist, searched for a pulse. She could not find any and his flesh was hard to the touch. It was as if rigor mortis was setting in and she realised he had probably died as soon as he had laid down the previous evening. She remembered with a stab of guilt her irritation at her called 'Goodnight' receiving no reply. He might already have been gone by then.

Regaining her feet, she went over and woke her sister who with an incredulous expression, seemed to have difficulty in believing the news. She in turn went across to check Bernard's pulse for herself but almost immediately let his wrist drop untouched. One look at the lifeless, wax like face made it all too clear the pair of them really were now on their own.

They retired a short distance from the body and spoke in a whisper about what to do next as if afraid that he would hear them. Their overwhelming feeling was one of helplessness at the loss of their guide mixed with one of guilt that their quest had been the cause of his death. Yet they quickly decided they could absolve themselves of any blame in that matter. After all, he had been looking for an excuse to retrace his wartime steps and at no stage had he shown even the slightest sign that he regretted his decision. And also, as their initial shock began to wear off a little, so did their feeling of being unable to cope without his help. They firmly reminded themselves they had overcome numerous setbacks since leaving The Rectory and there was no reason why they could not get out of this unfortunate situation with equal success.

Bernard had promised to travel with them a short distance into Italy to show them their route which now they would have to find on their own. But in one stroke of luck, the previous evening he had pointed out a triangular shaped rock on a ridge above them where the airmen used to rest before continuing on the next stage of their journey. This would at least give the sisters a correct starting point and with the way being downhill from then on, they would have a better view of how the land lay.

Having worked out their next step, they began to feel slightly better but then came the sudden realisation of what to do with Bernard's body. They could not take it with them and they could not just leave it where it was to be torn apart by wild animals. They owed far too much to the old man not to treat his remains with proper respect.

The only answer was to bury him or cover him with rocks until they could report his death and his relatives, if he had any, could decide what to do about reclaiming the body. Bernard had never spoken about his family and they, for their part, had seen no reason to inquire. Yet despite themselves, they could not help a flicker of irritation over the time and energy that would be required to carry out this necessary task. The route they had taken was a deliberately isolated one and border guards who might have helped, rarely patrolled the area.

Deciding on how to proceed, they realised that using rocks would be the easiest option. Yet the size needed would make them heavy to lift and carry and there was a real danger the sisters could damage their backs. They had become highly sensitive over what their aging frames could stand, for even a fairly minor injury shrugged off by anyone living a normal life at home, could bring their mission to an abrupt end.

Conscious that valuable time was passing, they spread out to try to find a patch of ground soft enough in the granite like terrain. The only implement they had to aid their bare hands when it came to digging, was Bernard's sharp but small spade. To their dismay, several promising looking places had to be discarded when the top surface, which was easy to remove, gave way to impenetrable rock. In the end, they found a spot higher up near the triangular shaped boulder which after careful probing, appeared to offer sufficient depth to cover a corpse of Bernard's size.

Without a thought of breakfast, the pair set about excavating down to the required level. Taking turns with the spade, they found it hot and tiring work and bruising to the hands. Some places were easier to dig than others and the roughly fashioned grave began to resemble a series of holes. But gradually as the hours passed, the stubborn pieces were eased out to leave a narrow and shallow trough.

The sisters thankfully sank to their knees with their exhausting labour over but there was to be little respite for they had somehow to get Bernard up quite a steep slope. It was a distance of about fifty metres and having regained a little energy, they first tried to carry him by his arms and legs but he kept sagging in the middle. Having made scant progress, and with their own arms aching, they came to the conclusion they would have to drag him.

Looking at the obstacle strewn path, they felt it would be best to pull him by his feet as his hands would be less likely to snare themselves on anything barring their way. Each therefore took a boot firmly in their grasp as they set about trying to synchronise their tugging movements. It seemed Bernard did not want to go anywhere and they ruefully learnt exactly what the term 'dead weight' meant.

Yet after much huffing and puffing, they finally reached the top of the ridge where they paused to rearrange his crumpled clothing before pushing him into what they hoped to be only a temporary home. To their great relief, it was just wide and deep enough although after filling it in, they had to reinforce the rather thin top layer with a coating of smaller stones.

Stepping back to admire their handiwork, they did not think they could have done any better in the circumstances. However their task was not yet over. There was still the problem of giving their late guide a proper Christian send off. They had no idea what religion he belonged to, if any, but suspected that being

French, he was a Catholic. And that faith, in the words of Miss Alice, was one that left them completely stumped. There was only one thing for it, there would have to be a compromise.

Standing facing each other, one each side of the grave with their heads bowed and hands clasped, they recited the Lord's Prayer. It had been part of the service of their local church every Sunday for as long as they could remember. Yet to Miss Mary, it seemed to have much more resonance when recited in such a wild and desolate place with the wind whisking their words up into the sky. Finishing their brief ceremony, they stuck the spade into the ground at the head of the mound to clearly mark the spot for any party sent to recover the body. Beside it, wrapped in his waterproof cape, they placed his belongings which they would be unable to carry.

With the sun slipping away towards the west, and the air becoming noticeably cooler, the sisters felt it was far too late to start walking that day even if they had had the energy to do so. They suddenly realised how famished they were, having had nothing to eat since their macabre discovery more than ten hours before. Munching hungrily on apples, cheese and chocolate, they decided against the effort of trying to light a fire.

They intended to make the earliest possible start in the morning and if the cold drove them from their sleeping bags then so be it. They turned in as soon as their supper was over but neither found it easy to get to sleep after the harrowing events of the day. Bernard may have been lying lifeless in his lonely resting place, but every time they closed their eyes his wax like face became their constant companion.

Chapter 9

The last of the stars were still visible in a clear sky when, numb with sleep and cold, the twins departed from what had become a depressingly melancholy place. Taking care to pass the triangular rock on their right as instructed, they began to make their way down a gentle incline into what was now Italy. The pair moved cautiously in the half light, discussing in low tones how shocking it was that fate could without the slightest warning, take somebody away. Bernard's death had reminded them of their own father who in an instant, had fallen dead at their feet. And what of their mother? Had she already succumbed to a similar end which was entirely likely at her advanced age? It was a sobering thought that their quest might have been a complete waste of time before they had even stepped out of The Rectory's front door.

The sun arrived, bringing warmth to their backs to cheer them up a little, but each continued secretly to worry about their own prospects of survival. Especially with the demands they were making on their far from young bodies. If Bernard's heart could suddenly give out then so could theirs. It was a most nerve- racking prospect.

The old man had explained the Italian side of the mountain range was more populated higher up and after they had been going two or three hours, the odd isolated building came into view although none lay directly in their path. Their destination that day was to be the first large village which their late guide had estimated they should arrive at shortly before nightfall if they were able to keep to the right path. Although in places travelling downhill could be as difficult as going up, in the main they believed it should make for much quicker progress.

One valuable lesson they had learnt since leaving home was that mental strength was as important as physical strength, and with a concerted effort, they managed to banish the all pervading feeling of gloom that had hung in the air like a dark cloud. They found the going was not only downhill but also free of the numerous enforced detours which had previously plagued their efforts to maintain momentum. This allowed the twins to abandoned their set timetable of resting every half hour, and to keep walking until they felt they had to stop. Without Bernard's wise counsel they occasionally overdid this, but by mid afternoon felt the still invisible village to be drawing them on.

The shadows had begun to lengthen alarmingly when they at last reached its outskirts. It was Miss Alice who was the first to glimpse the profusion of drab orange roofs that suddenly appeared to their left in the valley below. The vegetation was becoming thicker and the rutted track they were following turned into a dirt road as it wound its way through a belt of trees now in early summer leaf. The pair emerged into the fading sunlight to find themselves at the top of what seemed to be the main street although it was narrow and paved with uneven cobblestones. Bernard had warned there was no hotel, but that there was a police station where they could go for advice on where to stay. Little had any of them known at the time he said this, what would be their most important reason for visiting it.

Acutely aware of what they must look like, they paused to dig out their hand mirrors for a brief inspection of their weather beaten features. It was a ritual they had adopted when preparing to meet somebody, in a bid to look a little less like tramps. It resulted in barely more than pushing a stray hair back into place and became increasingly ineffective as the drawbacks of living an outdoor life took their toll. Yet they felt better for doing it and it reminded them of the way they had powdered their noses in more civilised circumstances when at home.

The village proved to be larger than it had seemed from above, but it did not take more than a few minutes for them to come across the station which they identified from the blue sign over its entrance. It was a square, solid one storey building, set a little apart from the others on a patch of spare ground. A few scattered plants gave the impression somebody had made a rudimentary effort to produce a garden, but overall the effect was spartan. The door was open and the twins on entering a reception hall, were confronted by a counter containing a large bell. Without further ado, Miss Mary banged it smartly and they waited to see what response it would bring. There did not appear to be any, and Miss Alice was about to have her turn when a side door opened and a uniformed figure materialised before them.

Capitan Morello as he was to introduce himself, was in his late thirties, of medium height, with dark hair and brown eyes which Miss Mary could not help noticing were less luminous than those of Le Grande Bandit's. Seeing his inquiring look, she announced in a voice that could not hide a certain amount of pride that they were from England and had just walked over the Alps. He held up his hand before she could go further. "It is fortunate you have come straight to me," he said in a pleasant voice. "I am the only one in this small community who can speak any English. I have been posted to many tourist resorts but now I am confined to this lonely spot. My wife's mother who lives with us, has bad lungs and needs mountain air. Come into my office," he added, leading them into the cramped room he had emerged from. "I can see you have a story to tell."

And what a story, thought Miss Alice as she and Miss Mary settled in chairs opposite his cluttered desk. She left the talking to her sister adding emphatic nods of confirmation at important parts. Capitan Morello listened in silence, occasionally jotting something down on a notepad in front of him with a silver pencil.

When she had finished, he picked up a telephone and spoke rapidly into it. Getting the reply he evidently wanted, he replaced the receiver. "That was my wife Gina," he explained. "I have told her to expect guests tonight. It will be rather a squeeze but I am sure you will find it superior to your previous sleeping arrangements." He held up his hand again to stem the sisters' flow of thanks. There now had to be an official procedure and he would like to inspect their passports. The twins handed them over and watched intently as he studied the contents. These proved to be in order and the officer could see no difficulties presented by their arrival although the route they had chosen was more often used by smugglers and fugitives from justice.

There was however, he went on to add in a more sobering tone, a problem with the body. It was of course obvious the cause of death had been the old man's heart giving out, but there would still have to be an autopsy. The question was, he continued, drumming his fingers on his desk, who should carry it out? The French authorities or the Italian? This completely unexpected dilemma perplexed the twins. Miss Mary respectfully pointed out that if he was buried in French soil then surely it must be the French ones. Capitan Morello's reply to this was to ask if they were certain that he was. He knew the area around the triangular rock well, and the border between the two countries there was far from a straight line and could deviate sharply in any direction. The corpse could well be under Italian soil or, and at this point he laid down his pencil and crossed himself, partly positioned in both countries. This would create enormous complications.

Seeing the shocked expressions of its two undertakers, who were struggling to comprehend what the outcome of their innocent search for a piece of soft ground might be, he hastened to reassure them. He had only been talking about a possibility. As a policeman, he had to consider every conceivable eventuality and be prepared in case it was the one that happened. Tomorrow he would take two of his men to discover the exact position of their late guide and make sure he was sufficiently buried until the time came for him to be recovered. They could not bring the body back because they had nowhere to store it. Had the sisters but known, a hut had been recently built within a few hundred metres of their final stopping place which he and his companions would use. Knowing the paths well, he expected his investigation to take less than twenty four hours and he would leave at first light.

Rising to his feet to signal their initial interview was over, he set about locking up the station while the twins waited outside on the front steps. Darkness was falling and the stars which had seen them on their way at the start of their long day, were reappearing one by one. Setting his cap firmly on his head and with his keys jangling in his pocket, Capitan Morello led the twins down an adjoining street where a house at the far end was ablaze with welcoming lights. Gina, who was hovering on the doorstep, proved to be a buxom woman, slightly shorter than her husband, with round placid features and a ready smile. Wiping her hands on her apron, she greeted her guests in a torrent of Italian while Capitan Morello busied himself pouring four large glasses of red wine from a newly opened bottle.

Soon the three were seated at a bare wooden table watching Gina spooning heaps of spaghetti onto their plates before ordering them to help themselves to mounds of grated cheese. There was no sign of Gina's mother but the sisters noticed a tray being taken to a nearby room whose door remained closed. They had not realised quite how hungry they were, and they eagerly accepted a second helping and a further glass of wine.

Aided by the warmth of their surroundings, nature was soon to do its work, and the twins, struggling to finish their final mouthfuls, were desperately trying to keep their eyes open. Seeing their predicament, Gina wasted no time in leading them to their quarters at the back of the house in which stood a large double bed covered by a counterpane fittingly patterned with thick bunches of grapes. Miss Mary just managed to switch the light off before they both fell upon it fully clothed and in an instant were fast asleep.

The following morning was well advanced before either stirred. It was Miss Alice who awoke first to be greeted by something repeatedly thumping the top of her head. Opening her eyes with difficulty, she began to wonder where she was until the previous evening's events gradually came into focus. Forcing herself up on one elbow, she nudged her sister who produced a muffled groan from the depths of her pillow. Finally making herself coherent, she too admitted to a distressing pounding sensation in her brain before lapsing into a strained silence. Although they had had an occasional drink before on their journey, they ruefully came to realise that for the first time they were suffering from what was known as a hangover. It was not a pleasant experience and, like many others before them, they vowed they would never touch another drop.

Sufficiently revived after a painful encounter with cold water, they emerged into the kitchen to find their hostess cheerfully scrubbing pans in an overcrowded sink. Gina's glass had been equally as full as theirs when she toasted their epic mountain walk during supper, but the alcohol appeared to have no effect on her. Despite being well aware they could not understand a single word, she kept up a constant chatter as she served them with several cups of much needed coffee along with fresh rolls and home made plum jam. The sisters in reply smiled and nodded at regular intervals, occasionally saying something in English to which, in turn, Gina would respond with a smile and a nod.

This maintained a most convivial atmosphere although her guests' thoughts were continually straying up the mountainside to where her husband was in the act of checking the position of Bernard's grave. They were profoundly grateful for not having to walk anywhere that day but just twiddling their thumbs meant they had nothing to help them take their minds off what could prove to be a most serious situation.

There was still no sign of Gina's mother, but when they moved outside to take advantage of the sunshine, they caught a glimpse through a window of an old woman sitting in a chair with a black shawl draped around her hunched shoulders. With the house being at the end of a row, its garden ran down to a small wood which was full of squirrels. Perched on a rickety but comfortable bench, the twins watched these jump with such ease from one branch to another, enviously wishing that they too had the same agility. Feeling at one with their surroundings brought a welcome surge of contentment but this did not last long as once again, worrying thoughts at what had been happening high above them came crowding in.

It was shortly after three o'clock that Capitan Morello finally reappeared. Summoned from their idyll, the sisters were told all business had to be conducted in his office and with pounding hearts followed him back to the police station. They waited impatiently on the front steps as he set about selecting the right key to gain entrance. At last they were able to reclaim their chairs opposite him and watch as he removed his cap and placed it neatly in a side drawer of his desk.

Putting his hands together and looking at the pair evenly over his fingertips he broke into a smile. He had made the most careful calculations he assured them, using a detailed map of the frontier and was happy to say their late guide was definitely buried a good three metres inside France. And he was quite safe from prowling predators, for he and his men had laid another layer of stones on top of the grave.

The air of relief that enveloped the room at this news was almost tangible. It was as if a great weight had been lifted from the minds of the twins. Yet they could not help thinking it would have been better if he had kept all his 'conceivable possibilities' to himself before launching his investigation. It was something of course they did not care to mention as the officer went on to explain what would happen next. He would contact the authorities in Brianco as it was the nearest regional centre, and provide them with details of the deceased's death and location of the body. He would also supply the address of the woman they had stayed with in the village in case she could give information which might help to trace any relatives.

He then leant forward and adopted a more serious tone. The normal procedure would be for the sisters to remain where they were until the body had been recovered and the autopsy carried out. However this could take a considerable time and he realised the urgency of their mission. So when he had taken down their statements, photocopied their passports and noted their own home address in England, he was prepared to let them continue on their journey. Before they could say anything at this most welcome turn of events, he added that he had further good news.

One of his men was going on a training course in La Spezia in the Liguria region and would be pleased to have their company on the long drive. The coastal resort and military centre was several hundred kilometres to the south and was a huge step in the right direction. They would find Fabio delightful company despite the language barrier. He was a lively, sociable fellow and a leading member of the village choir.

To catch their lift, the twins would have to leave very early in the morning so they immediately set about putting their statements down on paper. Reliving their relentless struggle, they marvelled how they had got so far and were overwhelmed once more with gratitude for the wonderful support Bernard had given them. When everything was completed to Capitan Morello's satisfaction, he invited them to supper and to spend a second night under his roof.

Fortified by a perfectly roasted chicken accompanied by just a single glass of wine, the sisters retired early and lay awake in the darkness knowing how fortunate they were to be able to continue their journey in a few hours. They knew little of officialdom in their own country having lived such a sheltered existence, but doubted if they would have been allowed to go anywhere until the cause of death had been established.

The pair were up and packed, and with mercifully clear heads, by the time they heard the sound of an approaching car. Its driver, looming out of the pre-dawn gloom, was in his forties with a completely bald head and a girth of impressive width. Unable to speak a word of English, Fabio enveloped his passengers in a huge hug before planting what they considered to be over effusive kisses on both cheeks. His exuberant greeting completed, he wasted no time in stowing their rucksacks in the boot of his white saloon and the twins, sensing his desire to be gone, said their goodbyes only too glad to avoid a lingering departure. They owed a lot to the couple bidding them farewell on the doorstep but with their reserved British character, found it hard to properly show their feelings.

Fabio saw them safely into the back seat before squeezing himself with some difficulty behind the wheel. He appeared to fight momentarily with the gear stick before the car moved off with a screech, giving the sisters barely time for a final wave to Capitan Morello and his wife.

Despite the early morning chill, Fabio wound down his window and drove with his elbow nonchalantly protruding out. He quickly reached a good speed and did not slow down at any crossroads leaving the sisters to think it must be the only car in the village. Their new companion remained silent apart from the odd tuneless whistle, but greeted the arrival of the sun with a burst of operatic fervour. Filling his lungs, he roared out aria after aria, scarcely drawing breath in between. His startled passengers found the sound alarming enough, but this turned to unremitting fear when he regularly took both hands off the wheel for what seemed an eternity to conduct an invisible orchestra.

As the road wound its way downwards, clinging to the side of the mountain for long precipitous stretches, Miss Alice, daring a glance out of the window, could see no safety barriers. There was nothing to prevent them from careering off the pot holed surface which was still unnervingly wet from overnight dew. With her own experience of being catapulted into the void so horrifyingly recent, she could only close her eyes and search for a suitable prayer. Irritatingly, for some reason, the only one that popped into her mind was For Those In Peril On The Sea, which somehow seemed inappropriate. Like falling over a cliff, she was discovering that travelling in a careering vehicle could be an effective remedy for ending even the most stubborn case of constipation.

Fabio, oblivious to the terror he was inflicting on those behind him, appeared to revel in the challenge the hairpin bends presented and saw no necessity to slacken his speed. The sisters, certain their last moment was coming, took to holding hands and keeping their eyes tightly shut every time a blind corner approached. The car seemed to veer round these rather than be driven, with its driver righting its path on the far side with a sudden wrench of the wheel. The pair were just thinking how unfair it would be to lose their lives so haphazardly after all they had achieved, when the land suddenly started to flatten out. And, as if on cue, the road began to move inland and took up a straight line between softly undulating countryside.

They were still travelling at speed, but the tension inside the sisters burst like a pricked balloon. It was as if they had got off one of those fairground roller coaster rides they remembered going on as children. The rest of the journey was uneventful as the endless kilometres took their toll of Fabio's exuberance and he lapsed into long periods of silence which were warmly welcomed by his passengers.

He dropped them in the centre of La Spezia in the late afternoon and they were sincere in their appreciation of how far he had taken them, despite their earlier alarms which, with their safe arrival, now seemed rather fanciful. Capitan Morello had refused to take any payment for their stay and after they had changed the last of their French money into Italian currency at the bank, they had enough left for overnight accommodation and a little food.

The twins could see no point in going further that evening and so began scouring the narrow streets in the old part of town in the hope of finding a cheap hotel. They discovered what they were looking for almost on the waterfront. It had few rooms and theirs on the top floor appeared to have been converted from an attic but was clean and tidy. They had dithered between that establishment and another across the street and were shortly to discover how this choice would have an extraordinary effect on their future.

Coming down for breakfast the following morning, they found only one other occupant of the cramped dining room. He was a small man with neatly parted ginger hair and bright, inquisitive eyes. Sitting at an adjoining table, the twins set about their omelettes with the concentration of those who are not sure exactly when their next meal will arrive. They took no notice of the other diner, but when they were starting on their coffee and discussing the most recent of their adventures, they sensed that he was beginning to stare at them.

In the end, Miss Mary could not resist looking over her shoulder and met his unwavering gaze. He reddened and looked away but then with a scraping of his chair, got to his feet. Placing himself in front of them, he apologised in a rather high pitched voice for his intrusive behaviour, but said he had become increasingly fascinated by what he was hearing. Introducing himself as Alfonso Ponti, he explained he was a teacher of English at a high school where his class were at that moment exploring the Iliad. From snatches of their conversation, he understood that they were undertaking what seemed to be an extraordinary journey. Obviously it was not quite in the same category as the Greek Odyssey, but there were

140

similarities and it was an interesting intertwining of the difficulties of travelling in both ancient and modern times.

He paused for a moment as if choosing his words carefully. He was, he finally went on, always looking for ways of stimulating his pupils and wondered if these two brave Englishwomen might be prepared to give a talk about their own experiences. It would help bring adventure off the dusty pages of history books and add a certain freshness to the subject.

The twins were, as usual, in tune with each other without even having to exchange glances. Such a comparison was completely ridiculous, but to hear of their efforts spoken of in such glowing terms produced a nice feeling and they began to warm to this rather intensive little man. Their natural reserve melted further when he said he knew enough about English accents to realise that theirs was of the best kind and would be of great advantage for his class to listen to. Miss Mary, who had taken a tentative sip of her coffee which was growing cold, put her cup down and asked. "Where is this school?"

Mr Ponti could not keep the eagerness out of his voice. "This is where I can help you," he replied. "It is in Terni, an ancient university town a hundred kilometres north of Rome. It is very much in the direction in which you wish to go and I can take you there. I have been attending an educational conference in La Spezia and will be leaving as soon as I have paid my hotel bill so you will have to make a quick decision."

This time the sisters looked at each other, and with a degree of hesitation for they had only just met this man. Seeing the uncertainty in their eyes, the teacher pressed his case further. "I have a two bed roomed flat almost opposite the school gates. You can stay there tonight and give your lecture in the morning. Then you can go on your way or stay a second night if you wish."

The prospect of speaking in public for the first time in their lives was a daunting one, but both knew in their hearts they could not afford to turn down such an offer. Conserving energy by travelling in the easiest possible way had to be their number one priority. After a nod of confirmation from her sister, Miss Alice said they would be ready to depart in fifteen minutes.

Squeezing themselves into the back of their new companion's compact green Fiat, they reflected over the recent change in their fortunes. After what the army would call long stretches of foot slogging, and hour upon hour of relentless pedalling, they were being given two lifts over a considerable distance in a row. As Miss Alice said. You never knew what was coming round the corner, although they both agreed it was not a phrase they would use for a while after enduring those horrifying hairpin bends. But at least the route that now lay ahead avoided most of the high ground and neither Alfonso, as he had asked them to call him, or his vehicle seemed to be associated with excessive speed.

And so it proved to be, with their driver keeping strictly to the inside lane where parts of the roads became a motorway. Human nature being what it is, the twins could not help beginning to feel restless at the pace they were moving for which they felt the best description would be 'chugging.' It was not that they wanted Fabio back behind the wheel, certainly not, but felt time was being wasted. Sensing a certain amount of fidgeting going on behind him, Alfonso explained their journey was being carried out to an exact schedule. Before they left, he had telephoned his cleaning lady and asked her to put a beef casserole in the oven at gas mark six at noon. At the speed they were travelling, they should arrive there exactly when it was ready.

And, he added, he did like to eat as soon as he got home.

At this, the sisters settled back in their seats mollified at the thought of a decent supper, but the hours that stretched ahead were not to be wasted. Mr Ponti wanted to hear a full account of their experiences and so help them to form the lecture they were now honour bound to give to his students. It was not easy, he warned, without practice to keep the attention of sixteen year-old minds. As the pair described each seemingly impossible obstacle they had managed to overcome, he listed the virtues they had displayed. These impressively included courage, determination, defiance, resolution, patience, resilience and enterprise. Although too polite to say so, the sisters could have added terror, anguish, despair, a tremendous desire to go to the loo as well as great hosts of butterflies in the stomach. Looking at themselves for the first time from another's point of view as it were, they felt a twinge of embarrassment at such a description. All they had done, as they had all their lives at The Rectory, was to get on with things.

Alfonso's carefully worked out calculations proved to be absolutely correct despite the travellers being caught in an unexpected traffic jam on the outskirts of Terni which led to much exasperated drumming of his fingers on the steering wheel. Leading the sisters up a short flight of steps to his second floor flat, he opened the door with a flourish and ushered them inside. A tantalising smell floated down the hallway to bewitch their nostrils and to remind them of how awfully hungry they were. Their host, with the air of a man on a mission, deftly lifted the lid of the casserole and after a thoughtful inspection of its contents with his nose, added a measured splash of red wine and a sprinkling of herbs before announcing dinner would very shortly be served.

It just gave his visitors time to settle into their room which, like the rest of the bachelor accommodation, lacked the slightest feminine touch. There were only the bare necessities of a large bed, a small chest of draws, a table and a chair with a single mirror hanging from a piece of string to enliven the empty walls. But to the sisters, it was another roof over their heads and with a decent meal to look forward to, they felt quite content. The only frisson of anxiety which occasionally entered their minds was the thought of the talk they would have to give tomorrow. Alfonso had alerted the school from La Spezia as to what was going to happen, and it had been arranged that it would take place immediately after the morning assembly which would give the twins less time to be nervous.

Supper, with the addition of a crusty loaf of fresh white bread left by the cleaning lady, proved to be every bit as appetising as the aroma that had preceded it. The sisters each had a second helping much to the delight of Mr Ponti who was clearly enjoying having such unusual guests. Once three very clean plates were lying piled in the sink, the replete diners again went through the sort of things the twins should concentrate on to prevent youthful minds from wandering. This only left them wishing they had had more time to prepare. By ten o'clock they were in bed with Alfonso promising to rouse them sharply at seven with a reviving cup of his special coffee containing just the right dash of cream. It was, he assured them, the absolutely perfect start to a day but led his guests to silently fear what the rest of it was going to be like.

The sisters, who were becoming used to sleeping in constantly changing surroundings, awoke feeling more refreshed than they had dared hope, and with their host's coffee and buttered rolls inside them, followed him with fluttering hearts across the road and through the school gates. Roll call was just finishing and soon the large, low building in front of them echoed to the clatter of hundreds of scurrying feet as the students dispersed to their various classrooms. The one the now increasingly nervous pair of lecturers were due to appear in was at the far end overlooking a play area and by the time they entered it, they found nearly forty expectant faces turned as one upon them. In the front was a small platform containing three straight backed chairs which the trio took with Alfonso seating himself between them.

During their earlier deliberations, they had discussed the need to speak slowly and clearly and that if there were unusual words which caused difficulty, he would intervene and translate them into Italian. That way it was hoped the pupils, who were in their fourth year of learning the English language, would be able to quite easily follow the events and to have their questions ready at the end.

The sisters had reluctantly promised to give the fullest account of their experiences after the teacher had gently pointed out that an adventure was only an adventure when things had gone wrong and there were daunting obstacles to overcome. If they were to just stick to the smoothest and less embarrassing parts of their journey it would not seem like one at all.

The pair had agreed that where one of them had taken a prominent role in any incident, then she would do the talking. And so it was that Miss Alice stepped forward to reveal the grave dilemma facing her when nature called with the greatest of urgency as she was confronted by a host of strange Frenchmen. The solution she chose, and described most candidly, resulted in an outburst of hastily smothered giggling followed by a wave of sympathy that seemed to engulf the room. Even at their young age, her listeners knew what it was like to be caught out like that at exactly the wrong moment.

From then on, they hung on to every word whichever of the two sisters were speaking. Miss Mary's dramatic encounter with Le Grand Bandit brought loud gasps of astonishment from the pupils who by then thought nothing more could have surprised them. The outlaw sounded so charming that it was no wonder that Signorina Mary, as she had been introduced, had made such a mistake. After all, it was something that anybody could do, as one or two of the girls murmured to themselves rather too wistfully.

By the time it came for Miss Alice to bounce her way over the cliff, it was as if the whole class had gone with her, such was the look of concern etched in their faces. She could not help making the precipice a little steeper and the rocks a little sharper, but then as she said to herself, that was only to artistically highlight the predicament she was in.

The twins had started almost with a stutter, but buoyed by their undeniably rapturous reception, were now in full flow. So much so, that Mr Ponti began to glance concernedly at his watch wondering if they would finish before the bell rang for the mid morning break. But then it was time for questions which the speakers, with their growing confidence, dealt with easily apart from one which caught Miss Mary unawares and gave her a very nasty moment. Although the pair had honoured their promise to give a complete account of their journey, she had not thought it necessary to reveal that Le Grand Bandit's grateful thanks for his rescue had included a most passionate kiss.

One girl, who appeared to be unusually mature for her years, asked if Signorina Mary still harboured a soft spot for the burglar who seemed to be much more attractive and exciting than the householder or, for that matter, the police inspector. Aware that her sister's inquiring gaze was fixed upon her as well as those of the whole class, she closed her eyes as she sought to conjure up an answer. This was a mistake, for immediately a familiar vision with its luminous brown ones above a luxurious moustache, came unnervingly into view. Bringing herself together with a start, Miss Mary realised she was blushing as she fought to control her rather flustered tone. No, she replied, she hadn't got a soft spot for him because she had been firmly brought up to know right from wrong. Yet she admitted that with the world being what it was, some wrong things were more appealing than some right things. But in her case, due to her upbringing, she would never let herself be affected by anything that was not morally and lawfully correct. She later consoled herself that this was only the smallest of white lies and had to be said to avoid setting a bad example to those of a younger generation.

Mr Ponti, who looked as if he could hardly believe how well everything had gone, was effusive in his congratulations and led a prolonged round of applause from his animated class which left the sisters, in spite of themselves, glowing with pride. They were dimly aware however that most, if not all, of their audience, would consider seventy to be a most decrepit old age, and looked on them as at best eccentric, or at worst, slightly mad. Yet Miss Alice knew that the pupils were not alone. On the day they had left The Rectory, she remembered the sight of Archie putting his finger to his temple and telling them they had taken complete leave of their senses. She wished he could see them now as they were given a guided tour of the school and its grounds by a beaming Alfonso who declared that afterwards they were to have lunch with the headmaster and senior members of his staff.

This took place in a side room just off the main dining hall with large windows which gave a commanding view of the well laid out sports pitches. Also well laid out, was a long table seating ten, covered by a spotless white tablecloth gleaming with silver cutlery and exquisitely shaped wine glasses. Mr Ponti explained the teachers did not normally dine in such splendour, but the visit of the sisters and the resounding success of their lecture, called for a special celebration. It was not normal to drink at lunch time he hastily added, but a small amount of the local grape could be sipped in responsible fashion as it was to be an afternoon of games with no lessons.

A salad, liberally adorned with olives, accompanied by thick slices of ham from the bone and hunks of crusty bread, were consumed in a most leisurely fashion. So it was, that before the diners had finished, clusters of young boys began to appear outside to prepare for a football match. A lone harassed figure in white shorts, forlornly clutching a whistle, was trying with little success to form the milling players into two teams with one position appearing to cause a particular problem. Alfonso, continuing in his role as interpreter, explained that what was happening was sadly a regular occurrence. Two of the more junior groups were playing each other and nobody on either side was prepared to go in goal. They were in fact, firmly refusing to do so. They all wanted to be among the attackers so they would get the chance to score goals and cover themselves with glory.

Miss Mary and Miss Alice later discussed endlessly how on earth they could have allowed each other to be part of what happened next and the calamity that followed. Whether it was the wine of which they had drunk two full glasses despite their promise to themselves never to over indulge. Or whether it was due to their elated mood which made anything seem possible they did not know. It was most likely a combination of both plus a desire to take any chance to repay their hosts for such wonderful and unexpected hospitality.

It was Miss Mary, taking another sip of her wine who raised the subject first with Alfonso. As they were such figureheads, she and her sister would each go and stand in one of the goals to set a good example. Mr Ponti, who was about to eat the last strawberry of his desert, put down his spoon and gave her a startled look as she urged him to translate. After a moment of startled hesitation, he broke into a smile of relief. Of course, he realised, it was one of those jokes that the English were so fond of making.

His version of their offer brought an outburst of merriment from their fellow diners including several loud guffaws but there was one serious face and it belonged to the headmaster. He was a tall, rather angular man with an air of authority befitting his role but he did not lack a sense of enterprise. Standing up, he leaned across the table and solemnly shook the hands of the two sisters who were sitting opposite him. He would take up their marvellous suggestion, he told Mr Ponti. They would indeed get the opportunity to go in goal.

This declaration brought gasps of surprise from his astounded companions, but he added, only before the match actually started. Their presence between the posts would create a wave of shame among the boys to cause a good number of volunteers for the position to step forward. When this plan was translated for them, Miss Mary and Miss Alice were already beginning to have second thoughts but realised with alarm that it was

149

too late to back out.

Without waiting another minute, the headmaster now in charge of what everybody agreed was a devilishly clever scheme, led the lunch party out onto the playing field. He waited until the sisters, almost unobserved, had reached their respective places at each end of the pitch before clapping his hands to gain the attention of the young footballers. Then, in ringing tones, he explained how the English ladies who were old enough to be their grandmothers, or, in some cases, great grandmothers, had volunteered to take the goalkeeper's jersey. They had felt sorry for such immature youths of the great country of Italy who were too selfish or cowardly to take up the most unpopular position.

The response, with his years of experience as a teacher, was just as he had expected. A forest of arms shot skywards with their owners making strenuous efforts to catch his eye so they could be the ones to be chosen. But one boy, who had wandered into the centre circle with the ball, gave it a mighty kick in his exuberance to get rid of it and join the crowd. It flew through the air and struck the crossbar under which Miss Alice was standing, before rebounding to strike her forcefully in the back, sending her sprawling. She uttered a loud, agonised cry and lay still with one of her legs stuck at a strange angle.

The sports master, who had been trying to marshal the players into two teams, was first on the scene. He knelt beside her, first feeling her pulse, and then putting his hand to her forehead. She was breathing steadily and appeared to be more stunned than unconscious but continued to make no movement or sound. As others began to arrive, he ordered somebody to immediately go to telephone for an ambulance. His eyes strayed to her extended limb and his expression became even more troubled. He had seen his share of sporting injuries and feared the prostrate figure before him could well have suffered a broken bone.

Instructing the growing crowd around them to step back and allow Miss Alice some air, he said that on no account was she to be moved until the ambulance arrived. Miss Mary, who had hurried from the other end of the pitch, pushed her way through the onlookers with her heart in her mouth. Ignoring the sport master's plea to give the still motionless victim space, she dropped to her knees beside her sister and anxiously called her name. At first there was no response, but when she repeated it, Miss Alice's eyes flickered open and after a moment she began to gaze around her in bewilderment.

"The ball knocked you over," explained Miss Mary in a voice of overwhelming tenderness as she took her sister's hand. "I don't think you are badly hurt but you must stay where you are until the ambulance is here. They will take you to hospital for a precautionary examination just to make sure you are all right." Miss Mary then became aware of a distraught Mr Ponti crouching down beside her. He profusely apologised on behalf of the headmaster, who stood, full of contrition behind them, more importantly of himself, and also the school for what had happened. It had been the most unfortunate of accidents and he was entirely to blame for organising their visit which had led to this dreadful situation.

Despite her anguish, Miss Mary was quick to make it clear that in no way did she hold the poor man responsible for their predicament and she felt certain that if she was able to, her sister would say the same. They had both learned since leaving The Rectory that anything could happen in this world to anybody at any time. At that moment she was handed a blanket and she busied herself gently tucking it around Miss Alice to keep her warm. Her sister seemed to look paler under her sunburnt exterior and she had closed her eyes once again. Miss Mary did not want to press her further, realising that she should do all she could to help her conserve her strength.

The crowd had now been dispersed apart from Mr Ponti and the head master who stood looking uncomfortably on from a few metres distant. The interpreter had explained the hospital was not far off and that help should appear within fifteen minutes. His predication proved accurate for barely had the time passed when the sound of a wailing siren heralded the arrival of the ambulance.

Directed by the frantically waving arms of Alfonso, it bumped its way across the turf to stop beside Miss Alice. Speaking in low tones he conveyed to its two occupants the urgency of the situation and the possible injury of their elderly patient. Seeing there was no immediate need to administer first aid, the men unloaded a stretcher and prepared to put Miss Alice on it. They first with the utmost care, straightened her leg but this brought a startled yelp of pain from the patient which sent a wave of terror through Miss Mary. What, she wondered, would happen to their mission if her sister would be unable to walk?

She forced herself to push this question from her mind as she watched her being manoeuvred into the back of the vehicle. Then after giving the forlorn figure of the headmaster a smile of reassurance which she did not feel in the slightest, she clambered in to sit alongside her twin together with Alfonso whose translating would be needed at the hospital.

The short journey through a series of quiet suburban streets was conducted in complete silence. Miss Alice showed no desire to communicate anything to anyone and her companions, who were fearful of disturbing her, could themselves think of nothing to say. The young doctor on duty at the accident and emergency department could not speak a word of English and Mr Ponti who had escorted the party through the swing doors into a brightly lit ante room, explained that Miss Alice had suffered a nasty fall, landing awkwardly on her leg.

As the two conversed, Miss Mary standing at his elbow, was surprised to see the normally composed Alfonso almost stuttering at one stage and then several times glancing uneasily out of the window. When Miss Alice was whisked away for a series of x-rays and the pair were left momentarily alone, he revealed exactly what had happened. The doctor, who had treated several elderly foreign tourists in the past, liked to guess what had befallen his patients. Had she, he'd asked, slipped on a wet floor while getting out of a hotel bath? Or stumbled on the steps of her coach while embarking or disembarking? Or, as so often happened, tripped on an uneven pavement she was not used to?

Having replied in the negative to each of these inquiries, he'd then been forced to reveal she'd been hit by a well struck football while standing in goal. This information had caused the doctor to sharply raise his eyebrows and a lengthy silence had followed while he digested it. He'd then asked Alonso to repeat once more Miss Alice's age and on receiving confirmation that she was seventy, had sorrowfully and slowly shaken his head.

The return of Miss Alice, pushed along by a young blonde haired nurse clutching a batch of negatives, meant the moment of truth was fast approaching for the sisters. The doctor, who had begun to look at his patient in a quizzical fashion, took them from her escort with an air of expectancy and held the first up to the light. Tracing a faint line slowly with his finger, he announced in grave tones that just as he'd expected, Miss Alice's lower left leg had sustained a hairline fracture of the tibia.

Having been told the twins were travelling on foot through Italy, he warned she would not be able to go anywhere for at least five to six weeks. Or maybe even longer. During that time she would have to lie flat on her back with the damaged leg in a raised position. What he was saying, he declared with considerable emphasis, was she would have to remain exactly where she was. With Italy's reciprocal health agreement with Britain, her treatment would be free and she would be well cared for. After her enforced rest, she should be able to walk again but only for short distances and certainly not for any length of time. There must be no strenuous activity of any kind for the heavy fall had taken its toll of her body which was no longer so resilient at her advanced age. His sincere advice, which, he added, he very much hoped would be taken, was that as soon as she could be moved, they should give up their journey and immediately fly home.

Mr Ponti appeared to be very close to tears as he translated what he knew only too well would be the most crushing blow the sisters could ever imagine receiving. Miss Alice, who had now begun to take an interest in things again, exchanged a defiant glance mixed with a strong hint of bravado, with her twin. Once more, both knew what the other was thinking but Miss Mary, seeing the condition of her sister lying prostrate on the trolley, realised this was not the time to raise what would be seen as irresponsible objections. Indeed Miss Alice, despite an irrational resolve inside her to keep going, was well aware she was incapable of standing up, let alone putting one foot in front of the other.

Chapter 10

The hospital, a series of low level white buildings on the outskirts of town, had extensive gardens backing onto a river with a wood running down to its banks on the far side. Miss Alice was given a single room overlooking a clear stretch of water which was home to several species of duck and a family of swans. Marooned on her iron bedstead with her leg held aloft by a pulley, she realised that, if she had to be held prisoner anywhere, there were a lot worse places. And most importantly of all for her morale and well being, her sister was close at hand. In all their long lives together, they had never been apart from each other for more than the odd day or two.

There was at first a great dilemma of what Miss Mary was going to do with herself while her twin underwent her extended convalescence. Mr Ponti offered to let her stay at his flat but that would have meant having to travel quite a distance to see her sister every day. In the end, after a suggestion from the head master which was almost a plea, the hospital, which had ample accommodation, agreed to find room for her as well. Provided with a bed in the nurses' quarters, Miss Mary was happy to earn her keep by being responsible for arranging flower displays in the wards. Selecting bunches from the colourful array of blooms in the garden, she could not help thinking of their own back at home and hoping Archie was carrying out their long list of instructions to ensure their survival until she and her sister returned.

Her occupation proved to be a busy one, but it still left plenty of time for her to sit beside her twin and discuss what the future was going to hold for them. The first thing they decided was they had no intention of changing their minds and going home once Miss Alice was on her feet again. They just could not contemplate such a move after coming so far and enduring so much in the search for their mother. Even after all these years their last glimpse of her remained clear in their memories. Her final wave at the garden gate, dressed in light brown corduroy trousers, a dark blue shirt and a pale yellow scarf adorning her slender neck which accentuated her high cheek bones of which she was so proud.

But at the same time they reluctantly realised that because of Miss Alice's ever more vulnerable condition, certain things would have to change. They would, for example, not be able to walk, or for that matter, cycle, if the chance arose again for any sort of distance. Instead they would have to travel by public transport all the way to Cairo and they were only too well aware this was going to cost money. And it was money which at that moment they certainly did not have. They would soon be forced to ask Archie to start wiring extra sums to help tide them over.

Whether the funds they had left him would be enough, and whether Shane was faithfully keeping up the repayments of the amount he had stolen from them, they simply did not know. But if the worst came to the worst, they had various items of furniture they had never really liked which they could instruct the caretaker to sell to raise more capital.

Despite the panoramic view from her bed through refreshingly wide windows, Miss Alice feared boredom would be her biggest enemy as she lay hour after endless hour, flat on her back. Miss Mary had scoured the well stocked hospital library for any books in the English language but had only managed to come up with a single volume. And it had left her wondering how on earth a 1946 edition of a History Of Boiler Making In Lancashire had come to find its way onto its shelves.

Yet Miss Alice was pleasantly surprised to discover she had been far from forgotten by members of Mr Ponti's English class. She began to receive a steady stream of visitors, many of whom arrived armed with pictures they had produced depicting various incidents from her and her sister's adventure.

These were put up in neat rows on the bare white walls to bring a welcome vivid splash of colour to the otherwise austere room. She particularly liked one of her clinging perilously to the bush that grew out of the sheer mountainside during her terrifying ordeal in the Alps. Her heroic look of determination summoned up by the artist, was just how she imagined she had looked although of course she had not been able to see herself. There was also an extraordinary lurid scene of Miss Mary freeing Le Grande Bandit from the cupboard which the misguided rescuer dismissed in a most offhand manner, saying they had not been anything like so close together.

Also a constant visitor was Alfonso who continued in his much needed role of interpreter as there was virtually nobody else at the hospital who could speak anything but Italian. Yet that was to change after three weeks when Miss Alice was able to get around on a pair of crutches and spend some time in the day room among other patients in a similar state of recovery.

Sitting near the door one day trying to work out the headline of a local newspaper she was glancing idly at, she heard shuffling footsteps coming down the corridor behind her. A bulky figure dressed in a pair of flamboyant, wide striped, red and blue pyjamas which were obviously not hospital issue, came into view. Drawing his open white flannelled dressing gown closer around him, he stationed himself by the window that looked directly down over the main gates.

157

It was a position, Miss Alice was soon to notice, that he regularly adopted when away from his ward. He was short with an almost square face and immensely broad shoulders that towered above his tapered body which gave him a sort of triangular shape. He had a mane of thick brown hair that looked as if it could have been dyed, and well manicured hands that were spoilt by his rather stubby fingers adorned with a set of gold rings. Yet she was to find his somewhat menacing air was easily softened by his wide, captivating smile and an infectious, if sometimes overloud laugh.

Discovering at their second encounter that she spoke English, he introduced himself as Luigi Capello in a heavy accent which had a distinct American twang. He had, he explained, spent several years in Brooklyn living with a cousin who ran a popular restaurant on Fourth Street. He had waited at table but when Angelo's two children had been old enough to take over, he had decided to come home. Hospital food was OK he confided, keeping to the subject, but nothing could beat Angelo's wife's macaroni with her tomato sauce made to her own special recipe. Nothing nowhere, he declared, could beat it.

Although Miss Alice had little interest in America or the various forms of macaroni for that matter, she felt attracted to her new companion partly because he was the only one around her who could speak English, and partly because she had never met anybody remotely like him before. He, for his part, had never come across what even he could see was a high class English broad of advanced years embarked on a most bizarre mission. Like all Italians, he greatly esteemed his mother, but as he gradually learned what Miss Alice and her sister had gone through, he could only shake his bullet like head in wonder.

With both of the patients having plenty of time on

their hands, their conversations grew longer and longer as their unlikely friendship blossomed. Yet Miss Alice, who was easily led into recounting her past life, began to realise that she was doing most of the talking. It was not as if Luigi was being exactly evasive but he was adept at steering subjects in different directions and rarely volunteered anything without being asked. There was for example, the large bandage around his waist which occasionally peeped out from under his pyjama top. It was obviously the cause of him being in hospital but what kind of illness he had, or, if an injury, how it had been sustained, he never revealed.

Finally, one wet afternoon when he was in his usual position by the window, staring down at the front gates, she could contain herself no longer and asked him directly. He did not reply immediately and only the sound of the rain beating in waves against the glass broke an expectant silence. Then, holding his hands up as if in surrender and with a reddening face, he explained he would have told her earlier but he was embarrassed because he had been such a fool. He had been out hunting a herd of wild boar in the forest with his friends and while climbing over a slippery fence, had accidentally caused his gun to go off. He had shot himself in the thigh and while no vital organs had been hit, he had lost a considerable amount of blood and with the wound not being clear cut, it was taking time to heal. Answering her next question before she had time to ask it, he admitted he should be spending more time resting in bed as the doctors had advised, but he had always been a restless guy and preferred the view from the day room.

Emboldened by the success of her inquiry, she asked another that had long been on her mind. Why was he always watching the hospital entrance she wanted to know. Was it because he was expecting somebody to come and see him? Again he did not reply straight away, first giving a vague shrug of his massive shoulders. He did not, he explained, like being cooped up and beyond the gates was freedom. And yes, he did have friends. She might remember he had gone hunting with them and there was always the possibility that they might decide to pay him a visit.

It was not long before their gradually improving state of health enabled the pair to take short walks in the grounds and they made an odd couple moving slowly along the paved paths: she being tall with a precise step, and he, being nearly a foot shorter, propelling himself along with almost a seaman's rolling gait.

The doctor's prediction that it would be six weeks before Miss Alice could travel again turned out to be an over cautious one, for after just five he announced she was fit enough to leave. But even then, he warned, she must continue to rest it as much as possible however keen she was to make up for lost time.

On her last evening having not seen Luigi in the day room, she went to his ward to say goodbye. She found him reclining on his bed immersed in a magazine with a scantily clad girl on the cover which he hastily put under his pillow as she approached. Hearing she was about to leave, he expressed surprise at her sudden departure and said she was a wonderful broad and he would greatly miss her company.

Discussing her route earlier with him, she had revealed her next destination would be Bari and he now inquired if that was still her plan. When she replied it was, he asked if she would kindly do him a favour. He had a sister who lived on the outskirts of the city by the coast. He had brought her a present from America but was likely to be detained at the hospital for another two weeks and then had business to attend to locally.

Would Miss Alice deliver it for him as she was going in that direction? He had thought of posting it but it was valuable and you could not always trust the Italian mail service.

Seeing a hint of uncertainty cross her face, he assured her he was not asking her to take anything illegal. The parcel contained a pair of pearl earrings he had bought on Fifth Avenue in New York. Obviously it would be more appropriate if a gift like that could be delivered in person.

Miss Alice did not know why, but she felt uncomfortable about taking part in such an arrangement. She wished she could discuss it with her sister because they always decided things together. But it would look silly if she told Luigi she could not make up her own mind. After all, she was hardly an immature teenager. Hearing no refusal, Luigi removed a package from his bedside locker and placed it in front of him. Miss Alice thought it looked rather large to contain earrings but realised they must be in a presentation box. Although still feeling uneasy, she could think of no reason to say no. Luigi had been a good friend and there was enough room in her rucksack for it and she would not be going out of her way.

Yes, she said, finally making up her mind, of course she would do it. And it would be most interesting to meet his sister. This produced one of Luigi's widest smiles and declaring his gratitude, he thrust his present firmly into her hands. She was surprised to find it wrapped in pig skin rather than paper and tied tightly with string with the address clearly written so she would have no difficulty in finding its new owner. Luigi once more rifled in his locker and his stubby fingers emerged clutching a large white envelope. Announcing that one good turn deserved another, he opened it and drew out a thick wad of new lira notes.

Miss Alice told her sister later she felt her eyes popping out of her head as she watched him with practiced ease peel a good number off the top and pass them over to her. The money, he said, was for their first class rail tickets to Bari, two nights in a good hotel there, and taxi fares to and from his sister's house. Putting a finger to his lips to halt her startled protest, he explained he was a rich man and could easily afford to meet any expenses they might incur while delivering the earrings.

Miss Alice, again discussing it with her sister afterwards, said she had been in a real quandary over what to do before commonsense for once prevailed. The money which appeared to be much more than would be required, was a godsend and she had immediately accepted it. She was only glad she had agreed to take the present before this had been offered. If it had been used as an incentive, she would have had an enormous tussle with her conscience. What the outcome would have been, she did not let herself dwell upon.

Miss Mary backed her decision to deliver the earrings but on meeting Luigi when visiting her sister, she had found him attractive but rather untrustworthy and she too wondered what was really inside the package. But their overriding priority was to reach Cairo and this unexpected major boost to their finances could never have been turned down. They both hoped they were keeping their much cherished integrity intact, but were finding this laudable aim much more difficult to achieve now they were away from The Rectory and living in the real world.

There was quite a party assembled to see Miss Alice and Miss Mary off at the station. They had been driven there by Alfonso accompanied by the headmaster while several of the pupils who had faithfully kept up their visits to the hospital, had followed by bus. Luigi, who was forced to stay behind, had escorted them to the car and three times wished them a safe journey. Miss Alice realised this was a common enough saying, but to her, he seemed to emphasise the word 'safe' and she wondered if she was becoming paranoid over her role of messenger.

The twins were relieved that Luigi's condition prevented him from coming to the station for they decided to buy, rather furtively, the cheapest tickets instead of travelling first class and for that matter, to stay in a guest house in Bari rather than a hotel and to travel by bus to his sister's house. That way they would save quite a sum of money and they could see nothing wrong in doing this as long as the earrings, if that is what they were, were safely delivered.

Installed in their carriage with their goodbyes said and their rucksacks stored on the rack over their heads, they once more turned their thoughts to the parcel. They had several times wondered if they should open it, and now being alone, this was the first chance they had without the risk of being interrupted. Yet they agreed it was something they just could not bring themselves to do. It was not their property and they were well aware Luigi had trusted them with this mission because of who they were. Two incorruptible English ladies of a certain class. And so it remained untouched, nestling in Miss Alice's luggage as the train pulled slowly out of the station and headed south.

Watching the buildings give way to the countryside as it started to pick up speed, they felt a surge of excitement mixed with relief that they were finally on their way again.

Chapter 11

Nobody among the patients liked their food more than Luigi despite the fact he could no longer have the special macaroni cooked by Angelo's wife. So when that evening he was not lying on his bed eagerly eyeing the approaching trolley as was his custom, eyebrows were raised. He had last been seen strolling along the path towards the river after saying his heartfelt goodbyes to the sisters in the car park. A nurse was despatched to search the grounds and going that way first, did not take long to find him. He was sitting down, leaning against a tree with the dying rays of the sun on his face a few feet from the water's edge.

Drawing nearer, she saw his arms had been thrust behind him and his hands tied behind the trunk with a rope restraining him around his middle. One eye was closed and the other appeared to be missing. His nose was crushed and stuck at a strange angle. A bone which seemed to be a rib, was protruding from his side and there was a large pool of encrusted blood which had stained his pyjama bottoms below his waist in a wide arc. The practiced eye of the onlooker, who found herself desperately gripping a nearby branch to stop her knees from buckling, could tell there was no need to feel his pulse to confirm he was dead. And that in his condition, he would surely have been very glad that he was.

Chapter 12

The single storey house, hidden discreetly behind tall evergreen hedges, stood alone just off the main highway that led to Terni. Thick velvet curtains of a deep red had been drawn across the dining room windows to keep out the last hour of remaining daylight. Inside, the air was thick with tobacco smoke which swirled in visible swathes in the beam of the single light which shone down upon six figures grouped around a solid oak table. At its head, Don Carleri, a bear of a man with beady, ferret like eyes, looked round at the assembled faces and gave a faint smile. "So he squealed good huh?"

A small man with a bull neck and flattened ears, stretched out a hand and carefully squashed the end of a cigarette into the ashtray in front of him. "Yes boss, he squealed good."

"But did he squeal true?"

"Yes boss," replied Beppe with reassuring conviction. "He squealed true."

His listener, whose smile had become a thoughtful frown, still appeared to be unsure if this was the case. "He has already double crossed us once. We should have killed him the first time." He turned to a taller man with hunched shoulders who was sitting on his right. "And what do you think Aldo? That he gave our pure heroin to two ancient English broads to deliver to his associates? I think there's a joke here."

"No boss," came the unwavering reply. "I was with Beppe. Luigi squealed good. He knew we were after him and that the women were the only chance he had of getting rid of it. He figured we'd leave him alone and go after them. Which we now can do. Luigi gave us the address they are going to."

Don Carleri tapped his fingers impatiently on the

silver cigarette case by his side and remained doubtful. "But is it the right one? Luigi was cunning as a fox as well as a fool." His brow furrowed as he came to a decision. "We need to make sure of the address. So we don't take the heroin off the broads. We follow them and then deal with everyone together."

Beppe's eyes gleamed. "We leave no witnesses eh?"

"Beppe, Beppe," replied Don Carleri sadly. "You don't rub out English broads. Think of the repercussions. The police would come down on us like a ton of marble slabs."

"But we show them we are upset eh?"

Don Carleri raised his eyebrows. "Upset? No, we are angry, very very angry and everybody connected with this will be made to understand that." He glanced at the expensively jewelled watch with its thick silver band on his wrist. "Contact Fat Toni and Ricardo and tell them to meet the train. Then Beppe, you take six men and get down there as fast as you can to join them."

As the room cleared to the sound of scurrying feet, Don Carleri sat scowling with his chin in his hands. Two English broads old enough to be grandmothers. On his mother's life could it be true? Yet it had all been checked out. They had been at the hospital. Were they innocent messengers or had they been sent to collect the package? Well, it would not be long before he discovered the truth.

Chapter 13

Miss Alice and Miss Mary settled back in their seats. There was something extremely gratifying about watching the countryside flash by at high speed when you were not moving your limbs yourself. Luigi, for whatever the reason, had been wonderfully generous and they were determined to make the most of the situation while it lasted. The steady rhythm of the train clicking over the rails sent them gradually into a contented sleep.

The train pulled into Bari station under a cloudless sky. It was another boilingly hot day and the sisters, stiffly lifting their luggage down from the rack, left the comfort of their compartment with some reluctance and joined the milling crowd on the uninviting platform. The bus station, although not far away, proved difficult to find and twice the pair came close to losing their resolve to go by public transport and looked longingly towards the taxi rank with its row of patiently waiting drivers.

Yet with the ingrained prudence of frugal travellers they had now acquired, they shrank from spending money that could well be used on more important things that were certain to come. Finding the station's information desk, they showed the address on the parcel to the cheerful woman manning it and were directed to Stand Twelve where a study of its timetable revealed they had half an hour to wait.

There were no seats in its basic shelter, but mindful that Miss Alice should rest her leg whenever possible, they proceeded to sit on the pavement and lean their backs against it. It was a posture they would not have been seen dead adopting during any exhausting excursions from The Rectory. But they were no longer the shrinking violets they had once been in what now seemed a long, lost cosseted existence.

Surrounded by a jostling crowd, the twins had failed to notice two men in crumpled, black serge suits standing by the barrier when its passengers had emerged from the train and made their way through it. The tallish upright figures of two elderly women with greying hair, each with a well filled rucksack strapped to her back, had not been hard to spot and the waiting watchers, with a nod to each other, began to follow at a discreet distance.

Now the two rather sinister males, with their felt hats sporting wide bands, were sitting at a window table in the station's café which gave a good view of the Stand were Miss Mary and Miss Alice were patiently waiting. Their two observers were taciturn by nature with little to say whether to each other or anybody else. Yet in a surprised and somewhat mystified tone, Fat Toni could not help wondering aloud to his companion if there had been a mistake. Or maybe, he thought, somebody was playing a joke on them.

Ricardo, after cautionary glance at the next table where a young woman appeared to be staring aimlessly into space, said he agreed. One look told you that their quarry were not slick broads belonging to the mob. It was like you was staking out your own grandmother, he said. It was Fat Tony's turn to agree to that but, being faithful foot soldiers, an order was an order and so their unflinching gaze remained firmly on the unsuspecting sisters.

By the time the bus had pulled up and the twins had climbed awkwardly to their feet, a lengthening queue was beginning to form. Taking advantage of their position at its front, they managed to gain seats directly behind the driver who, after having his attention drawn to the address on the package, indicated he would alert them when their stop arrived.

Also getting to their feet, after seeing the two women disappearing on board, were Fat Toni and Ricardo. Hastily throwing a handful of coins on the table for their coffees, they stepped outside and looked around anxiously for the back up party they were expecting after their phone call to Don Carleri revealing the sisters' movements.

It was Ricardo who caught sight of Bebbe first, standing by the station's exit. Looking strained after his long drive south and in a white suit that seemed at least a size too small, he had seen the pair and was beckoning to them urgently with a podgy hand. Joining him, they eagerly identified the vehicle to follow before getting into the back of a black Mercedes parked by the curb with its engine idling. Its five occupants, invisible through the tinted windows, sat in silence until the bus emerged to enter the stream of slowly moving traffic. With a swing of the wheel, the driver edged the Mercedes out to fall in behind while parked fifty metres to the rear, another of similar appearance containing four shrouded figures, began to move in the same direction.

The sisters, blissfully unaware they were the cause of so much attention, started to discuss what Luigi's relative would be like. Miss Alice regretted her natural reticence that had prevented her from inquiring a little about his sister. She had not even bothered to confirm her name, taking it for granted the Tina Portello on the address must refer to her. Was she younger or older than her brother? Was she for that matter, married or single? And did she live alone or with her parents? As Miss Mary said, they did not want to know everything about her personal life, but it was disconcerting to find themselves delivering a mysterious parcel to somebody equally mysterious.

Yet whoever she was, they imagined her living in one of the neat suburban houses they were now passing which lay in never ending lines on either side of the road. At every stop they half rose in expectation that it would be theirs, but the driver, keeping his back firmly towards them, drove relentlessly on until the dwellings began to thin out and stretches of open scrubland began to appear. They had been travelling for over half an hour and, fearing they had been forgotten, were debating over whether to tap him on the shoulder when he pulled up by the side of a small rock face and indicated it was their turn to get out.

Alighting with relief into the fierce sunlight, their first impression was of a deserted landscape with no sign of habitation anywhere around them. Yet, adjusting their eyes to its glare, they eventually noticed a battered green mail box tied with wire to the top of a short iron post on the other side of the highway. From it, a rutted track covered in stones, led away through more scrubland before disappearing at some distance, into a grove of scattered olive trees.

When stepping down from the bus, the twins, busy fiddling with their rucksacks, had barely noticed the two black limousines which had overtaken them to vanish over the brow of a small hill which lay directly ahead. But once over it and hidden from view, these too had pulled up on the verge and Beppe, emerging from the front passenger seat of the leading car, made his way cautiously back to the summit. Crouching behind a bush, he extracted a pair of binoculars from their black leather case and proceeded to study the scene below.

It did not take him long to pick out the two women who stood, necks craned intently forward, beside the mail box. One of them, who held a package in her hand, appeared to be checking to see if the address on it matched the one scratched into the flaking paint. It seemed that it did, for after a moment's hesitation, the pair began to make their way slowly up the drive. Having discovered their intended destination at last, Beppe replaced the glasses with an air of satisfaction and flicking a particle of unwanted dirt from the knee of his spotless white suit, he returned to his companions.

The sisters plodded determinedly on in the searing heat, picking their way with difficulty along the uneven surface. Miss Alice in particular, was taking extreme care over her progress, only too conscious of what had happened to her the last time she had suffered a fall. Twice they stopped to rest leaning against a convenient boulder, dabbing their perspiring faces with the sodden rags which their constantly used handkerchiefs had become.

Eventually they reached the trees to find these to be much more widely spread than they had appeared from the road. The drive ran on through their gnarled and stunted trunks for a further hundred yards before ending at a solid two storey stone farmhouse with a roof of discoloured orange tiles. At least, that is what the twins presumed it to be, because there were several outbuildings including an enclosed yard with water troughs but there was no sight or sound of any animals. Nor for that matter, did the main dwelling show any signs of activity. Its windows in the front were heavily shuttered and it had an almost neglected air.

The sisters agreed in nervous undertones that it was hardly the place they had imagined to find Tina Portello living in. But having come this far, there was only one thing to do and that was to knock on the front door. This was made of a dark wood and seemed to be as solid as the rest of the house.

Miss Mary's knuckles had little effect when it came to alerting anybody who might be inside of their presence. So picking up a nearby stick, she gave it several sharp raps. The intruders, which is what they felt themselves to be, listened intently only to be greeted by a long uninterrupted silence. Miss Alice was just thinking that she ought to have a go as well, when they heard a scraping noise coming from somewhere level with their heads. The hinge of a deep set peephole they had failed to notice, had been pulled back and they were startled to see a rather yellowish eye staring at them.

"Hello, we're English," Miss Alice found herself calling out brightly as if the voice was not her own. "We've brought a present for Tina Portello."

The response was a guttural growl that sounded something like 'uno momento' and the hinge was snapped shut. The sisters exchanged perplexed glances at this latest development, but at least they could console themselves the place was inhabited as they waited to see what would happen next. This time they were not left in suspense for long. A series of rasping noises indicated bolts inside being drawn back: one on the top, one on the bottom and one in the middle. The door was pulled open to reveal a slim youth of around eighteen whose well groomed appearance with his neatly trimmed fair hair and perfectly tailored pink shirt and slacks, was greatly at odds with his all too obvious rustic surroundings.

"Yes," he said, noticing their surprised expressions. "I know I look out of place here." Holding out a languid, pale hand which the sisters tentatively shook in turn, he added, "I have come home from my university in Rome for a few days before I start my examinations. It is a fortunate coincidence that our visits coincide for nobody else here can speak your language. My father and his friends only converse in the local dialect which even when you know it, grates on your ears. Pedro, whose eye you saw appraising you, thought you were French, but as soon as I saw you I knew you could only be English."

"We are here because we have brought a present from Luigi for his sister," interrupted Miss Mary who feared a long introduction and wanted to get out of the sun which she could feel beating remorselessly down on her neck. "We met him in a hospital in Terni where my sister was recovering from a fractured leg, and he asked her to deliver it as he would have to remain there for some time after accidentally shooting himself while out hunting."

This was the signal for Miss Alice to delve into the rucksack at her feet and produce the package which she gratefully handed to the youth being happy to no longer be responsible for it. Turning it over slowly in his hands, Dino, caught sight of the address and gave a half smile before following it with an incredulous shake of the head. "Luigi is my uncle," he explained. "He is always the funny guy."

"What is funny?" asked Miss Mary with a frown.

"Luigi has no sister. Tina is the name of a pet dog we the Portello family used to have, but you have certainly come to the right place for this is for my father." He tapped it with a forefinger showing a neatly clipped nail and gazed intently at its messengers. "Do you know what is in it?"

"We were told expensive pearl earrings from Fifth Avenue in New York," replied Miss Mary who was beginning to feel increasingly uncomfortable.

"If only that was so," replied the youth. "No, it is pure heroin worth many, many thousands of liras. You have got yourself mixed up in something you should have kept out of."

When it came to making an understatement, thought Miss Alice, who felt herself going cold inside as he spoke, that had to be the best she had heard. "But we are innocent victims," she declared. "We had no reason to believe otherwise."

Dino looked at her quizzically. "You had no suspicions?"

Miss Alice frowned a second time and paused before replying. "Not really, only that he might have been expecting visitors it appeared he did not want to see. He spent a lot of time away from the ward watching the front gates."

Dino nodded sombrely. "I am sure by now you have realised my father is involved with the Mafia and that my uncle was bringing him a shipment of drugs. There was a dispute over payment with a rival organisation and he was shot during a heated confrontation. That is why he was in hospital and may have feared they would come after him again." It was now the speaker's turn to frown as his thoughts raced ahead of him. "I am surprised Luigi did not telephone to warn us that you were coming. I wonder if anything could have happened to him." Once more, he treated the twins to his sobering gaze. "Do you think you could have been followed?"

"Good Lord no," exclaimed Miss Mary. "Why would anybody want to do that?"

"Because if they were watching the hospital and knew of your association with my uncle, they might suspect that you had become his couriers."

"Well they didn't," declared Miss Alice. "I am absolutely certain we would have noticed if there had been anybody around us who was behaving suspiciously."

"That may be so, but you were not expecting that somebody might be, and they are very professional when it comes to the art of surveillance."

Despite their growing nervousness, the sisters

thought privately that Dino was becoming over dramatic in a typically Italian fashion as, like a dog with a bone, he would not leave the subject alone. "Think hard," he said ignoring their rather pained expressions. "Did anything at all odd stand out on your journey?"

It was Miss Alice who, after a moment or two, came up with the only thing she could think of. "There was not much traffic about," she said. "But as we were getting off the bus to walk up here, two large black limousines drove slowly past in close formation. We only caught a glimpse but imagined they were part of some sort of funeral cortege."

This information had an electrifying effect on their young listener. Stepping back over the threshold, he let loose a torrent of Italian into the darkened interior of the house. Almost immediately the twins heard the sound of somebody moving about on the roof above them followed by more activity by the side of the house where a man emerged to jump over the low wall of the yard before disappearing hurriedly into the trees in the direction of the highway.

Dino meanwhile had turned back to face his visitors. "It is important I make clear to you I am not a member of the Mafia and my father has accepted this. That is why I have kept you out here. I wanted you to return to your bus stop without becoming further involved but now it is no longer safe to let you go. That funeral cortege you saw will be carrying members of the mob my father is in dispute with who have followed you. I very much fear now for my uncle's safety."

With that, he ordered the pair to pick up their rucksacks and to come inside without delay. They did as they were told and waited in the hallway while he shut the door behind them and slid each of the bolts firmly home with a clang. Then the two thoroughly frightened English pensioners who once more were wondering why on earth they had ever left home, were led into a large kitchen with a stone flagged floor.

Despite the presence of four grave faced men in earnest discussion around a wooden table in the middle, the room had a strangely disused air. A large casserole dish stood beside an old fashioned iron stove but a long row of pots and pans hanging from a rail above it, did not look as if they had been used for a long time, and crockery lining the shelves in a glass fronted cupboard, appeared equally dusty and untouched.

Dino had not mentioned his mother and the sisters had not seen fit to ask about her, but they doubted if she was there for to their eyes there was a definite lack of a female presence. The youth was talking to his father who, after giving the package a cursory inspection, opened a cutlery drawer in front of him and wedged it at the back among the knives and forks. His unshaven face, shock of unruly silver hair and baggy corduroy trousers held up haphazardly by a thick leather belt, were in stark contrast to the almost foppish figure of his son.

Cesare, as he was introduced to the twins, stood up and shook each solemnly by the hand but said nothing before resuming his seat to continue conversing with the other three who had done little more than favour the newcomers with the briefest of glances.

Motioning the pair to take the two unoccupied chairs by the nearest of the two windows, Dino explained a council of war was taking place to decide on a course of action if the vehicles the sisters saw did contain members of the mob, and if they decided to approach the house. The answer to these questions were answered almost immediately when the man they had seen vaulting the wall of the yard appeared in the doorway breathing heavily and wearing a grim expression. Translating his hoarse and hurried account, Dino said he had seen a group of eight men walking slowly and openly up the drive and had noticed no attempt by them to fan out among the trees or take advantage of any cover.

This meant, he told the twins, there would be a parley before anything else would be allowed to happen. The Mafia always liked to try to settle things peacefully first. If they couldn't, they would then set out to kill everybody.

This last sentence was uttered in a facetious tone but it did little to improve the morale of his listeners with Miss Alice for one being on the point of tears. She had faithfully kept her promise to deliver safely what had turned out to be a most dangerous parcel for which she had not even received a perfunctory 'Thank you.' Instead it was as if she and her sister, far from being greeted with gratitude, were the most unwelcome of visitors. She was beginning to realise that they were being blamed for leading whatever rival gang it was to this hideaway and, now there was going to be trouble, they would undoubtedly be in the way.

A muffled shout from the roof announcing that Cesare's unwanted visitors had arrived and had business to discuss, broke into her troubled thoughts. Emphasising that she and her sister must remain exactly where they were, Dino followed his father out to the front door after carefully closing the kitchen one behind him. The twins were left alone apart from the last occupant of the table, a tall, heavily jowled man with a receding hairline and a brooding countenance.

Rising to his feet without a glance in their direction, he proceeded to open a cupboard set in the wall behind him and tentatively stroking his chin, appeared to be considering which of its contents to select. As he stooped to take a closer look, the shaken sisters saw over his shoulder, a two tier rack containing a variety of telescopic rifles each held in place by a short metal chain.

Having made up his mind, the now decisive figure deftly and quickly extracted six and laid them side by side on the table. Then he sorted through a lower compartment to bring out four hand guns along with several cartons of wax proof paper containing ammunition. Slowly and methodically, as if he had all the time in the world, he inspected each weapon in turn to make sure that it was ready for action. His calm, deliberate movements, reminded his onlookers of Dino's words that nothing would happen until every effort had been made to find a peaceful solution. This gave the pair a measure of comfort as they watched with a mixture of sheer disbelief and morbid fascination at what was taking place in front of them.

Ordered not to move, Miss Mary and Miss Alice could only wonder what progress, if any, was being made outside and the occasional sound of raised voices that reached their straining ears despite the thick walls, did not bode well for a successful outcome.

Nearly an hour had passed before Dino reappeared alone to report that the discussions so far had been mainly about the sisters and that he had a proposition to put to them which, for their sake, he very much hoped they would refuse. His father had declared that they were innocent couriers who had not known what they were carrying and Don Carleri's men, as they had revealed themselves to be, agreed this was so after keeping the pair under close surveillance. Therefore they were offering to ferry the sisters back to the centre of the city in one of their limousines so they would no longer be involved in what was clearly none of their business.

Dino said that his father had agreed to this and had

taken him aside to say they would be perfectly safe because if any harm came to two elderly English tourists, it would cause a blaze of unwelcome publicity for the mob. Yet his son had protested the mafia did not like to leave any witnesses to their operations and were well known for being experts at arranging fatal accidents when necessary.

After a heated argument, Cesare had relented and said he would allow the twins to make their own decision and Dino was now strongly urging them to refuse to leave with their pursuers. He added there was another possible solution that he would explain later, which he admitted was far less pleasant but very much safer.

The twins, who by now were feeling completely overwhelmed by events, could only nod their assent to his suggestion whereupon he asked in which direction they were heading. Miss Mary replied in a dull voice which betrayed her feeling of utter helplessness that they were making their way towards Greece. Apparently satisfied with this answer, Dino abruptly left the room and a short time afterwards they heard him make a telephone call from the hall.

Left on their own again except for their solitary taciturn companion who was inserting cartridges into one of the handguns, the mystified pair began to greatly fear what could be in store for them. Despite being in a state of constant apprehension, they began to feel pangs of hunger for they had not eaten all day and nobody had offered them any food. Miss Mary longingly eyed the casserole beside the stove but did not possess the nerve to go and see if there was anything in it.

Another hour had passed and dusk was approaching by the time Dino reappeared. Once again he was on his own and his sombre face warned the sisters that he was not bringing good news. He briefly explained that the besiegers were claiming part of the money exchanged for the heroin was in counterfeit bills which his father was vigorously denying. They were demanding compensation by nine o'clock in the morning or they would have to take matters into their own hands. They were at this moment surrounding the house while his father in response, was stationing his men inside at a variety of vantage points and would be arming them with the weapons now being made ready.

As if on cue, their brooding companion picked up two rifles and a box of cartridges and disappeared from view to hand them out. Seeing the look of fear in the sisters' eyes, Dino added that with luck they would be long gone before any violence erupted. If indeed it did. Therefore it was of the utmost importance that they got as much rest as possible. He hoped their chairs were not too uncomfortable for they had to stay where they were because it was the safest place in the house. He had to help his father over the next few hours but would look in on them from time to time. Whether he did or not the twins never discovered for the light was switched off and in the growing darkness they fell into a fitful sleep exhausted by the dramatic events of the day.

It seemed only five minutes later to Miss Mary that she was roused by Dino's hand being gently laid on her shoulder. Yet a glance at her watch showed that it was shortly after four o'clock. Nudging her sister awake, she noticed Cesare was also there. Dispensing with any pleasantries, his son told the pair to cover as much of their hair as they could with their head scarves and to tuck the bottom of their trousers into their socks.

The light had been turned on and feeling completely bemused, they did as they were told as the two men gripping an end of the table each, proceeded to drag it sideways. Then kneeling down, they levered up a flagstone with the help of a knife blade to reveal a cleverly hidden wooden trapdoor. It took several tugs on its heavy brass ring to lift it clear in a billowing cloud of dust.

The room was immediately filled with the most foul air which came seeping out in visible grey waves that had the twins groping frantically for their handkerchiefs. Waiting for their coughing and his own spluttering to subside in the fetid atmosphere, Dino explained the tunnel below had been built as an escape route but had not been used for more than fifty years. It ran for over a hundred metres before coming out into a hidden gully.

The sisters, who did not like closing the door behind them when in the darkened cellar at The Rectory, were prone to attacks of claustrophobia, but realised they were not being given a choice as to whether they wanted to go or not. Suddenly the thought of being driven back to the city in a limousine, however frightening their escort, was a wonderfully appealing idea compared with what lay ahead down such a terrifying black hole.

It was then they noticed that Dino was no longer the dapper figure who had greeted them on their arrival. He had changed into a pair of old blue jeans and a matching windcheater zipped up to the neck and even as he spoke in an attempt to lift their spirits, he was pulling a woollen hat down firmly over his ears.

There was, he emphasised, nothing for them to be afraid of. He would go first and clear any thicket of cobwebs that might be blocking their path. All the insects they might encounter were harmless apart from the odd scorpion which would scuttle out of the way on hearing any approaching footsteps. If there were any bats, he added, using the tunnel for a home, they would most likely still be outside on the wing at this hour. And as for rats, well none had ever been seen. Their little party, he emphasised, would have to move cautiously but if they managed to keep to a steady pace, the journey should not take more than a mere ten minutes.

He then ordered his fellow travellers to put on their rucksacks and checked there was nothing protruding from these and that they firmly rested in the middle of their backs. As soon as this was done, Cesare stepped forward with an outstretched hand and the twins shook it for the last time realising that in a hurried departure, they were being given no chance to have second thoughts.

A feeling of panic welled up in their throats as they watched Dino, a torch held tightly in his grasp, disappear into the darkened void about to devour them. After a moment's hesitation, Miss Mary began gingerly to descend the short flight of stone steps followed by Miss Alice who was keeping hard on her heels as if afraid of being left too far behind. No sooner had she reached the bottom than the welcome shaft of light vanished as the trap door was dropped back into place with a loud thud.

Now, whatever their terror, the sisters knew there could be no turning back. Dino was waiting a little distance from them and the beam from his torch, casting terrifying shadows, lit the way to his side. But from then on, he had to hold it out in front of him and they would be left in the pitch black to follow its evasive bobbing light. The tunnel was disconcertingly narrow and they often found themselves brushing up against the sides of its uneven walls. The roof too was barely high enough for them to stand erect, and they had to walk with their heads sunk on their chests to avoid snagging their scarves on parts of its jagged surface.

Dino's exhortations for them to keep as close to him

as possible were entirely unnecessary as they stumbled on as quickly as they could in his wake. The lack of air made breathing difficult and the uneven floor had to be negotiated with extreme care to avoid tripping. Long stretches of the way were damp, with water in some places running freely down the walls which again called for great caution as everything was slippery underfoot. Despite their strenuous efforts to keep up with the wavering light, the twins found themselves shivering with the all pervading cold which enveloped them in its icy grip as they plodded on far below ground.

Their escort tried to keep to his pledge of maintaining a steady pace, but several times had to stop to dislodge dangerous pieces of rock hanging loosely above his head and then to warn the sisters to step over the fallen bits. Unable to see anything other than the pin prick of light ahead, the pair could not prevent their imagination from running out of control. They continually heard the patter of rats' tiny feet scuttling past and regularly brushed themselves down to dislodge spiders although Dino kept declaring forcefully over his shoulder that his torch was picking out nothing.

After what seemed like an eternity, the air slowly became noticeably fresher as it wafted towards them and then the pitch black turned into a ghostly grey in which their hunched silhouettes at last became visible. The tunnel took a sharp turn to the right and then narrowed leaving a gap the sisters had to almost squeeze through as they emerged from the shadow of a small overhanging cliff that hid the entrance into a boulder strewn gully.

They immediately sank onto their knees with a feeling of tremendous relief, drinking in the wonderfully sweet and cool atmosphere. Dawn was beginning to break but the stars high above them were still shining brightly and to the grateful watchers, had never appeared more beautiful. Savouring their escape from the horrifying bowls of the earth, it took them several minutes to become aware that they were alone. There was no sign of Dino anywhere in the gloom and they realised he must have slipped away through the thicket of bushes that covered the entrance to the gully.

Not knowing how distant the farmhouse was, they felt unable to call out in case they alerted the men besieging it and their feeling of exhilaration quickly turned into one of nervous uncertainty. They had no idea where they were or in what direction they should be heading. It was Miss Alice who put into words what they were both bitterly thinking. They had been unceremoniously dumped because they had outlived their usefulness. It had been obvious from the start they had not been welcome despite the parcel they brought and had been treated accordingly.

It was at this point they thought they heard a whistle. It was low and short and barely audible. They stopped talking and strained their ears but it was not repeated and they put it down to the breeze which had begun to spring up. Finally coming to the decision that it made no sense to sit there doing nothing, they had just climbed to their feet when Dino emerged from the thicket in front of them. Putting a finger to his lips for silence, he waved them towards him before disappearing once more into the undergrowth.

The pair, suitably ashamed for having felt they were being abandoned, followed him, pushing their way through a forest of leaves to come out onto a wide open plain. Waiting for them, outlined against the brightening sky, was a tall figure sitting astride a pony that appeared almost too small for his bulk. He held the reins of two others of similar stature who stood patiently cropping the sparse grass on either side of him.

Dino, having received a nod of confirmation from the rider that he was ready, turned to the twins to say this would be their form of transport for the next stage of their journey. Time was of the essence he warned, for they had to be long gone before it was fully daybreak. He then reached into his windcheater pocket and withdrew a thick grey envelope which he proceeded to hold out to Miss Alice who remembering the problems caused by the last one, instinctively took a step backwards.

Producing a rare smile, Dino thrust it into her hands assuring her that it contained nothing whatsoever that was dangerous and did not need to be delivered because it was for them alone. Then answering her unspoken question, he said that no, he would not be going back into the tunnel. As he had explained earlier, he was having nothing to do with his father's business and would watch the outcome, whatever it was to be, from afar. Then after wishing the pair good luck, he shook each briefly by the hand before turning on his heel and striding off.

Their new companion had dismounted and on a closer inspection, they could see he was in his early fifties with a swarthy, heavily lined face crowned with a drooping moustache above a set of almost uniformly white teeth. Strands of black hair escaping from under his wide brimmed felt hat, ran down to the collar of his tightly fitting leather jacket. He looked each sister slowly up and down with grave eyes but said nothing before holding out the reins for them to take charge of their mounts. Neither had ridden for many years but they had been brought up with horses and had hunted with hounds regularly as teenagers so had no qualms about getting into the saddle again.

Miss Alice, conscious of her recently broken leg, led

her pony to a small mound from which she could climb aboard without putting undue strain on it. Miss Mary, opting to mount from where she was, had just put her foot in the stirrup when she felt herself suddenly being lifted up by an unwanted and certainly unasked for hand placed firmly on her bottom. What was it, she wondered crossly as she hit the saddle with a thump, about men with moustaches? And it was at that moment she knew for an absolute certainty that the camel driver who her mother had run off with, would have had one.

Their guide, who was now back on his own mount, glanced quickly to see that they were in control of theirs before setting off at a brisk walk. Their way led down through a wide, gently sloping valley, dotted with trees and clumps of bushes. There was no sign of any habitation although every now and then they would come across a pathway or beaten track.

They rode in single file behind the solitary figure who showed not the slightest sign of wishing to conduct any form of conversation with them and after initially seeing them mounted, had barely acknowledged their presence. The only sound to break the silence apart from the flight of an occasionally startled bird, was the rhythmic pounding of the ponies' hooves upon the hard, sun baked earth. Gradually the landscape changed to become more cultivated and this produced the first signs of life with one or two farm labourers visible in the distance as they set off to begin their backbreaking work in the fields.

It was fully daylight and the sisters had been travelling for well over an hour, when the first hint of sea air reached their nostrils. As if on cue, their leader, who had maintained a walking pace as if reluctant to test their unknown riding skills, broke into a steady trot. The twins began to wonder if they were being taken to a port with a ferry but their surroundings, which were becoming desolate again with large patches of scrub grass and rock, gave a distinctly different impression. The ground began to slope steeply and the party slowed to a walk once more as the ponies had to pick their way down carefully being given a free rein by their riders.

The sisters could now actually taste the salt in the tangy breeze which meant the sea must be close. But how close they did not know, for its presence continued to be hidden from view. At the bottom of the small hill they had negotiated, the terrain evened out again and they began to follow a long line of windswept trees whose deformed limbs hung low over the pathway. At the end of these they came out onto a patch of clear land and to their right they saw far below them a tiny isolated cove hemmed in on three sides by a continuous sheer cliff face. Swaying gently to and fro, just off the small sandy beach sheltered from the elements, lay a motor launch whose sole occupant they could just pick out.

The only way down was by a narrow precipitous path cut into the rock which was entirely unsuitable for ponies and these, after the party had dismounted, were tethered to the lower branches of the nearest tree. Then, once more led by their morose guide, the sisters began their nerve-racking descent. At the sight of the figures gingerly making their way high above him, the boat's occupant brought its engine into life and edging it as close to the beach as he could without grounding it, he dropped anchor and leapt ashore.

As the twins finally reached the bottom, thanking God for their safe deliverance, they noticed they were going to be in the hands of a youth so young, he looked as if he should be at school. Dressed in a white singlet and dark blue knee length shorts, he had a mop of black hair that reached almost to his slender but wiry shoulders. His conversation with their guide, although conducted in serious tones, lasted barely a minute before he was waving the twins urgently towards the boat. Speed as usual, the pair ruefully realised, was of the essence which they had to admit, was the way they liked to travel as long as they were given the chance to catch their breath.

Doing as they were told, they took off their boots and waded through a short stretch of shallow water to clamber on board. Looking back, they could see their former guide was already a third of the way up the path on his return journey without so much as giving a glance over his shoulder.

The youth, who looked to be no more than fifteen, having retrieved the anchor, gave them a fleeting smile as he steered the launch out into open water. Yet otherwise he showed no more inclination to communicate with them than had their previous escort. It seemed, as Miss Alice whispered to her sister, that having delivered their parcel, they were now being treated like a pair of parcels themselves. So where were they going they wondered as, seated in the prow, they felt the spray springing up to splash their faces as they began to breast increasingly larger waves. Were they being taken down the coast of Italy, or out towards Greece which lay somewhere over the distant horizon? That after all, was where they had told Dino they were heading although there was no reason why he should be responsible for getting them anywhere near that far.

Yet their sturdily build launch with its single sail backed up by a powerful engine, was capable of making such a voyage despite it only having an open deck. They attempted to put the question to the youth who obviously could speak no English but appeared not even to be bothered to listen, instead busying himself with checking his navigational aids. But it was one that was quickly answered when Miss Alice remembered the envelope that Dino had pressed upon her.

Extracting it from a pocket of her rucksack, she slit it carefully open with one of her few fingernails that was still unbroken, to discover that it contained a thick wad of drachmas. Looking at the Greek currency, the sisters who had been greatly upset by the aloofness of Cesare and his men, began to understand that in the fashion of their kind, they might just be returning one favour for another. And if they needed confirmation of this, it came from another beckoning motion from their young companion. Reaching his end of the boat, they found a large open locker stocked with all kinds of food. There was fresh salad consisting of lettuce, cucumber and huge round tomatoes, cold chicken and ham, three kinds of cheese, a long, flattened loaf of bread, fruit, and a square sticky cake with thick icing. Also, tucked away at the back was one bottle of rose and another of medium dry white wine.

Suddenly with a pang of guilt, the twins began to see Cesare in an even better light. He was no longer the cold, uncaring figure they had thought him to be who did not know how to treat his guests. No, he had been far too preoccupied with defending his farmhouse from his enemies to find time to look after their welfare. Now they were free, he had been in a position to do so and had shown true Italian hospitality.

Finding knives and plates in a side drawer, they set about filling their desperately empty stomachs for the first time in three long days. Gone were the genteel manners they had always displayed at The Rectory as they literally fell upon the feast before them, completely oblivious to the bemused gaze of the watching youth. Nor was the wine forgotten with Miss Alice pulling the cork out of the rose with her teeth. Now was not the time to honour their promise to be careful over how much they drank.

As the reaction to the terror they had been forced to suppress, first at the farmhouse and then in the tunnel, set in they realised how close they had come to having nervous breakdowns. And like many others before them who had somehow survived the most horrifying trauma, they felt incapable of showing any restraint during whatever celebration took place afterwards.

The launch was now out of sight of land, surrounded by a sea of deep blue with the sun shining brightly from the clearest of skies in which not a solitary cloud lingered. Miss Alice poured the last drop of rosé into the only glass which they had been able to find, and which had frequently passed between them, and took a sip. Their previously animated conversation had given way to an occasional remark that was not always distinct and they were struggling bravely to keep their eyes open. Their sitting position on the gently heaving deck gradually became a horizontal one as they manoeuvred their rucksacks under their heads to act as much needed pillows. Then, as the last vestiges of the tension that had gripped their bodies ebbed away, sheer exhaustion took over and they sank into a most welcome state of complete oblivion.

At one stage, as the boat battling a strong wind shook them awake, they opened their eyes briefly to see thick, grey clouds gathering overhead. Another time they felt gusts of rain sweeping over them and later, as these appeared to intensify, that some sort of sheet was being laid on top of them. But their deep, dreamless sleep was always swift to reclaim the pair before at last an urgent hand on their shoulders finally brought them back into the world.

Coming to their senses slowly, they wondered how long they had been blissfully unconscious. Had it been for just a few hours or a longer period? However long it was, it was not long enough. Their eyelids still felt unpleasantly heavy and their heads were aching alarmingly as a result of their drinking the whole bottle of rose. Taking in the gloom around them with difficulty, they realised they did not know if it was morning or evening. The stars were faintly visible in a sky that had cleared once more, but it was hard to see whether these were fading or beginning to make their appearance.

The youth, who was standing beside them, pointed ahead and following the direction of his outstretched arm, they understood why they had been so cruelly roused from their blissful slumber. Just visible on the horizon was a long, dark, rugged coastline which signalled land was fast approaching. And as the launch ploughed on through white tipped waves toward it, the sisters noticed the light was slowly but surely improving which meant they would be making a dawn landing.

Rising stiffly to their feet, they realised that despite the youth's kind act in trying to protect them from the worst of the weather, they were soaked to the skin. Their clothes were sticking to their bodies and the brisk sea breeze they were now subjected to, seemed to whip through them and they began shivering uncontrollably. But soon they were struggling into their rucksacks and the young sailor was handing them a paper bag containing some of the remains of their feast.

A minute later he was cutting out the engine as the boat drifted in close enough to the shore for the twins to negotiate a short patch of water reaching no higher than their knees. As soon as they found themselves safely on land, they heard him call out in English 'Good luck' before the engine burst into life and he began heading back into deeper water leaving them once more completely on their own.

Chapter 14

It was now nearly broad daylight and they were able to take stock of what seemed to be their rather intimidating new surroundings. They had been set ashore at a bay which at first glance looked remarkably like the one they had left in Italy although slightly larger. It looked equally as remote, hemmed in as it was by cliffs without any sign of a pathway to enable them to get in or out. It appeared to be an inlet that could only be reached from the sea which could cause great difficulties for them in the future. Yet at that moment they had neither the strength nor the desire to move on anywhere. Their only priority was to become warm and dry.

The first faint rays of the sun, which was now beginning to warm their backs, decided them on their course of action. They once more carefully inspected their surroundings. The cliff face enclosing them, although not of a great height, was almost sheer, and the narrow beach, far more shingle than sand, was not the sort people would chose to picnic on even if they were able to get there. There was in fact no sign that humans ever visited what was obviously an isolated and desolate part of the coastline.

So without further discussion, the castaways as they now viewed themselves, stripped off their clothes apart from their knickers and laid them out in a neat row on a flat section of rock. Sheltered from the worst of the offshore wind and with the sun's heat steadily rising, the pair were confident it would not take long for them and their sodden garments to become dry. What little was left of the breeze circulating round their bodies was refreshing and choosing a sandy patch of ground, they sat down to admire a gloriously uninterrupted view of the gently rolling ocean. Yet it was not long before their eyelids began to droop and the rhythmic sound of the waves lapping the shoreline at their feet, broken only by the occasional cry of a passing seabird, lulled them once more into sleep.

The sun had not climbed much higher in the sky when Miss Mary came to with a start, imagining she had heard a cough. Her eyes alighted, barely a metre from her, on a pair of shining black knee high boots and travelling higher, took in a pair of dark breeches and matching blue shirt before coming to rest upon a serious, partly outraged face beneath a close fitting helmet with the visor up. The man was writing with measured strokes on a notepad but stopped when he saw she was awake. Pointing with a no nonsense finger towards the clothes, he turned his back with an exaggerated movement and began staring studiously out to sea.

Blushing to the roots of her hair, a panic stricken Miss Mary hastily covered herself before pulling her startled sister to her feet. She in turn let out an astonished gasp as she too rushed to hide her nakedness. The twins were in a considerable state of shock when once more fully dressed, they faced their intruder who began speaking to them in a distinctly admonishing tone although they could not understand anything he was saying.

It was at this point that a young fair haired man in his mid twenties, dressed in a pair of white shorts and a yellow T shirt, suddenly came round the corner of the cove. "Hi," he called out. "I'm Paul. I live in a villa overlooking the bay and I saw you come in. I would have come earlier but I could see that you were in a state of undress." The sisters, still nonplussed, stared up at the cliff top and noticed the square white outlines of a building they had somehow failed to spot in the early morning light. The pair found themselves briefly ignored as the two men held an animated and at times intense conversation before Paul turned to them again with a grave expression. "I am afraid you must prepare yourselves for a shock."

"A shock," said Miss Mary. "What kind of a shock?"

"This is police patrolman Tollick," came the reply. "He is placing you both under arrest for sunbathing topless in a public place."

Miss Mary opened her mouth but nothing came out. Miss Alice kept hers closed but shut her eyes. Acute embarrassment swept over them. It came in waves each time turning the twins more scarlet as the realisation of what was happening began to sink in. Miss Mary opened her mouth a second time and managed to find her voice. "But we are old women. There was nobody around. We just wanted to dry ourselves before we caught a chill."

Miss Alice was also pulling herself together and had a different question as if trying to ignore their predicament. "Why did you immediately speak English to us? How did you know who we were?"

It was the young man's turn to blush. "I was watching you through binoculars. It was obvious from your appearance you could only be English. And certainly not the kind who would undress in public without good reason."

"I hope you told the officer that," said Miss Mary.

"Of course I did. I said you were on a walking holiday and had been caught in a storm and with nobody around, thought you would not be seen. I'm sure your passports are in order but I didn't think it was a good idea to tell him how you entered Greece."

"Well now he knows what happened will he let us off?" she asked anxiously. "He can see we are not young girls flaunting ourselves. We are just a pair of silly old women."

Paul regretfully shook his head. "To our friend here exposed flesh is exposed flesh however young or old it is. Like most policemen he has the mind of a traffic warden. An offence has been committed whatever the extenuating circumstances."

"Can you try once more?" pleaded Miss Alice.

"I'm afraid it would be a waste of time. It is always the way with officialdom whatever country you are in. Once you've started filling in a form you have to complete the process. And anyway he says he was genuinely shocked to see you had removed your clothes in such a wanton manner."

"But how did he see?" exclaimed Miss Mary. "We are so tucked away here."

Paul looked at her in surprise. "Tucked away? There is a main road just out of sight running along the top of the cliff. Unfortunately for you Officer Tollick stopped his motorcycle to have a cigarette and when strolling off to look at the sea, could not help seeing you in a state of undress."

"But how did he get down here?" Asked Miss Mary who was still bewildered by his sudden appearance.

"The same way as I did. There is a well used path round the corner of the cove which leads straight up to the highway. And," he added, "that is where we are going to go now. So please pick up your rucksacks."

As they began to walk, he explained what was going to happen next. The most important thing, he emphasised, was to cause the authorities as little work as possible. What would normally occur in a case like this would be for the officer to telephone for a police van to come out and collect the offenders. But he had offered to drive them to the police headquarters in the nearest town which was fifteen kilometres away to save a lot of bother. As it was still quite early, they would all, including officer Tollick, go to his villa for a quick breakfast to allow the sisters to tidy themselves up.

Concerning what would happen to them, it was not easy to say. The worst they could expect was to be fined but they might even be let off with a warning. It could help, he added, that he knew the police chief well having acted as an interpreter and translator on occasions. He was fluent in both languages through his father being Greek and his mother English. It was his parents who owned the villa, but at the moment they were away in Athens where they worked together for a publishing company. He was writing a book about the German invasion of Crete, and always started his stints early in the morning when his mind was at its clearest which was why he had seen them land. He had, he said, witnessed many strange sights along the coastline but their arrival had been by far the most intriguing.

Sensing the question he wanted to ask but appeared too polite to, Miss Mary said friends in Italy who owned a boat, had taken them across saying it would be much nicer than travelling on a crowded ferry. They were making their way to Egypt but travelling as simply as possible because of a grave shortage of funds. Aided by her sister's discreet silence, she decided that was quite enough of their plans to reveal at this time to a complete stranger however helpful he was appearing to be.

After gaining the road, a further short climb followed before they entered a pair of wrought iron gates into a gently sloping and well tended garden full of early summer flowers. Reaching the top in front of the house, they paused to take in the breathtaking view in which their previously imagined invisible cove could be plainly seen. Then, handing the remains of their food to Paul, they had a shower and quickly washed their hair while he laid out breakfast upon a long table on the terrace which ran down the whole length of one side of the villa. The twins emerged to find bread rolls, fruit, cheese and coffee awaiting them but having over indulged the day before and with their meeting with the police chief looming, they had very little appetite.

Officer Tollick had isolated himself at the far end from the other three and although courteous, continued to treat the sisters to a series of disapproving looks. Without his helmet, he appeared to be about forty five with the measured air of a solid countryman. The twins, conscious of his attention, were still struggling to understand why they had been arrested at their advanced age for something only young women did.

Paul put down the coffee cup from which he had been thoughtfully sipping to explain that was exactly the reason why. Officer Tollick had told him that at their stage in life, they should have known far better than to indulge in such immodest behaviour whatever the circumstances. Greece, their host added, was a conservative country which tended to frown heavily on such antics and they would be seen as setting a bad example.

It was in a sombre mood that the pair climbed into the back of Paul's open top jeep and with Officer Tollick leading the way on his motorcycle, set off for the nearby town. On their driver's advice, they reluctantly agreed to hide any indignation they might feel over what they perceived to be the unfairness of the situation, and to apologise and be full of remorse. They felt that by doing this, they would be admitting guilt, but being out of their depth in a foreign country, they bowed to what they hoped was his superior knowledge.

The police station was an unimpressive single storey concrete building which was set back from the road on the edge of the main shopping district. Paul followed

Officer Tollick's motorcycle into the yard and parked behind it. Instructing his passengers to get out, he explained they would have to wait in the reception area while the report was being made and that he would go in with them to act as their interpreter if the police chief was available to see them straight afterwards. If not, he warned, it could be a long wait, something that would do nothing to calm the twins' increasingly strained nerves.

Officer Tollick, notebook in hand, had already vanished into the interior by the time they took their seats next to the counter manned by a young man whose friendly nod to Paul showed they were on familiar terms. In the event, barely ten minutes had elapsed before Officer Tollick reappeared from a door to their right wearing his usual sombre expression which gave nothing away as to what had taken place inside. Catching Paul's eye, he gave an affirmative although somewhat curt nod as he proceeded to make his way out into the yard. "No clues there then," murmured their escort as, rising to his feet, he ushered the pair through the door Officer Tollick had just left into a short corridor. Knocking on another door at the far end, he received what the sisters took to be a gruff command to enter.

The owner of the voice proved to be a stocky man with dark brooding eyes and sparse tuffs of grey hair who rose from a creaking chair behind his desk to shake Paul warmly by the hand before waving the twins towards two empty chairs. And there they sat for what seemed to them an interminable length of time as the two men held a prolonged and sometimes tense conversation. No sooner had this finished than the police chief who had virtually ignored their presence, began to slowly look them up and down in a manner which the sisters found to be extremely disconcerting.

"He's sizing you up," explained Paul who had taken a seat on the far side of the desk. "I've stuck to the story I told Officer Tollick that you entered Greece through the nearby border with Yugoslavia and are on a walking holiday. Luckily he accepts that without question, but just cannot understand why, with your obviously cultivated background and age, you are not travelling by air conditioned coach and staying at the better off hotels like the rest of your kind. In reply, I said you are a pair of typically English eccentrics and spent much of the time in trying to translate what that actually means into Greek."

The sisters ruefully agreed that this description was the right one. When first attached to them, it was a label that had made the twins feel uncomfortable. Yet now they were beginning to see it did have its advantages. Eccentrics were a little odd and deserved to be given a certain amount of leeway. At least that is what they prayed the captain was thinking, if indeed he had understood what Paul meant.

Yet this hope was quickly dashed when he warned that although the police chief was intrigued by this description, eccentricity could not be used as a defence for undressing in public. The pensive figure behind the desk finally shifted his gaze away from the twins and once more onto Officer Tollick's report which lay open in front of him. In the silence that followed, the twins could feel the growing tension in the air before he suddenly looked up and began speaking in a rapid manner to Paul. Their young friend listened intently, nodding from time to time as if in agreement, before with a half smile, turning to the waiting pair. "Captain Tolon," he said, naming their interrogator for the first time, "wants to make it clear that Officer Tollick did exactly the right thing in putting you under arrest. However taking into account the reasons you had for discarding your garments, the early hour at which this happened, and the relative obscurity in where it took place, a warning in this case should be considered sufficient."

The overwhelming sense of relief was clearly evident in the faces of the sisters who found themselves clutching the arms of their chairs as Paul went on. "I have thanked Captain Tolon once again on your behalf and offered your sincere apologies for any distress that you may have inadvertently caused. There will be no record of this kept in any file and you are free to go. He emphasises he hopes your stay in Greece will be a very pleasant one from now on, and that any undressing you do in future will be in private."

Sensing that Paul had finished his message, the police chief got to his feet and breaking into a smile, thrust out his hand which the sisters in turn gratefully shook before departing with joyful steps into the corridor. Outside the station, in the blessed fresh air and with the threat of a possible terrifying court appearance lifted, only their upbringing in which emotions had to be kept in check, prevented them from throwing their arms round their saviour. They were only too well aware that his relationship with the police through his interpreting, had been a significant factor in the decision not to take the matter any further.

In a jubilant mood, they insisted on treating Paul to lunch despite his protests, that from what they had told him, they would need to conserve every penny of their finances. Not at all, replied Miss Alice, they were well supplied with drachmas at the moment and he must let them repay him for all the help he had given two such helpless women. Acceding to their earnest requests graciously, he led the pair across the road to a little taverna shielded from the sun by bright red awnings which overhung the pavement above a cluster of tables draped in matching covers. These were all taken, but inside there was an empty one in a corner by the window which the three promptly occupied.

The sisters, buoyed by their escape, suddenly found their appetites had returned and each ordered a Greek salad to be followed by meat balls in a tomato sauce which Paul said was perfectly adequate for him too. The pair realised they owed it to their benefactor to reveal their whole story which would help to explain properly their bizarre arrival on the beach below his villa. So between mouthfuls, they told him of their attempt to find their mother and of the ill winds of fate which were unceasingly buffeting them along the way.

Their companion, who found his credulity being stretched to its limit more than once, realised he was being given the truth, but felt 'eccentric' was not nearly a strong enough word to describe the old girls busily eating opposite him. They had shown the most extraordinary resilience in getting as far as they had, but he was doubtful they would ever reach Egypt and as for finding their mother after fifty years, well, any sane person would say that was impossible.

The arrival of a young waitress to clear away their plates was the signal for Miss Alice to delve into her envelope to extract a handful of Cesare's generously provided crisp drachma notes. The other two remained in their seats, finishing the last of their coffee, as she made her way to the proprietor who was installed behind his till under a slowly revolving fan. Flicking through a sheaf of bills, he pulled one out and placed it in front of her. Seeing the total at the bottom, she passed over three notes which would just cover it, intending to leave what was leftover as a tip. Taking them between his fingers, he turned them over carefully before holding each up to the light. Then as if not satisfied with what he had seen, he lifted his bulky frame off his stool and striding outside, held them up again, this time to the sun. Hurriedly resuming his position, he leant down and pressed a button in the wall by his knee. Paul, having noticed the unusual proceedings taking place, appeared at Miss Alice's side to inquire if anything was wrong.

The owner, whose expression was becoming increasingly disgruntled, muttered something darkly and showed one of the notes to Paul who in turn began to frown. Miss Mary had joined Miss Alice and he addressed the sisters in a tone of weary resignation. "These notes are counterfeit," he said. "As will be the others your Italian friends with the boat gave you." Taking out his wallet, he proceeded to pay the bill himself, adding that as the proprietor was not being left out of pocket, he would not be pressing charges but that the matter was already out of his hands. The bell he had pushed was connected to the police station and an officer would be coming across the road at any minute. There had been a spate of forged notes being passed around the town which had put shopkeepers on the alert and enabled them to quickly spot one.

"Most of the customers who had passed them on were innocent," Paul added. "Which the owner in this case readily concedes that you are. It will be just a matter of making a statement, trying to pin point where you were given them, and handing over any others you have, to be checked." It would be better, he told Miss Alice, if she gave him the rest of them to destroy and to declare the only ones they had were those offered to pay the bill. And that having made many transactions, they had no idea how they had come to be in their possession. Handing over the envelope which Paul swiftly put in his back pocket, she asked the question which her sister had already thought of. "Will we," she said in a rather faint voice, "have to go and see the police chief again?"

"No, no," Paul replied sensing their growing anxiety. "Whoever is on duty at the front desk will do it and the whole process will only take a few minutes. Especially as the owner here who is keen to attract foreign tourists, is more than happy to vouch for your innocence."

At that moment, an officer appeared in the doorway and after a short discussion with the two men, beckoned politely to the twins to follow him as he set off back across the road. Striding by their side, Paul did his best to raise their spirits by pointing out their second visit was a really simple matter compared to the ordeal they had gone through earlier the same morning. The officer, with an encouraging smile, handed them over to the young man who had been on duty at the counter previously and who, if he had felt any surprise at seeing them again so soon, did not show it. He produced a batch of forms for them to fill in which they quickly set about doing with the help of Paul.

They had just completed these, and were adding their signatures, when they heard the sound of heavy foot steps entering the main entrance behind them. Whoever it was, appeared to stop short and after a moment's silence, there followed a raised, distinctly questioning voice which with sinking hearts, the sisters immediately recognised.

The police chief, newly returned from lunch himself, was staring at them with arched eyebrows while Paul, hastily stepping into the breach, began a hesitant explanation. Cutting him short, Captain Tolon waved commandingly for them to follow him and marched off down the corridor to his office. Once inside, the twins discovered this time that they were not to be offered chairs. Standing slightly behind Paul, they tried to make out what he was saying as he sought to convince the police chief that even more extenuating circumstances were attached to this second visit than there had been to the first. Captain Tolon's reaction was to start tapping his foot impatiently on the floor and to subject the twins to a series of increasingly baleful glares which they found anything but encouraging. But then suddenly, as if he'd already heard more than enough, he dismissed them with a finger thrust towards the door.

Safely out in the yard, Paul revealed he had explained that the taverna owner had vouched for their innocence, that the forged notes had been handed in, and that they had completed their statements to the desk officer's satisfaction.

"And what did the police chief say?" asked Miss Mary as the twins began to digest this information. "Well," replied Paul after a moment's hesitation. "To translate it as pleasantly as I can, he said get those two idiot women out of my sight."

Chapter 15

The sisters were sitting on the terrace in wicker chairs with their feet up on the surrounding rail while far below, the sea was lapping lazily against the rocky shoreline. The weather was perfect and the gentle breeze was wonderfully cool as it ruffled their new, thin cotton dresses of a fetching light blue pattern. They were thinking of home and for the first time either could remember, they were not wishing they were there because of some awful catastrophe that was afflicting them. That morning Paul had taken the pair into the town so they could wire Archie to remit whatever funds were readily available and with instructions to take the chest of drawers on the landing to the local auctioneering firm which held fortnightly sales. The proceeds from this ancient piece of furniture, which neither of them really liked, was to be transmitted at a later date with the hope it would see them through to Cairo without further requests.

With that accomplished, they had exchanged their few remaining liras before Paul took them to the busy street market where he insisted, they kit themselves out with a complete change of clothes because the temperature, as they moved ever eastwards, would only become hotter. As they would now be doing no long distance walking, they replaced their sturdy boots with a pair of canvas shoes while their thicker blouses and trousers gave way to the lightest replacements, mainly of cheesecloth, that could be found. And when their money had run out, Paul had chipped in with his, saying they could repay him when theirs arrived, and could also, as the twins had made clear they were determined to do, give something for their keep if it helped them feel better.

The sisters expected to be staying at the villa for

about a week to ten days and Paul was adamant that, to conserve their energy, they must not lift a finger. His early morning writing stint which began at four o'clock, was usually finished by the time they rose around nine, which he said, left him free all day to look after them. It was a situation they could not help taking advantage of after their constant struggles against exhaustion and their feeble protests were easily brushed aside. Their host turned out to be an excellent cook and every dinner, eaten out on the terrace in the glow of a fading sunset, was accompanied by a plentiful supply of the most delicious, expertly chilled, dry white wine.

The twins had to admit that, if nothing else, their journey had turned them unashamedly into drinkers. But who wouldn't need a glass or two they told themselves with the clearest of consciences, after what they were constantly having to put up with?

At the end of eight days they were ready to depart at last. Their money had come through and they were feeling fully refreshed. And the impatience which they always felt after an enforced stop, was rising rapidly to the surface. Their biggest problem as ever, was how to travel as cheaply as possible over the next stage of their journey which was to take them to Athens.

It was on their last evening that Paul, who had already more than surpassed himself in the help he had given them, revealed what he called his master plan. He had gone shopping alone and when he returned, he summoned the sisters in from the garden and placed before them on the table two long cotton scarves bearing red and white stripes.

Asking the pair to put these round their necks, he inspected them from different angles before declaring that, yes, they did look exactly the part. In answer to their mystified expressions, he explained they were now supporters of the local football club whose colours they were so proudly wearing. Its team were playing a match outside Athens the next evening and several coaches were being provided to take the large number of followers who wanted to watch the game. The fare would be far less than travelling on normal public transport whether by bus or a train. He had, he said, bought two tickets for them for the journey which would last around six hours and the departure time had been set for noon. They should have no trouble mingling with their fellow passengers who would have food parcels with them so the pair's rucksacks would not look out of place. Once there, it would just be a simple matter of disembarking from the coach and slipping away from the crowd as it made its way slowly into the stadium.

The sisters' first reaction was to baulk at the prospect because of the language barrier which might well expose them as interlopers wanting a cheap ride with the most embarrassing consequences. Yet they had become nothing if not pragmatic when it came to the chance of saving money, and thanking him for what they called his brilliant idea, they said they would be more than happy to take advantage of it. They were put further at ease when he explained that once the coaches were underway with such a long journey ahead, the majority of people would soon try to sleep so they would not be expected to converse with anybody.

That night at dinner, Paul finally broached the subject which he had repeatedly put off from raising. He did not want to undermine what by any standard was a most gallant mission, but how on earth could they really believe they would ever find their mother? Cairo was a densely overcrowded city and they did not even know where to start. The twins' reaction was to truthfully admit that this was a very good question. It was one they had asked themselves over and over again without coming up with an answer. There had been several others on the way before Paul who had asked the same thing. And they had seen it on the faces of several more who could not bring them selves to raise such a delicate subject. Something inside themselves had told them to leave their happy, comfortable lives at The Rectory and start out on what they agreed was an extraordinary quest. And once on their way, they had found it impossible to turn back however intimidating the circumstances. Whatever it was, it just kept drawing them on.

Paul looked at the pair quizzically. "Maybe it is your mother who is driving you on."

Miss Alice frowned. "What do you mean?"

"She must have had a restless streak hidden inside her which you have come to inherit."

"Yes, that's the mystery of it," ventured Miss Mary. "She seemed very happy and content at home and we all loved each other. She was only meant to be going for a short holiday."

"It was such a great shock that it happened so quickly," added her sister. "We know people can turn native when the East gets hold of them, but usually after they have been living there a long time. She'd barely been there two weeks when the telegram arrived."

"And this camel driver," went on Miss Mary. "To be honest, mother was really quite a snob. Although always very polite and charming, she was extremely careful over whom she mixed with. It just doesn't make sense for her to give up her family and lovely home which she adored for a life of what?"

"We could only think that with the kind of person she ran off with, she must be living in a tent in the desert," intervened Miss Alice.

"If that is the case," replied Paul. "There is not the

remotest possibility that you will ever find her. She may not of course, even still be alive which I am sure you will have thought of. If I may be allowed to ask, what took you so long before deciding to begin to search?"

"That is another question that we have asked ourselves countless times," replied Miss Mary. "At first, I think we were too overcome by the death of our father and then for a long time we waited in the hope that mother would eventually contact us. Then when nothing arrived for our birthdays or at Christmas, we came to believe that she wanted to cut herself off from us completely."

"For some reason we just retreated into our shell and the years slipped by so quickly," said Miss Alice taking over again. "I suppose it's because we are twins, but the restless feeling suddenly appeared in both of us at the same time and kept getting stronger. We can only think the desire to see our mother again was lying dormant, and that as we were rapidly approaching seventy, we subconsciously realised this would be our last chance before our aging bones made the task impossible."

"I have to say they have held up very well so far," replied Paul with a note of admiration. "But we have to be realistic; you are not there yet. I can only wish you all the luck in the world, which judging by what has happened to you so far, you are certainly going to need."

Chapter 16

Arranging their scarves around their necks as tastefully as they could, the sisters critically examined their appearance in the long mirror that hung in the hall. Although they had provided goal posts for the village pitch at home, try as they might, they could not see themselves looking like genuine supporters of a football team. Yet the die was cast. Paul had already put their belongings into the jeep and was calling to them to hurry up or they would be late. Excited though they were to be moving on again, the thought of the coming journey was an intimidating one and it was a wrench to be leaving the beautiful villa which had become their much loved sanctuary.

The drive to their destination was short and soon they were disembarking to join a large boisterous, but good natured, crowd milling around in the car park of the stadium. To the left, stood a row of four large coaches beside which orderly queues were already beginning to form.

On Paul's advice, the twins were happy to wait until the very last moment before attempting to board the final coach which was unlikely to be completely taken and would give the pair a chance of finding places with empty seats around them. Their prayers were answered when it proved to be barely half full with the majority of their fellow passengers choosing to congregate mainly towards the back. This allowed the twins to claim almost isolated seats and settling into them, they just had time to look out of the window and wave to Paul as the coach moved off.

Their grateful thanks to the young man for all he had done could not have been expressed more sincerely or have been more heartfelt. Twice he had saved them from ignominy or worse when it came to dealing with the law, and they had reached the point where they wondered whether they could get along without him. But get along without him they would have to, as was only too evident from the sight of his figure disappearing into the distance behind them.

Paul's prediction that after an early buzz of conversation, it would not be long before eyes began to close, proved to be up to the mark. And as silence descended the sisters, after studying the passing landscape for a while, could not stop nodding off themselves.

As Athens neared, they shook themselves awake and began in whispers to go over their carefully laid plan to escape from their fellow supporters. Paul had said it would be best if they waited to get off last. Being in the final coach, this would leave them at the very back of the crowd moving slowly down the short avenue towards the stadium.

Along this stretch were several narrow side roads leading off it, and it would be a simple matter for the twins to quietly slip away into one of these. There were a good number of hotels in the area and it should not be difficult for them to find suitable accommodation for the night before departing on the next stage of their journey. As they would now be going by public transport due to Alice's vulnerable leg, they had ditched their camping equipment along with their old clothes and would be travelling lighter than at any stage since leaving home. Looking back, they realised how dangerously close they had come to wearing themselves out by climbing the Alps and that it was an incredible silly thing to do. Their achievement made their hearts swell with pride, but they both knew that whatever the circumstances, they would find it impossible to make a physical effort of such intensity again.

The sisters sat quietly in their seats as their companions from the back of the coach filed past to join the swelling crowd whose bobbing heads could be plainly seen through the window. The pair were relying on remaining where they were for at least five minutes so as to be able to open up a gap between themselves and the rest of the supporters. But these hopes were quickly dashed by the driver whose urgent promptings for them to depart, made it clear he was waiting to lock the vehicle so he could join the throng.

Forced to disembark much earlier than they intended, the twins discovered to their dismay that the nearest coach to them, having been full, was still unloading its passengers. As they struggled to put on their rucksacks, they were unceremoniously swept into the nearest group that was almost fifty strong. Wedged in the middle, they were carried along for quite a distance before managing to work their way out towards its fringe. Never having been part of a large crowd before, they marvelled at how smoothly it was flowing when they had feared they would be trampled underfoot. But on reaching its edge, they found to their horror exactly why they were moving in such an orderly fashion. They were being expertly marshalled by a cordon of policemen spaced just a few yards apart, who were shepherding anybody who strayed from their companions, firmly back into line.

Coming abreast of the first side road, the twins attempted to break away only to receive the same treatment being meted out to all the other stragglers. They could see from the grim expressions on the faces of the officers that even if they could speak the language, any explanation or entreaty would be entirely a waste of breath. Miss Mary, standing on her toes, saw a similar line of unbending uniformed figures on the far side of the road and realised they had become trapped.

They were like so many corralled horses being herded towards the stadium that was their holding pen. And which was now close enough for its giant floodlights to be seen standing stark against the night sky. Another side street came into view, but even as the sisters took a step towards it, a policeman marched forward to swiftly bar their way. It was now obvious to the badly rattled pair they would have to watch the match and hope to make their escape as soon as it was over.

Since setting out from The Rectory, they had become used to being confronted with sudden setbacks but this one seemed to be so particularly cruel and unexpected. After all, Paul had been so clever in astutely solving their problems and never once had he put a foot wrong. It was true he had made it clear he was not interested in football himself, but surely he should have known crowds of such a size were bound to require controlling by police? As they reached the gates to the stadium feeling completely helpless, the twins had to admit with shame that, despite all he had done, if they had come face to face with him at that moment they would have found it extremely difficult to be civil.

Their one faint hope was, having tickets only for the coach and not the match, they would be turned away. Yet they discovered as they were swept effortlessly through the clicking turnstiles that being part of an organised group, these were not being asked for. They found themselves at the top of a sweeping row of terraces running down, step by step, to the perimeter wall which separated them from the pitch. They were among the first to arrive in this section and those coming from behind, pushed them to the bottom were they were able, much to their relief, to lean against it.

They had barely settled themselves before the two opposing teams came running out to be greeted by huge roars of encouragement from the excited crowd which was rapidly filling the few remaining gaps in the stands. By matching the colour of their scarves to the shirts of the players, the sisters were able to pick out which side they were meant to be diligently supporting. Although feeling impostors and terribly out of place, they could not help being affected by the animated and partisan atmosphere heightened by the floodlights blazing down from a now pitch black sky. With the game underway, a continuous wall of sound engulfed the twins, rising and falling in line with the dramatic events being enacted on the field.

There had been narrow escapes for the defences at both ends but no goals had been scored when the controversial incident happened with half an hour left to play. The referee awarded the home team a penalty when one of its players appeared to fall over in the area without being touched by any of his opponents. This so incensed some of the younger supporters around the sisters that when the kick was successfully taken to put their team behind, they climbed over the wall and ran onto the pitch to protest. Others who were in better control of their emotions, seemed to be waving to them urgently to come back. A middle aged man who had heard the twins talking and spoke English, explained the fools on the field of play would be ejected from the ground and so miss the rest of the match.

This news electrified the pair who realised they were being offered an entirely unexpected avenue of escape. To the speaker's astonishment, Miss Mary responded by asking for what in the horse world would be called a leg up. In no time she and her sister were straddling the five foot high wall and it was Miss Alice, giving no thought to her vulnerable leg, who was first to land on the other side. The two had barely joined the dozen or so group of protesters, when they were encircled by a ring of match stewards who converged on them from every part of the stadium.

The warning of their fellow spectator quickly proved to be right, for instead of being urged to climb back over the wall, they were marched without delay towards the main gate. As they approached and saw it was open with the street lights visible on the far side, the twins' spirits soared. For once, entirely using their own initiative without advice from anybody else, they had extracted themselves from an extremely awkward situation. In a moment they would be free to search for an hotel and it was still early enough for these to be open. The escapees, as they now saw themselves, developed a spring in their step as they were escorted through the gate and it was only their rucksacks that prevented them giving each other a congratulatory pat on the back.

At first they failed see the three black vans parked neatly in a row with their small grill windows and back doors wide open. They could only gasp incredulously as they were shepherded into the first one along with four other protestors. It was but a short journey to the police station and they were still numb with shock as a female officer behind the reception desk made a list of their belongings. Picking up their passports, she shouted in the direction of the corridor and an English speaking colleague stuck his head round it. "You are charged with pitch invasion," he said to the sisters. "You will be held here tonight to appear in court tomorrow." Then he disappeared. The officer, having done her duty to explain to the foreigners their predicament, could only gaze at them in disbelief as they were led away to the cells.

Lying on the hard, narrow cots in the darkness, the sisters had a distinct feeling of deja vu after their nights spent in France in similar surroundings. Yet then they were guests being kindly provided with free accommodation. Now they had an overwhelming feeling of being incarcerated as bona fide criminals even though they had yet to appear before a magistrate. The shock of having their fingerprints taken and their belongings locked away, brought home to them just how amazingly stupid they had been.

They had promised themselves after earlier rushes of blood to the brain, that they would not take any decisions without first carefully and soberly examining all the possible implications. It would only have taken a minute or two of thought to realise disrupting any public event would almost certainly lead to an arrest. They had been brought up to never indulge in self pity and for the greater part of their lives they had triumphantly succeeded in doing this. Yet on this one night, there were probably not two other people in all of Greece who felt more sorry for themselves than they did.

Chapter 17

He was a small man with a bald head and a rather long suffering, sour expression, who did not even bother to introduce himself. He merely said he was to be their interpreter and that their case was the next one to be heard. And before they could question him, the sisters had been called from the spartan waiting room where they had been nervously twisting their hands and found themselves standing in the dock while he took a chair beside them. The somewhat small chamber with high windows and a slowly revolving ceiling fan, was dominated by an ancient wooden bench on a platform from where an elderly man with thick, grey hair was studying the defendants with a slightly bemused expression.

He began speaking in measured tones which the interpreter in a listless almost sing song voice dutifully turned into English. The two women, the magistrate said, must have been well were aware of the murmur of surprise that had swept round the courtroom on their appearance. English football supporters had a well deserved reputation for hooliganism but not normally in the form of two ladies of such a mature age. He had at first wondered if the court papers had become muddled and they were actually involved in something more genteel.

"However," he declared, "the court is not concerned with who you are or why you were attending the match. Only with what you did while there which is clearly documented in the signed statements of several experienced witnesses I have before me.

"According to one seasoned steward, your determination was such that you implored a bystander to hoist you up as the barrier was too high for you to climb on your own. Fortunately the majority of supporters nearby had enough self discipline and sense not to follow your quite shameless example of what can only be described as the most delinquent behaviour. As you can see from the facts, there can be no verdict other than one of guilty. Therefore, I have only to ask before I pass sentence, whether you have anything to say in mitigation."

The sisters, being so attuned to what the other one was thinking, had no need to consult. The court, they knew, was right. It was only concerned with events inside the stadium and whatever reason they gave for being there would not be accepted as an excuse. And it could well cause more speculation and prolong their excruciatingly uncomfortable presence in the dock. Holding herself erect, Miss Mary replied in a calm and steady voice that they had nothing to say while Miss Alice, with similarly straightened shoulders, nodded her assent.

The magistrate took off his steel rimmed spectacles and gave them a thoughtful polish with a silk handkerchief while this information was being translated. Propping them carefully back onto his nose, he turned his gravest expression upon the defendants and declared they would be fined four hundred drachmas each which would be deducted immediately from the money they had in their possession.

The interpreter beckoned them to step down with a disdainful glance that portrayed his complete disinterest in their fate. Leading them out to a cramped side office where their belongings were being held, he pointed to a manned desk in the corner before favouring them with the slightest of bows and disappearing. The twins had to reluctantly admit that any further conversation was unnecessary as they painfully counted out eight hundred drachmas under the watchful eye of the clerk from their rapidly dwindling pile. Their overwhelming feeling of relief that their ordeal was over, was tempered by the fact they would soon be in financial difficulties again and by the awful realisation they now had a criminal act recorded against their names. And as the full implication of this gradually began to sink in, they wished the ground underneath would open up and swallow them.

Once outside, they started to almost run along the street as if subconsciously trying to put as much distance as they could between themselves and the courthouse which had been the scene of such a harrowing humiliation. The sky overhead was for once overcast with a blanket of thick, grey cloud that summed up their mood which was turning from abject despair to something akin to outright panic. For the first time since they had left home, the unshakeable equilibrium they had relied upon to sustain them through so many crises, had completely disappeared. They felt as criminals, every eye was being turned in their direction and that wherever they went, accusing fingers would be pointing them out. Even as they strode blindly on, they became gripped by an all consuming desire to flee from the Greek mainland with all possible speed. It would not matter where they would be heading as long as it was towards their ultimate destination of Egypt.

Before leaving home they had discarded any idea of sightseeing for which they would have neither the time nor the energy. Their one exception would have been a visit to the Acropolis, that incredible wonder of the ancient world they had avidly read about in their youth. Yet now it was the last thing on their minds as they took a bus to the bustling seaport of Piraeus and immediately began to search for any imminent sailings which they might be able to join. Their choice fell upon a pleasure cruiser leaving for the island of Rhodes within the hour that would allow them just enough time to wire Archie with instructions to remit the money from the sale of the chest of drawers there. For this, they picked out the mail delivery office in Lindos whose name was short and easy to spell which would make the message cheaper. After paying for this latest voyage, they found to their dismay they were now virtually destitute.

Chapter 18

"So what have the two biddies been up to then?" Eric Parsons the postman was helping Archie to manhandle the chest of drawers down the stairs from the landing before putting it into his friend's van to take to the auctioneers.

"I wish I knew," replied the caretaker puffing slightly as he took a firm grip on his end of it. "But whatever it is, you can be sure it won't be doing them any good. They keep asking for more money so they must be in some sort of trouble."

"If you ask me, they should never have left home."

"You can say that again. If losing their passports before even setting off wasn't a dire warning, I don't know what is. They just refused to see sense."

Eric nodded gravely "I always said they were stubborn biddies didn't I?"

The two men put the far from light piece of furniture down in the hall while they took a much needed breather. "You and I are as stubborn as the next man," responded Archie mopping his perspiring face with his shirt cuff. "But the difference is we know when to be and when not to be. They just close their eyes to anything they don't like and keep going."

"Well according to your wire they have managed to reach Greece. I wonder what the locals there think of them. I know people round here have always thought them a bit strange."

Archie took on a profound air. "Human beings are funny aren't they?"

Eric gave a slight frown. "What do you mean?"

"Well, take those two old girls. Of all the people you and I know in the world they would be the last you would think to go off like that. I mean look at their age, and it's not as if they are experienced travellers.

They've hardly been more than a couple of miles from The Rectory in their whole lives."

Eric nodded. "As I said, they're strange biddies. You never know what a woman is going to do, but I agree you'd never expect them to do something so daft." He gave his nose a ruminative scratch. "We all get urges but there are urges and urges and the older you get they should become more sensible."

"That's the funny part," replied Archie. "I've known them for fifteen years and they'd always been sensible. You couldn't get anybody more sensible. As I said when I heard they were going. It was as if they'd been struck on the head by a thunderbolt from the heavens."

With the chest of drawers finally secured inside the van, Archie closed the doors and thanked the postman for his help.

"Let me know if they want to sell anything else," Eric replied. "I just hope it won't be the grandfather clock for we'll never fit it in."

The caretaker watched the postman drive off to continue his round before retracing his steps to lock the doors of the house which would soon be empty and silent again. Although he mowed the lawns regularly and did his best to tend the main flower beds, the garden was too large for one person to manage properly. Especially as he was only able to make one or two visits a week. With the weeds beginning to sprout unchecked, and the unclipped privet hedges becoming more ragged with each passing day, nature was slowly but remorselessly undoing all the hard work of the sisters to keep everything pristine. They had been gone over four months and the house itself with its drawn blinds only added to the air of desolation that hung over the deserted property.

Pocketing the key for the front door lock, Archie had a final look round before climbing into his van. He had not realised just how fond of his employers he had become until they were not there. Wondering what was happening to them as they travelled through those strange foreign lands was a constant worry. But he realised there was absolutely nothing he could do other than faithfully carry out their instructions and to hope for the best. The trouble was, he just could not get rid of the thought that it would all end in tears. Not just any tears, but floods of them.

Chapter 19

Once the port of Piraeus had disappeared over the horizon, the sisters' spirits, aided by a bracing sea breeze which seemed to cleanse their souls, slowly started to revive. But after a gratifyingly uneventful voyage, they landed on Rhodes at Prasonis to find themselves immediately confronted by another major mistake they had unwittingly made. Lindos, where they had chosen to pick up their latest addition of desperately required funds, turned out to be nearly a hundred kilometres up the coast and their pitiful supply of money was not even enough to pay a local bus fare. Despite Miss Alice's vulnerable leg, which they had to say, had not been giving the slightest trouble, they had no option other than to grit their teeth and walk. They could only hope with it still being the holiday season, there would be a reasonable amount of traffic which would give them a chance somewhere along the highway of obtaining a lift.

The early arrival of their cruiser allowed the pair to set off in a confident manner before the sun began making its formidable presence felt. But it soon turned into another scorchingly hot day without a breath of wind to cool them, and they quickly found the going hard as they tramped along the unforgiving tarmac stretching endlessly away beneath their feet. Walking had once been second nature to the experienced travellers, but they had hardly done any seriously since their epic climbing of the Alps and their limbs were soon starting to protest at such unaccustomed exercise. Yet their determination had not deserted them and they plodded grimly on although they could not prevent their progress from becoming slower and slower.

It was Miss Alice who caught sight of the stream, winding its way a few metres from the road at the bottom of a gentle slope. On its far side, two trees cast their branches over a crumbling stone wall, offering a welcome chance of shade to the freely perspiring twins. When staying with Paul, he had taken them to a popular village beach where they had seen its elderly female inhabitants clad in black dresses, cooling off in the shallows. With one thought between them as usual, and without saying a word, they made their way down to its edge and peered into the silently gliding current. It appeared to come barely up to their knees and ran over a patch of inviting sand.

The sisters had learned their lesson over the danger of taking off their clothes however remote a spot seemed to be, but saw no reason why they could not safely follow the example of the natives. After a cautionary look around, they slipped out of their knickers to keep them dry, and entered the stream's refreshing embrace. Sitting side by side, they carefully knotted their dresses around their waists to keep as much of these out of the water as possible, and revived by the deliciously cool flow, they proceeded to splash their faces and necks and to run wet fingers through their hair. They remembered how difficult it was to get out of a hot bath in winter at The Rectory while here it was the complete reverse.

Yet they knew reluctantly they could not afford to linger. Without money they would not be able to eat or pay for somewhere to stay and they had long since lost the desire to sleep out of doors. Untying their dresses, they climbed awkwardly to their feet and moving to the nearby stone wall, perched their bare bottoms on its warm surface in a bid to dry out before retrieving their underwear. It was a most blissful feeling after the heat and the dust of the road, and Miss Mary was beginning to nod off when she was startled by a piercing shriek from her sister who leaping to her feet, began to execute a kind of dance while flapping madly at her dress.

She said later it was as if someone was sticking red hot needles into her and then as the searing pain spread, as if she was sitting on the hotplate of the Aga at home. Miss Mary, who had jumped up too, looked at the spot that had been occupied by her sister to see a dislodged stone from under which several black forms were scuttling out.

"Oh my goodness," she cried. "You've been sitting on a nest of scorpions. You've disturbed them and they've stung you."

Miss Alice, who found this information superfluous, had ceased to move and was leaning against one of the trunks of the trees. She was feeling faint and could not stop her eyes from watering from the pain which seemed to intensify with each passing second. She pulled up the hem of her dress in a desperate attempt to stop it touching the inflamed area which now felt literally as if it was on fire. Her sister, kneeling with great concern beside her, counted no less than five puncture marks on the rapidly reddening skin and knew they had to find help immediately.

Swiftly pulling on her knickers and stuffing her sister's in her own dress pocket, she picked up both rucksacks and set off back up the slope urging Miss Alice to follow her. Gingerly, step by agonising step, her twin at last arrived at the top to find Miss Mary frantically waving at two passing cars whose drivers barely gave her a glance as they carried on their way. Miss Alice was now affected by dizziness and with eyes closed, was beginning to sway dangerously. Her sister, waving one hand at an approaching third vehicle, hastily pulled down the front of her twin's dress with the other to maintain her modesty for she was now incapable of doing anything herself.

The last car, which had driven past like the others, suddenly stopped a few metres down the road and reversed with a squeal of tyres until it drew level with the now almost hysterical twins. A young man of slender build with blond hair got out and then they heard the blessed sound of an English voice. "Hello, what is happening here then?"

Miss Mary, indicating the forlorn figure of her sister, revealed their desperate situation in a few terse sentences.

"Obviously there's no time for introductions," came the reply. "But I'm Roger Taylor, a rep for a holiday firm in Lindos where there is a small hospital. We must get her there for treatment as soon as possible."

Miss Mary opened the rear door of the blue saloon and helped her sister to climb in where she crouched on hands and knees across the back seat, carefully keeping her dress above her hips. Miss Mary then eased herself into the front one, barely having time to close the door before the engine burst into life and they were off. If their rescuer was intrigued by their bizarre presence at the roadside he did not ask, instead explaining he was returning from taking two tourists to the airport for their flight home for his company which ran six villas in the resort.

Miss Mary kept glancing over her shoulder at the motionless form of her twin whose eyes remained closed and who did not reply to any of her solicitous inquiries. Seeing her worried look, Roger said although victims of such attacks could fall quite seriously ill, the stings would certainly not prove to be fatal. The conversation then ebbed away as he concentrated on driving as fast as he could along the winding road whose corners frustratingly conspired to keep his speed down. The one saving grace was it was virtually empty but on one open stretch, they were overtaken by a uniformed rider on a motorcycle who slowing down once he was safely past, motioned for them to pull over.

"A traffic cop," explained Roger. "I wonder what he wants." Doing as he was ordered, he got out and went to meet the officer who was parking his machine on a nearby grass verge. Watching through the windscreen, Miss Mary could see the two of them in an animated but short conversation with Roger continually pointing in the car's direction. Hurriedly retracing his steps, he revealed they were in luck for the officer, understanding the urgency of the situation, was going to escort them to the first aid centre. Again they set off with her new companion firmly gripping the wheel as they began to move at a faster pace. After a while, Miss Mary asked the question which had been troubling her. "Why were we stopped?" she said. "Surely we couldn't have been speeding?"

"No, the officer thought we were breaking a different kind of law."

"Really? She replied. "What was that?"

"There's a craze that's been sweeping the island and he thought your sister was taking part."

"A craze?" responded Miss Mary who was none the wiser for this rather puzzling reply. "What craze?"

"Have you ever heard of mooning?"

"No, I haven't."

"Young people, mainly men, do it if they've been knocking back the drink and are riding around in cars or coaches. They drop their trousers and bare their backsides to passers by."

Miss Mary took a gulp of air and began to speak. "You don't mean-."

"Yes," interrupted Roger. "As the officer passed us, he saw your sister's bottom displayed in the back window. My Greek isn't much good, but as soon as I managed to explain what had happened and that she was an elderly woman, he could not have been more helpful."

Miss Mary took time to digest this information, but then despite the seriousness of the situation, her lips began to quiver slightly. Once this was all over, she would delight in telling her sister how her backside had halted their emergency dash to Lindos.

Chapter 20

It was the third day Miss Alice was having to spend lying on her stomach and she prayed it would be the last. The swelling had almost disappeared, with the pain become nothing more than an occasional dull ache, although the affected area was still sensitive when poked by an exploratory finger. She had been told at the hospital she was lucky the scorpions were young ones but that she had a most impressive cluster of stings. Roger, having delivered his passengers safely, had waited discreetly outside the cubicle where she was being treated to translate any instructions that were necessary.

Yet the cheerful young doctor, despite being unable to speak a word of English, had clearly expressed his feelings by giving a long, low whistle on first inspecting the burning behind. With the greatest of care, he administered the first of two creams which Miss Alice was to take away with her while giving Miss Mary, who was standing by her side, a reassuring thumbs up with his spare hand. The victim's early faintness and dizziness he explained, was due to shock, and it was just a case now of complete rest and of regularly applying the ointments. It was not a good idea, he added rather superfluously, to sit on stone walls in Greece without giving them a careful inspection first.

Helped to her feet and with her sister feeling like a bridesmaid as she held the back of her dress up, Miss Alice again tottered to the car and crouched in the back as Roger drove them the short distance to a two room apartment overlooking the sea. With the holiday season coming to an end, he said he would let them stay in a spare villa at a cut price which they could pay for when their money arrived. Waving away their thanks, he pointed out it was better for the company than leaving the place empty and hearing they were virtually destitute, gave them what cash he had in his pocket.

Now there was less work for him to do, he paid the twins periodic visits, joining Miss Mary on the verandah while her sister lay on her bed by the open window so she could join in the conversation. But once she could get into her underwear again and her bottom had recovered enough to take her weight, all three of them would sit outside looking down at the sandy beach where an occasional figure was still sunbathing. As they got to know their new companion better, the sisters once more found themselves, as always with slight embarrassment, telling him what they were trying to do without revealing too much of what had happened to them so far. Of one thing they were certain. Their lips would be forever sealed over their incredibly distressing appearance in court.

Roger listened, as Paul and others had before him, with an air of bemusement mixed with a certain admiration for their courage which could only be described as foolhardy. Yet they had got this far, and he would do what he could to get them on their way again. With Miss Alice fit enough to travel, their sense of impatience which was never far below the surface, was beginning to rise to the top. This only increased further when their money came through and they were able to pay what they owed and had no reason to stay any longer.

It was on the following day around noon that Roger appeared and said he had a piece of good news for them. They had a chance to get off the island and if they took it, would be heading for the best possible of all destinations. He had been making inquiries on the harbourside and discovered an English couple who would be setting off in their boat tomorrow for the port of Alexandria on the Egyptian coast. From there, the sisters should have no trouble in catching a bus to take them across the desert to Cairo.

His hearers looked at each other as if they could not quite believe their ears. At long last a rare stroke of good fortune seemed to be smiling upon them after all their setbacks. Hastily they asked what they would have to do to get themselves on board. Roger explained that he had briefly mentioned they wanted to get to Cairo but would leave it up to them to give their reasons. The boat owners were a retired couple in their sixties from London who were called John and Peggy Sanders. He had been an engineer and she a teacher and they now spent their summers sailing around the Mediterranean. They seemed to be very pleasant and no doubt from time to time were pleased to have some company. As they were due to sail in the morning, he had arranged for them all to meet at a waterfront café at four o'clock that afternoon.

Miss Mary and Miss Alice arrived to find the couple already settled at an outside table with Roger, shielded from the sun by a vast parasol. Getting to his feet, their benefactor made the introductions before saying he had things to do but would return later. The twins looked upon him as an ally and would rather he had stayed, but realised it was up to them to portray themselves as agreeable travelling companions. Feeling rather like school leavers attending a first job interview, they could not help experiencing a flicker of anxiety as they took their seats. The pair opposite, burnt a deep brown by the sun, looked considerably younger than their years. They both had neatly cropped grey hair and lean figures which were the product of their active life in the open air. They gave the impression of being inseparable and this was heightened by their attire, for their blue shirts, white shorts, white socks and leather sandals, perfectly matched each other.

It was Peggy who spoke first, saying how nice it was to meet others of their generation who were being adventurous. That was the trouble with England today, not enough people of any age were prepared to get out and about. John enthusiastically agreed, adding that he was impressed when Roger told him about their long overland journey to reach Cairo, and he and his wife would be delighted to give them a lift over the final barrier.

The twins, taking it in turns to say how grateful they were, immediately offered to pay for their berths but this was dismissed by a wave of the husband's hand. They could contribute to the food supplies if they wanted, but that would be all that was required. Their new hosts then rose, explaining they had to make the final preparations for sailing and would meet the pair at the entrance to the local market at ten o'clock the following morning.

They had barely left to mingle with the crowd strolling along the waterfront when Roger reappeared. The buoyant twins told him they would indeed be leaving Rhodes in just a few hours and were amazed they had been accepted in such a short time without revealing anything of themselves.

He gave a short laugh in response. "You're the sort of people they like to associate with and I had already given you a decent reference. As I said before, when there are just two of you out here all summer it's nice sometimes to be entertained by somebody else. Most people of their kind have got their own boats so can only get together when they meet on dry land. No," he added thoughtfully, "I was more interested in their characters and capabilities rather than yours. I have checked with the harbourmaster who says they have been around for a while and do appear to be competent sailors. I did not want to be responsible for sending you off to a watery grave. They are apparently a very fastidious couple as you can detect from their appearance and keep their yacht spic and span, but you should get on well together as the voyage is only likely to last three or four days at the most."

The sisters assured him that they most certainly would. At that moment, with Egypt's coastline at last tantalisingly beckoning from just over the horizon, they would have happily sailed with that most notorious of all pirates, Captain Blood himself.

Chapter 21

The twins arrived at the market entrance the next morning five minutes early to find John and Peggy already waiting for them. They were again wearing matching outfits although now they were in yellow polo shirts with white collars and light grey socks. They guided the pair deftly in and out of the stalls, picking up fresh fruit and vegetables along with loaves of bread, cuts of meat, an enormous slice of feta and a mound of green and black olives. The new crew members insisted on contributing their share and with arms overflowing, the boarding party made their way through the shoppers down to the quayside. Bobbing gently against the jetty was the Eastern Lady, a thirty six foot, four berth yacht in the pristine condition that Roger had predicted and whose highly polished fittings sparkled in the morning sun.

Having said goodbye to Roger the night before as he had to be at the airport to collect people, there were no emotional farewells to be said as they climbed aboard. Peggy cast off the ropes while John brought the engine to life and in no time the craft was nosing its way out into the open sea. Watching the land slowly recede into the distance, the sisters for the first time had the sensation that Cairo really was coming close.

The Sanders continued to ask no questions about the reason for their journey but behind their politeness, the twins sensed a growing curiosity. So once again, as the four of them sat in the cabin over a lunch of salad and cheese, they explained how a mysterious restlessness had forced them to leave the comforts of home to go in search of their mother. Yet instead of the bemused or astonished reaction this would normally engender, their revelations were greeted with unbridled enthusiasm. As somewhat restless characters themselves, John and

Peggy said they fully understood what it was like when something inside got hold of you that you could not get rid of. But their hosts, being practical, wanted to know the practicalities.

It was Peggy who posed the question that had worried the sisters from the very start. "How are you going to go about it?" she asked, eyeing each twin in turn and they, put on the spot, could think of no immediate reply. The four of them had been discussing the odds of their mother still being alive at eighty seven in a hot climate and had agreed they would be very long indeed. So if they couldn't find her in the flesh what then? asked John. There were dozens of cemeteries in the city and they could not possibly search them all. And, as he gravely pointed out, most of the inscriptions would be in Arabic. But again, if she was alive how would they recognise her if they saw her? She had probably not spoken English for years and may not even recollect her former married name. So what did they have to go on?

Miss Alice drew out a small waterproof wrapper that had never left her pocket. Why she decided to do so now, having never shown it anybody else, she did not know. Maybe it was because they were nearing their destination at last or because the Sanders were being the most encouraging. Inside was a small passport sized photograph of a youngish woman. Although faded, it clearly showed a rather striking face with clear grey eyes beneath neatly tied shoulder length fair hair. "This was the last picture we had of our mother," she said. "It was taken shortly before she left. We have looked at it so many times over the years. She has always stayed the same in our heads but of course she would be a complete stranger by now."

She passed it round. Peggy, holding it gingerly, stared at it for a long time. She had had her ups and downs with John but what, she wondered, had induced this woman to give up an apparently secure and happy home with two wonderful children? It was such an intriguing mystery that she almost felt like joining the search herself. Not that there was any hope of an outcome. A subdued silence followed as the reality of it all hit home to each of them and it was a subject that was mainly skirted around for the rest of the voyage.

It was on the morning of the fourth day that the outline of Egypt's coast came into view, being only just visible through the haze. And by late afternoon they were edging slowly into the crowded harbour looking for a place to berth. It took an hour for them to find one and safely tie up and then another to go through all the paperwork formalities. The sisters, standing among the mass of humanity thronging the wharves, soaked up the exhilarating and also slightly intimidating atmosphere. They were now well and truly in the East with Europe lying far behind them.

They had decided to spend a last night on Eastern Lady and to catch the first bus to Cairo in the morning. After a frugal supper of the voyage's leftovers, the four sat on deck listening to the never ending hum of activity around them and looking up at the stars beginning to appear in a clear night sky. Everybody's head was bursting with thoughts concerning the twins imminent departure, but there was a distinct lack of desire to put these into words. Despite their initial enthusiasm and genuine admiration for what the sisters were trying to do, John and Peggy, had come to realise just as much as Miss Mary and Miss Alice, what a formidable task awaited the pair. The dense crowd thronging the shore by their boat, was but a microcosm of the teeming streets of Cairo and its outskirts.

So in a bizarre fashion, the conversation turned to England and the homes they had both left behind, with the sisters discussing the wonders of The Rectory with an intensity that was driven by the fear they might not see it again. Even as they spoke, the wide lawns, the fruit trees, the shrubs and the ivy creeping up the back wall sprang to life before their eyes and they felt a desperate yearning to hear the sound of Archie's mower and the blackbirds singing by the kitchen window.

The decision to start their journey in the morning rather than straight away, had been taken to ensure they got a good night's sleep and so would awake suitably refreshed. But once they had turned in, they found that hard as they tried, blissful oblivion just would not come. They tossed and turned repeatedly in their narrow bunks with the sounds and smells of a strange new land already invading their senses.

The grey light of dawn greeted their sleepless eyes and they were soon up, readying their rucksacks before being ordered by Peggy to force down several biscuits with their coffee despite their complete lack of appetite. They had often confidently imagined in their mind's eye how they would feel when at last approaching Cairo, a thrilling mixture of mounting excitement and a tremendous sense of achievement. But now that moment had arrived, the reality was proving to be very different. John and Peggy had offered to go with them to the coach station and as they followed them down a series of narrow streets, the twins' mouths were dry from anxiety and they felt a distinct fluttering in their stomachs despite an outward show of calm. John bought their tickets with Egyptian currency left from a previous visit and they paid him with some of their drachmas as they did not have time to change their own money before the bus left. That would have to be their first job when they got to Cairo.

They had become adept at saying heartfelt farewells

over the past few momentous weeks but none had felt harder to make than the one they were having to undertake now. Like others before them, the Sanders had been unfailingly kind and helpful but the sisters needed friendly faces like never before as their journey was inexorably approaching its climax. After all the difficulties they had defiantly overcome, they wondered if at last their nerve was beginning to fail them.

Yet once the bus had left the city centre behind and stretches of desert and clusters of palm trees began to speed by, their spirits once again gradually began to revive. As far as they could tell, they were the only foreigners on board but a constant chatter arose from their fellow passengers who were mainly middle aged women clutching large bags and the atmosphere was warm and convivial. There were no hold ups along a fairly empty highway and their early start meant that the pair arrived at their destination shortly after midday.

Disgorging from the vehicle, they stood uncertainly, envying those being greeted by friends and relatives or who knew the direction in which they were meant to be going. Feeling lost, the twins wondered where to find suitable cheap accommodation, either lodgings or a small self contained flat or, if the worst came to the worst, a single room.

The big question of course, was how long were they likely to be staying? Even if they did not find their mother, they knew they would have to go home at some time. The money they had left to exchange should last them for a week or two if they could discover a reasonable rent. Yet they had no idea about the cost of living in the city. It would just be a case of being as thrifty as possible but as insurance, they had already selected the next thing at The Rectory to sell if it became necessary. This was a large painting of a seventeenth century country squire surrounded by his hunting dogs which hung above the desk in the study. It was reputed to be quite valuable, but neither of the sisters liked it much because the man's baleful eyes seemed to follow them round the room.

But that was in the future. First they would have to replace their Greek currency and then search for a tourist office that hopefully could provide a list of addresses from which they might be able to choose somewhere to stay.

Despite having made an attempt to iron their dresses while on the boat, the new arrivals were well aware that living out of a rucksack made them look considerably more scruffy than the average foreign tourist installed in their air conditioned hotels. The bus's system had been intermittent, and they felt terribly hot and sweaty as well as tired after their sleepless night. The one advantage of being in a distant land was you could do things that you would never dream of doing at home. And so knowing that she was completely in the company of strangers, Miss Mary lifted her elbow and risked a good sniff under her arm. She was immediately shaken to hear a booming English voice that came from somewhere over her shoulder. "What ho my dears. Need a shower do we?" The speaker, who had the reassuring accent of their own class, was dressed in a spotless, expensive looking white suit under which a shirt of the palest pink stretched over an impressive expanse of stomach. Its owner took a handkerchief that was as florid as his face from his top pocket and patted his forehead carefully with it. "My name's Augustus Prentice-Jones. It's most awfully hot isn't it?"

Their new acquaintance said he was an antique dealer who regularly travelled between Cairo, London and New York and was on his way to inspect some vases somebody was keen to sell. "But what are you doing in this den of iniquity? I must say you do look like a couple of lost souls."

The pair privately agreed with this verdict and Miss Alice explained they had come to find their mother and were in desperate need of a place to stay. Their new friend, if that was what he was going to be, gave her a quizzical look. "In what part of the city does she live?"

"Actually we don't know," came the reply.

"My goodness, you have set yourselves a task. Look," he said as if suddenly coming to a decision. "Why don't you let me buy you lunch? I'm feeling a bit peckish and I know a really decent watering hole not far from here."

"But what about your vases?" asked Miss Mary.

"I have arranged to see them anytime today so they can wait until later. You are a curious pair and I want to know more about your search. If I feed you, that will be my bribe."

It was a most tempting offer but the twins looked at each other and for a moment they hesitated. Yet several times before they had put themselves into the hands of total strangers and here they were, having survived the experience to tell the tale. "We would be delighted to accept," replied Miss Mary. "But we feel that we should pay our way."

"I won't hear a word of it," responded Augustus obviously delighted with their decision. "It's not everyday I get the chance to entertain my own countrywomen." Telling the pair to call him Augie like all his friends did, he beckoned to them to follow him and set off with a purposeful stride down the street.

Gradually the pavements became wider and less cramped and the shop fronts more elegant with expensive goods on display in their windows. It was becoming obvious to the sisters that they were entering a more affluent part of the city. Finally they came to a halt before a tall four storey, narrow fronted building set back from the road with the flags of several nations fluttering from poles on its roof. The twins could see at a glance it was an international hotel of the standard that in England would be called five star.

Ushered up its short flight of marble steps by their ever genial host, they entered the blissfully cool embrace of the foyer feeling uncomfortably like a pair of tramps. Augie, gracefully acknowledged the brisk salute of the uniformed doorman and told the twins it was the best place for lunch in the whole of Cairo. Pointing to a rest room on their right, he said he would wait at the bar if they would like to take the opportunity of refreshing themselves. Accepting the offer with alacrity, they were greeted by a row of glistening basins, spotless white towels and ample bars of exquisitely perfumed soap. Setting to with a will, they washed as much of themselves as they could in the circumstances, marvelling over how their fortunes had changed once again. The odds of accidentally meeting what they were calling their knight in shining armour in a city of several million people, must have been astronomical. Yet as they said, they had long ago become well accustomed to the vagaries of fate.

Emerging if not well groomed, at least clean and tidy, they made their way to the bar where Augie, perched on a high stool, was sipping a large whisky and soda appreciatively. In front of him stood two slim flutes of very pale dry sherry. "I hope you don't mind me choosing your drinks for you," he said greeting them heartily. "I thought it was the sort of thing you'd like and I didn't want to waste time. Mind you, the barman had to go and find a bottle in the cellar but they've got everything here."

The sisters in turn took an appreciative sip and glanced with growing anticipation at the beautifully laid tables which were visible through the glass fronted restaurant doors. The biscuits they had forced down on the boat on Peggy's orders seemed a long time ago and with the butterflies in their stomachs now having vanished, there would be plenty of room for food.

As if divining their thoughts, Augie picked up his glass and instructing them to do the same, led the way to a table of three by the window he had decided upon earlier. He had also decided what they would drink with their meal and this arrived swiftly on their heels, a bottle of the house's best champagne in an ornate silver bucket with a leaping lion depicted on its side. While one silent figure in a white coat busied himself uncorking it, another similarly attired, was handing out menus containing an impressive array of dishes described in both French and English.

The twins stared at these without really taking anything in. Their elevation from being part of the teeming crowd outside whose heads could be seen passing by the window, to the rarefied atmosphere of their current surroundings had been so swift, they were having difficulty adjusting their minds to it. Augie, seeing their struggles, suggested that he should chose for them. "The trouble is, when you're spoilt for choice it's so difficult to make up your mind," he said. "But I'm quite good at being decisive." So with the waiter standing attentively by his elbow, he adroitly pointed out what he wanted.

The fresh quail's eggs were the first to arrive followed by the most delicately cooked monk fish in a tangy sauce and then an exotically spiced lamb stew. The sisters made short work of these and by the time the fresh mangoes and ice cream were placed before them, their spirits were rising inexorably like the bubbles in their champagne glasses which were constantly kept topped up.

They said they dared not think what the final bill

would be but Augie airily waved away their concerns. Their tongues had loosened as they began to unwind, and he had listened with astonishment to some of their more colourful exploits. What they had so far achieved, he declared, deserved the best possible celebration and he could easily afford it. The drink and the occasion was beginning to make the twins feel quite light headed so they were grateful for the pot of black coffee that finally arrived along with a plate of hand made Belgian chocolates in the form of little pyramids.

They felt life could not possibly get any better but then to their amazement, it did. Calling for a cigar, Augie with an experienced eye, selected the largest and what looked to be the most expensive. Lighting it with great care, he took a deep puff and watched the smoke curling towards the ceiling. "I have been considering your accommodation problem," he said gravely. "With the funds you have available, you will almost certainly end up in a most ghastly back street hovel. There will be a danger of bed bugs and lice which can cause very nasty infections. You do not want to be ill for the task that awaits you. I have a Dutch friend who has a nice clean apartment with its own roof garden overlooking a quiet street in a good part of the city which is very near here. He has a spare room and I am sure he would not charge an exorbitant rate if I recommend you. He normally pops home at this time of day so we could go now and see if we can catch him in. It is only in the next street."

The sister attempted to rise to their feet with their host but he quickly held up his hand. "No, no. I meant of course that I would go. You deserve to let your lunches settle. I'm sure you don't get much of an opportunity to relax during your amazing travels. It will only take me a minute or two."

"But if we need a deposit to take up the offer

immediately we only have Greek currency," pointed out Miss Alice.

"Look, let's kill two birds with one stone," replied Augie. "There is a bureau at the side of the hotel. I can exchange yours on the way and probably get a better rate than you could." He took a long puff of his cigar and placed it at the right angle in the ashtray to prevent any smoke drifting towards the diners. "I shall be back long before that's finished," he said carefully counting the notes Miss Alice had given him before depositing them in an inside pocket. Watching him amble off towards the foyer, the twins' eyes shone brightly with gratitude and admiration. At that moment, they would not have been at all surprised if he'd said he would be returning with their mother.

There could hardly have been two more contented souls in all of the city than Miss Alice and Miss Mary as they forced themselves to have another chocolate while they discussed the latest upturn in their fortunes. They had been in similar situations before, if not quite so grand, but this time they were no longer facing another stage in their increasingly painful journey. Oh no, they had arrived and already it seemed that they had somewhere decent to live which would leave them buoyant and refreshed to start their search. It was right, they agreed, that an Englishman should always help his compatriots abroad and indeed they had a reputation for doing so. But Augie, in the words of their late lamented father, had really pushed the boat out and they could not thank him enough.

Chattering away, they had not realised how time was passing until suddenly they noticed more than a quarter of an hour had gone by. Obviously, they thought, there must be a queue at the exchange and of course Augie was quite a talker. It was then they saw the waiter approaching. He was carrying a small silver tray upon which lay a thick sheaf of papers. Placing it carefully on the table between them, he announced. "Your bill madams."

The diners watched his performance in horrified disbelief. "But, but," stammered Miss Alice putting her hand to her mouth, "we are the guests of Mr Prentice-Jones."

"I am under the impression madam that this is not so. He was quite clear that he was your guest. I have included a large cognac he had on the way out. He also told me to give myself a decent tip."

Miss Mary looked incredulous. "On the way out?"

"Yes madam, he left about twenty minutes ago. He asked that I allow you plenty of time to finish your coffee and chocolates before disturbing you."

Miss Alice found her fingers reaching out numbly for the contents of the plate. The total leapt out at her from the bottom of the last page. She did not understand the currency, but what seemed to be a never ending line of numerals showed that the amount was huge. The blood drained from her face as she let it flutter to the floor. Miss Mary snatched it up, took one long horrified look and went as pale as her sister. The whole thing was a bad dream. Augie would come marching through the door at any moment. But however hard they stared at it, there was no sign of him. "I am afraid there has been the most awful mistake," said Miss Alice who was slowly regaining her colour. "We are quite unable to pay this bill."

The waiter looked from one to the other with a perplexed air. "Excuse me if you will kindly remain seated, I will call the manager."

As he disappeared, the twins, feeling completely dumbfounded, sat in silence. Each knew what was whirling round inside the head of the other and in their dire situation words seemed superfluous. Looking around the restaurant which was now empty apart from themselves, gave them a modicum of comfort for they knew the confrontation that was to come would be extremely embarrassing. They did not have long to wait before their waiter reappeared accompanied by a tall, thin man with slicked back grey hair above a high forehead. "I am Raymond Delors the manager at your service," he said with a hint of an accent that betrayed his French origins. "Haji here tells me there has been a misfortune."

Miss Mary who could not have agreed more with this description, explained how they had met Mr Prentice-Jones and how he had taken them under his wing and had most clearly promised to pay for their lunch. But then, she said, blushing deeply at their own stupidity, something worse had happened. They had given him all their Greek currency to exchange and now they were completely destitute.

"He is just running an errand for us," interrupted Miss Alice who was still finding it difficult to accept the situation. "Look, he has left his cigar unfinished. I am sure he will be back at any minute."

Mr Delors produced a faint knowing smile. "Sacrificing a cigar however expensive is a small price to pay to ensure you have enough time to make good your escape. You will not find him now." His brief show of mirth gave way to a slight frown accentuated by his long face. "There are many such tricksters in Cairo. They wait around bus and train stations looking for new arrivals like yourselves who appear lost and uncertain in a strange city and who become easy prey to their schemes as you have discovered. But this man has paid you the compliment of bringing you here because not all victims would fit in at our hotel and we have not had a case like this before."

It was a compliment the sisters could have done

without for both knew what the next question was going to be and so it proved. "It is a delicate inquiry I have to make of you and I apologise for doing so, but how are you going to pay the bill?"

"We have money in England," broke in Miss Alice again. "We are going to send for it and will soon be able to settle with you. We are not fly-by-nights. We are in Cairo to search for our mother so will be here for quite a time."

The Frenchman uttered what sounded like a mournful sigh. "Hotels listen to many offers to pay later but these are never acceptable to the management." He picked up the sheaf of papers from the tray and slowly shifted through them. "You owe a large amount. The champagne alone comes to nearly two hundred pounds in your currency. Your Mr Prentice-Jones, if that is his real name, had an excellent eye for the good things in life." The twins in their state of shock, were again unable to think of anything to say and waited for him to go on. "We have to consider what the options are. The bill is too large to be written off and in normal circumstances we would call the police, but the prisons are not nice places to be in here and there would be no guarantee that the hotel would get its money."

Picking up a teaspoon, he began to tap it meditatively on the tablecloth while turning his eyes first upon one sister and then the other. There was a long pause before he put the spoon down and adjusted a shirt cuff. "This is an unusual situation and calls for an unusual solution. There are those guests who deliberately try to avoid paying but I can see this does not apply to you. You have been unwittingly caught up in this man's fraud. What I propose will ensure the hotel is not out of pocket and will provide you with free accommodation which you will no doubt be pleased to accept at the moment as you are without means of support."

He paused to stare steadily at each again. "The hotel will employ you as chambermaids until the debt is paid or your funds arrive from England. Unfortunately the rates of pay are low which will extend your stay but of course you will be provided with meals which although filling, will not be quite what you have experienced in the restaurant. We regularly have English guests staying and most of our room staff struggle with the language so your presence will be a welcome advantage. Your hours of work will be in the morning only which will leave the rest of the day free for your own pursuits. I hope you will agree to this solution for you seem fit enough for the task and really you have no other option."

The sisters sat there in a daze but their brains were active enough for them to realise that however reluctantly, they would have to agree. The alternatives of being handed over to the police or evicted penniless into the streets did not even bear thinking about. Mr Delors pronounced himself satisfied with their answer and said there were just two more formalities to complete. The first was to sign their contracts which Haji would organise before showing them to their staff quarters. The second was for them to hand over their passports to the hotel for safe keeping. He emphasised they must not feel this was in any way a slight on their integrity, but the hotel needed some insurance they would remain at their posts until the matter was resolved. Then he wished them success in their new positions and watched as Haji escorted the two still shocked women from the room. They had entered it as pampered guests and were leaving it as part of the workforce.

Chapter 22

The small cramped room on the top floor had a sloping ceiling and contained two narrow beds. There was a small hand basin in the corner with a bathroom and lavatory outside in the corridor. The sisters were relaxing on their skimpy mattresses after their morning's work which had left them tired but far from exhausted. They found the effort required was no more than they were used to in keeping The Rectory neat and tidy. They had each been given three bedrooms to clean. These were large with their own terrace that also had to be swept, but were sparsely if elegantly furnished and had king sized beds. The guests were so far proving to be tidy people although they had yet to meet one in the flesh.

All in all, they considered, things could have been a good deal worse. The Frenchman had a made a pragmatic and sensible decision to hire them. He could have caused a scene and called the police. It was true he had confiscated their passports but they could understand any manager acting this way in such a situation. As for Mr Prentice-Jones, they trembled with indignation at the mere thought of him. How could such an obvious gentleman act like that? They agreed he was a complete and utter scoundrel. Even worse than those they had read about in lurid Victorian novels back at home. However they would waste no more time on such a distasteful subject. They would cast him completely from their minds.

The one big problem was their empty pockets which meant they could only explore within a few streets of the hotel and so greatly hampered the start of their search. Most of the drivers who gave camel rides to tourists and might have valuable information, were outside the city centre as were most of the cemeteries.

All of these were too far to reach on foot in the heat and the twins' penniless condition meant public transport was out of the question. And when they did venture forth, they could not even afford a simple glass of freshly squeezed fruit juice from a roadside vendor to combat the humid conditions. It was a most depressing feeling for throughout their travels they had always had some money, however little it had been. They had borrowed a small amount from the hotel, which was added to their bill, to wire Archie to send more funds. But these would take time to arrive while they waited for the painting to be sold. And they could not get an advance on their wages which were all going to pay off their incredibly expensive lunch.

It was then Miss Mary thought of the packet of expensive looking postcards a departed guest had either forgotten or left behind as a tip. These were large and colourful, and showed a succession of Cairo's most famous ancient landmarks. They seemed to be superior to the best of those seen by the twins in the hotel foyer or in shop windows. The big question was could they be turned into cash? They were the only things among the sisters' entire possessions that could possibly be sold. The pair had seen a variety of postcard sellers at work in the streets around them, but these were operating from jealously guarded pitches. Could the twins pluck up the courage to find their own space and offer theirs in the middle of a teeming crowd?

They could certainly not have done if they had just been setting out from home. But the Miss Mary and Miss Alice of those days were not the same Miss Mary and Miss Alice who found themselves at seventy years of age chamber-maiding in a Cairo hotel.

Once the heat of the day had begun to subside, they decided they would set off into the hostile streets to try their luck. Resisting the idea of conserving their energy, they spent the afternoon washing and ironing their dresses to make their appearance as pleasing as possible. Realising they would have to position themselves where most of the city's visitors congregated, they took a tourist map from the foyer which highlighted the most promising venues. The problem, they were soon to discover, was that other postcard sellers had long ago come to the same conclusion and were firmly established at all the best vantage points.

After an hour of being in the thick of the fray, as Miss Alice put it, the sisters retired to a bench in the corner of a quiet square to reassess their strategy. It was not in their nature to vigorously accost passers-by like the mainly young male Egyptian sellers did. They had reasoned their potential customers would be almost all middle aged or elderly European tourists who appreciated a more gentle, conservative approach. The result of this, was they had one less card than they had started with, and not a single pilaster, the lowest of the local currency, to show for it. They had stood side by side smiling brightly, while displaying their offerings in their outstretched hands. Most of those thronging the busy pavement had ignored them, but one man, deftly taking Miss Mary's card from her fingers, had muttered a polite response and walked on.

When the twins' indignation had subsided, they realised he must have thought, that by standing mutely, they were giving them away free like people they had seen handing out leaflets for night clubs and restaurants. From now on, they decided, they would be more forceful in accosting passers-by.

Having found a new site by a museum of ancient history, they proceeded to put their plan into action. Their more vocal efforts caused several people to stop and look, although not one of them showed any interest in buying. It was most frustrating because across the road, another group of young sellers seemed to be getting rid of theirs without the slightest difficulty. This mystery was finally solved by a neatly dressed elderly Egyptian man, who noticing the sisters' predicament, gave them some valuable advice in perfect English. Their cards were indeed beautiful, but of the kind that could be easily purchased in almost any hotel. To sell cards successfully in the streets of Cairo they needed to be, and here he paused, well, more interesting, more explicit of nature, more colourfully exotic.

It was Miss Alice who was the first to understand what he was discreetly indicating. "You mean they have to be rude?" she said.

"Yes madam."

"And that is what they are selling?" interrupted Miss Mary, pointing to their rivals who were surrounded by a jostling crowd on the opposite pavement.

"Yes madam. But they are more dirty than rude. Indeed they are very, very dirty postcards."

Back in their room once more, a subdued Miss Mary placed the contents of the almost unused packet in the drawer by her bed. There, she declared, they would stay until they finally had some money when they would send a nice picture of a pyramid to Archie.

Chapter 23

The morning had gone particularly badly. It was, Miss Mary ruefully said to herself, jolly unfair. Her first two bedrooms had been unusually untidy with bits of rubbish left in awkward places such as under tables or beds which had meant a lot of stooping and bending. So it was getting towards eleven o'clock when, not in the best of humour, she approached her third and final one and knocked softly on its door.

Hearing no response, she turned the handle and entered to be greeted by almost total darkness. The mottled green curtains which she had thought to be in the poorest of taste, had not even been opened. Padding across the thick carpet, she gave a deft tug at their cord to begin to pull them apart. A shaft of sunlight shot across the room picking out a previously undetected figure lying prone in the king sized bed that dwarfed it. A feeble female voice arose plaintively from the pillow. "God, no, no, please no light." Miss Mary hastily drew them back together leaving a small enough gap so she could see through the gloom. After a lengthy pause it came again, sounding even more agonised. "I'm dying. Do you know any psalms? I have not long to prepare myself. There's one that goes Closer My Lord To Thee or something."

"No, I'm afraid I don't," replied Miss Mary.

At this response the speaker raised her head slightly to reveal a deathly white face ringed by a mass of black curls. "Thank God I can see you clearly now. At first I thought you were an angel and I was already dead." The distressed figure paused again. "But I must say you spoke awfully good English. I can't normally understand a word the chambermaids say. I told the manager that teaching them to communicate properly should be a rule of the hotel."

Miss Mary drew nearer. "But I am English."

The head slowly rose again from the pillow and she felt herself being peered at intently. "My God, you are."

"You don't sound very well. Do you want me to call a doctor?"

"No, no. What I need is a large brandy. Hair of the dog and all that."

"Will the bar be open at this hour?"

"No, no, there's a bottle by the sink. There should be enough left if I remember rightly. Not that I can remember anything anyway."

Miss Mary threw a glance in the desired direction and could immediately see that the source of her salvation was empty. Without saying a word, she filled a glass with water and handed it to the prostrate victim who struggled into a sitting position and took a gulp. "Ugh, horrible, is this all there is?" Miss Mary nodded, realising she was coming under scrutiny again as the woman's mind slowly began to creak into action. "You certainly look like the right sort of English girl. What on earth are you doing here?" Before the newly installed chambermaid could reply the voice came again. "Wait! Please soak a flannel under the cold tap and place it on my forehead. Then I will be more in a fit state to listen."

Miss Mary, feeling more like a nurse, did as she was told and then, invited to sit on the edge of the bed, related the sorry story of their first hours in Cairo which had led to her and her sister wearing the hotel's uniform. The face on the pillow wore an anguished look which Miss Mary could not decide was due to sympathy for their plight ,or to the thumping headache that must be going on inside her listener's head. When she had finished there was a long pause before a voice, strengthened with indignation, rose from the covers.

"That Prentice-Jones sounds the most frightful chap. What a dreadful, dreadful cad. Mind you," it added. "I've met an awful lot of cads in my time. I've been married to four of them."

She suddenly sat up. "Good God, I haven't introduced myself. I'm Cissie St Clair. We must meet when I'm feeling a little more compus mentis and you can tell me more of your story. There is a café directly across the street. I will treat you and your sister to afternoon tea so please be there at four o'clock." With that, she sank back again and Miss Mary, aware that an unbroken silence took precedence over her cleaning activities, left the room in the state it was and slipped quietly out of the door.

When the sisters arrived at the appointed hour, they found their hostess already there sitting at a table in the dimly lit interior. She was wearing a wide brimmed black felt hat despite being out of the sun, and sported a pair of large dark glasses which she removed briefly to greet her guests revealing a pair of rather puffy eyes adorned with dark circles. Yet despite her fragile appearance, she seemed alert and interested as the twins, over cups of lemon tea sweetened with brown sugar, told of their long journey and the coming search for their mother. When they had finished, Cissie again removed her glasses to stare at them briefly in turn with raised eyebrows. "Over the years I have heard many quite extraordinary stories," she declared. "Mainly from men of course. But this is the most extraordinary of the most extraordinary of them all."

"Do you think we are mad?" asked Miss Alice.

"Utterly, utterly insane," came the immediate and firm reply. "There is absolutely no doubt at all about it. Yet you most certainly must look for her. And as I have nothing to do at the moment, I have already appointed myself as leader of the search party." Sensing a protest coming from her startled new companions, she swiftly went on. "I know Cairo well and if I may say so without appearing to be rude, you are like two lost helpless souls adrift in this strange land."

As the sisters sipped their drinks and listened, Cissie in turn explained in rather wrought tones her own personal circumstances which showed exactly why she had time on her hands. She had just divorced one Ralph de Vere, a financer who had been husband number four. And like all the rest, he had been completely charming but the most dreadful rat. But like all the previous bounders before him, he had given her a hefty payoff. It was odd that of all the men she had come across in life, the poor ones had all been nice, while the rich had proved to be jolly nice. Even if only for a short time. Which is why she had always ended up with them.

Looking at the twins with approval, she said how very, very wise they had been never to have entered into a marriage. But then the lavish gifts of jewellery she had received and the handsome settlements had been a wonderful help, along with a decent amount of brandy, in healing her repeatedly bruised heart.

Yet enough of her, she added as if the successive partings had been too ghastly and painful to be mulled over. They had to plan for the future. And the first thing to be done was to end the sisters' employment at the hotel. It was the nineteen seventies for God's sake. The white slave trade had been banished many years ago. Cissie said she had contemplated inviting the pair to be her guests there but realised such as situation would be uncomfortable for all concerned in view of their previous existence. So she would pay off the outstanding amount they owed for their lunch, which, she said on hearing about it, she would have liked to have sampled herself. Then she would rent a small flat where they could all stay. It would be in a central position and an ideal headquarters from which to start their search.

Once more she acted swiftly to head off any of their protests. She could easily afford it, she announced with an impressive air of authority. She was actually rolling in money. To be fair to those dreadful cads who had ruthlessly taken advantage of her, they had come up trumps magnificently when having to atone for their evil ways. And anyway, she added, taking off her glasses again and tentatively rubbing her forehead, the pair could help out with expenses when their money arrived.

The dominating personality of their new companion despite her obvious suffering, overwhelmed the twins who gazed at her with a mixture of astonishment and gratitude. They were no longer alone. They appeared to have gained a powerful ally but for how long, and to what benefit, remained very much to be seen.

Chapter 24

The flat was on the first floor in a quiet road with its own balcony and side entrance leading to a short flight of steps. It was simply and plainly furnished but was ideally suited to what was going to be required. Its new occupants would be out for most of the time, and would need it only as a place to recoup their strength after what they expected would be many long hours spent tramping the streets. The sisters from the outset had only had a hazy idea of what they would do when they reached Cairo, and it was Cissie who led the way by saying they must assimilate all possible information so they could put together a coherent plan.

The first and most important question to be considered was what did they know about their mother? The answer of course was not very much as they had not seen or heard of her for more than fifty years. "But she must have been head strong and impulsive," ventured Cissie, who was already warming to the distant figure because she felt a growing affinity with her. "People say we're the sort who fling ourselves at a man," she went on. "But that is absolute and utter nonsense. What really happens is the men can't stop themselves from making every effort to grab us. And by the sound of it, that is exactly what happened to your mother. Of course she had to be attracted to him as well, but these Arabs are frightfully cunning at getting you to like them."

She gave an involuntary sigh. "Oh he must have been so terribly handsome otherwise, with her civilised background, she wouldn't have done it. Those desert Arabs have such wonderful physiques and bright and merry roving eyes to go with them." She had of course noticed them herself, she added, before suddenly becoming thoughtful. But Mrs Harrison had run off so long ago. Fifty years was a lifetime in Egypt. And hers would not have been one of luxury if she had ended up with a native who had little means of support. Oh no, far from it. Arabs were wonderful wooers and were difficult to fend off. But once the courtship was over, they kept you at home washing and cooking. It would be a very hard life. Especially for a white woman in such a hot climate. Under such conditions their mother could not have possibly survived into her eighties. Her remains could have ended up anywhere. Even on a rubbish dump.

Suddenly Cissie pulled herself together. "No, no, that's not like me. I'm becoming far too morbid," she said in an effort to sound brighter. "Look, a good pointer will be your family's history. Did her parents - your grandparents - live to reach a ripe old age?"

Miss Mary averred that they certainly had. At least into their early nineties as far as she could remember.

"That is an excellent sign," replied Cissie approvingly as she felt her confidence returning. "But we do have to compare the climates of England where they lived and Egypt. It can be a lot hotter here and as I have already said, I expect her living conditions to have been much harsher. But now, the talking has to stop and the action begin. The first thing we will do tomorrow morning is to hire three camels and take a ride round one of those pyramids."

"But we can't waste time doing that," exclaimed Miss Alice who was feeling impatient after their discussion. "We have to start searching immediately."

"Waiting another day after fifty years will not make any difference," Cissie replied calmly. "That's what you and your mother were originally going to do so it is really important that you fulfil your destiny. I am a great believer in unseen forces and it would not do for you to tempt fate. Anyway, we shall have to go to all the places where they offer camel rides to see if anybody can provide any clues. Whoever your mother ran off with will be retired by now so only the older ones among the owners are likely to have any knowledge of him."

"Wait a minute," replied Miss Mary with a hint of indignation in her voice. "He would only be around our age and we are still very active."

"Good God, I know you are. I still can't believe how you managed to get this far and by slumming it as well. Travelling like you do, I couldn't go five miles without having a hot bath and a manicure and I'm only forty nine. But Arab men are not the hardest workers and I doubt if he would still be out in the glare of the midday sun." She was suddenly struck by a thought. "Talking of physical activities, your mother would still have been of child bearing age when she met him. You may well have a brother or sister, or indeed both."

This was an eventuality that for some reason, had never ever entered the head of either sister and it came as a most unnerving shock. It was something they did not want to contemplate at this stage because they already had so many things to think of and they tried to push it firmly from their minds. Yet when they retired early to get as much rest as they could before their foray into the desert, the possibility of such a thing happening kept returning to keep them awake. Were they, they wondered, members of a mysterious and extended family?

Chapter 25

Emerging into the street after a breakfast of spicy bread buns, fresh fruit and thick black coffee, they realised being under Cissie's wing did not only provide them with decent accommodation. Normally in such circumstances they would be resigning themselves to squeezing onto an overcrowded bus or tramping along the unforgiving pavements in the scorching heat. Instead, their benefactor, dressed in perfectly fitting jodhpurs, a silk blouse and scarf, and her wide brimmed felt hat, ushered them into a taxi she'd hailed with a commanding wave of an elegant hand.

Seating herself in the front beside the driver, she immediately showed she was going to be in charge of their operation. As the pyramids would be one of his popular destinations, she said, did he personally know any of the camel drivers? The recipient of this question was of late middle age with glossy black hair and a sallow complexion. The twins, catching a glance of his expression in his rear mirror saw him wince. No, he did not know anybody who owned camels, he replied in a forceful manner. They were dirty, ugly brutes and he much preferred his nice clean vehicle which did not veer off in different directions without warning or try to bite you as soon as your back was turned.

Inveterate talker though she was, Cissie could tell when a conversation was going to be a complete waste of time and this was certainly one of them. So she lapsed into a rather sulky silence for the rest of the forty minute journey with the sisters following suit.

No sooner had they stepped out of the taxi than they were surrounded by a jabbering throng with each member loudly declaring his camel was the best behaved and the easiest to ride in all the kingdom. Two tourist coaches parked in the shadow of the pyramid were on the point of departing, leaving the search party as they had christened themselves, to the undivided attention of every driver as well as those of the souvenir stallholders. These were offering every kind of artefact from exquisitely fashioned wooden boxes to toy figures in local costumes all adorned with the traditional red fez.

Miss Mary and Miss Alice felt a little overawed and intimidated by their reception, but Cissie appeared to revel in the attention. Singling out a tall, rather grave looking man who seemed to have better command of English than most, she called him over and asked Miss Alice to produce the picture of her mother. Turning it over curiously in his hand, he listened as Cissie explained who the fair haired woman was and why they were looking for her. Holding it high above his head, he proceeded to translate her appeal in a strident voice that to the ears of the searchers carried a pleasing sense of urgency.

The effect on the motley crew of onlookers was immediate. An astonished murmur swept through their ranks and they surged forward to get a better look at the photograph with several towards the back, forced to stand on their toes. The result however was disappointing as the sisters in their hearts knew it would be. Nobody stepped forward to offer information of even the most vague kind. Instead, there was much shaking of heads interspersed with occasional guffaws and sly grins as the crowd savoured the prospect of such an unusual union.

"As of course I expected, we've drawn a blank," said Cissie stating the patently obvious. "I'm afraid we're going to get a lot more of this."

With the photograph safely returned to Miss Alice, Cissie began haggling over the price of their ride as beast after beast was paraded for inspection. In her opinion she declared, they were all frightful creatures but she finally selected three who appeared to be among the quietest. These at a word of command, knelt down with a series of groans on their bony knees in the sand while their riders clasping the pommels of their saddles with clammy hands heaved themselves on top.

Rearing to their feet, the animals shook their gangly heads and began plodding in single file behind the leading beast of Herat, their youthful guide, who Cissie had hired to take them on their foray into the desert. He looked about eighteen with sparkling brown eyes, and proud of his growing knowledge of English, keen to talk. Most of his conversation was carried out over his shoulder but he regularly reined back to ensure his charges were coping with their new and strange form of transport. Having been an avid listener to Cissie's appeal he was determined to continue with the same subject. He too, he declared with barely concealed eagerness, would like to marry an English girl and now was his best chance. His present party were such pretty ladies they must have pretty daughters who in turn, would have pretty daughters they could introduce him to. As the owner of three hard working camels, he would make an ideal husband for one of them. Or indeed all of them.

"I'm frightfully sorry but you will have to look elsewhere," replied Cissie firmly. "My companions, Miss Mary and Miss Alice, despite being incredibly attractive, have never been married. They were never able to find anybody remotely good enough for them. And myself?" she added catching Herat's inquiring eye. "I have had four husbands but they were all without question dreadful rascals who led me badly astray. I thought I could improve them but it turned out to be an absolutely impossible task. Yet fortunately there were no offspring so I do not have a constant reminder of the ghastly mistakes I made."

"But why do you want an English girl?" asked Miss Alice. "We have seen many pretty local girls in the short time we have been here. They must be much easier to meet and to get to know."

"It is true," agreed Herat with a serious expression. "And much easier to marry. But then what does that bring you?"

"Hopefully happiness and contentment and a loyal friend," ventured Miss Mary who had read a lot about the subject in historical novels at The Rectory.

"That is a good answer," replied Herat. "But I say again what does this loyal bride bring with her?" There was a perplexed silence from his three female companions which he finally broke in a loud but heartfelt voice. "A mother-in-law. They are always around the house in our country telling you what to do. If I married an English girl, she would be far away in England which would be very good."

A stiff breeze was blowing up and flying sand began to sting their faces. The sisters, bowing their heads, were hanging onto their reins with grim resolution but Cissie St Clair seemed completely unfazed by the bumpy ride and sharpening wind. When the party slowed momentarily she took out her hand mirror to inspect her complexion and return a wayward strand of hair. The twins looked at her enviously. They believed they had learnt to take most things in their stride but not with such aplomb. And she had been married four times!

After a while the wind dropped as suddenly as it had arisen and the sisters, becoming used to the undulating motion of the camels, for the first time began to enjoy their ride. The flowing robes of Herat beckoned them on as now his quest for an English bride was over, he kept a yard ahead occasionally tapping his beast with his long cane to keep their little convoy going at a steady pace.

Miss Mary and Miss Alice suspected that if they had undertaken this ride when they were seventeen as was originally intended, they would probably have liked to have gone faster but in their more advanced state of life, a rhythmic trot was quite enough for them to handle. The vast structure of the pyramid overshadowing them as they circled it, stood stark against the clear sky and was a vivid reminder of the ancient world and the vast eons of time that had passed since it was built. Their fifty year wait to finally see it might feel like an eternity to them but it was not even a blink of an eye in its long history.

Their ride took more than two hours and when the camels knelt for them to get off at the end of it, the twins wondered if their legs would work. They felt stiff all over and their hands were numb from constantly grasping the reins. But they had to admit that Cissie had been right. It was important that they had carried out what was in some way a rite of passage. The pair dimly remembered how, long ago, they had enthusiastically discussed with their mother what would have been the highlight of their holiday. And now, however late, they had completed it. Of course it had not been with her, but somehow they felt they had accomplished something which in a way brought her closer although they were not quite sure how.

Herat bid them a fond farewell, once again reminding his little party that if any of their friends had daughters or granddaughters that would make suitable brides, they would always find him at the pyramid. Promising they would bear this in mind, they climbed awkwardly into a waiting taxi hoping the temperamental hot water system in their flat would allow them to ease their aches and pains with a decent

266

hot soak as soon as they got home.

The next morning Cissie called a conference saying it was time for one of their appraisals although in truth, everybody agreed there was nothing to appraise. Yet one thing was clear. Despite their failure to pick up any clues during their ride, they would have to visit every place in the city where there were camels for hire. It was the only way their mother as a tourist, could have met the man she ran off with.

So their first venture would be to visit every tourist office they could find to try to compile a list of these. And they would also draw up a separate one of every British institution from the Embassy downwards in case she had ever felt the need to get in touch with her former countrymen. In doing so the pair were acting as if she was still very much alive. If at the end of their search they had drawn a blank then so be it. They would make a start on the numerous and densely crowded cemeteries. It was a task that at the moment they could not bear to think about and Cissie actively discouraged them from even attempting to do so. Be positive, that was her motto. With the daunting task that lay before the three women, they knew only too well they could not afford to have any other attitude.

It took two days to collect the information they required and on the morning of the third, they set off on the first of their searching expeditions into the bustling and colourful city which fifty years ago had swallowed up Mrs Harrison. One by one, they crossed off their destinations as they mingled fruitlessly with the camel herders on what Cissie called an unending question and answer session. The query, always accompanied by a display of the photograph, was very simple. Have you ever seen this woman or heard anything at all of her?

The answers were varied and delivered with an array of gestures and tones, but all in the end were depressingly negative. Some of the older men after staring into the distance in a show of concentration, said they might have heard a rumour in the marketplace but when pressed, could not provide a single detail however vague.

But among the head scratching and frowns and the thoughtful tugging of ears, one man gave them an unexpected ray of hope. Dark haired with an intelligent face, he showed a great interest in their quest, listening intently to what they had to say before squatting on his haunches in the sand and picking up a short stick. They watched spellbound as he carefully drew the outline of first a man and then a woman who appeared to be holding hands as if they knew each other, although from the crude picture the sisters had no clue as to their identity. He then rose to his feet and without saying a word or favouring them with as much as a backward glance, walked off into the crowd before they had a chance to question him.

"Do you think he was trying to tell us something?" asked Miss Alice looking in astonishment at the retreating figure.

"I don't think so," replied Cissie shaking her head. "It looks to me as if he is the sort of chap who just likes doodling."

To break their days, the search party spent one half talking pidgin English with the Arabs and the other conferring with the more cut glass accents belonging to those manning the offices of the various British outposts dotted around the teeming city. And the result sadly, was exactly the same despite everybody being most helpful although the subject did tend to raise more than one or two eyebrows. Records were poured over, memories searched and word was passed around so that anybody who might know something was not missed out. Among those who had visited the institutions over the years and signed the guest books were several people called Harris and, among others, a Harries, a Harrity, a Harrington and a Hamerson. But never once a Harrison. It was as if the sisters were chasing a will of the wisp or as Cissie said, looking for a needle in a haystack while blindfolded and with one hand tied behind your back.

Finally after seventeen fruitless and depressing days, they regretfully realised they would have to abandon their investigations into the living and begin to concentrate instead on the homes of the dead. And as they began to list the most likely cemeteries, it began to sink in just how many members of the human race had gone before them and they wondered how many had been laid to rest without any of their friends or relatives knowing. And on the same subject, Cissie wondered how many people had vanished in Cairo never to reappear or to be rediscovered in the most joyful, or in some cases, fraught circumstances.

With the passing of each day, the sisters began to appreciate more and more the support they were getting from Cissie. They were so worn out after their long journey that they found her enthusiasm and determination invaluable in helping them to keep going. They had feared she would soon give up on what had always looked to be a lost cause, but their friend quickly proved to be the sort of person that stuck to her guns. As she said, producing one of her encouraging smiles, it gave her something to do. The twins' money had by now arrived and they insisted on making a modest contribution to the rent and the living expenses which made them feel a little more like equal partners.

After yet another conference, it was decided to start looking in the parts of cemeteries where Europeans were buried although the sisters were well aware that if their mother had gone native as the saying went, she was unlikely to be there. But as Cissie said, they had to begin somewhere and the sooner they got started the better.

So began another long ordeal that every evening left them exhausted and desperately trying to revive their flagging spirits. Miss Mary and Miss Alice had always found looking around the well kept village graveyards at home with their ancient churches and sheltering yew trees, a pleasurable experience which was a far cry from their perspiring treks beneath a pitiless sun among the vast valleys of the dead with their dust choked tombs and great variety of scuttling insects. Miss Alice in particular, after her encounter with the scorpions in Rhodes, was most careful not to disturb any of these long established and numerous inhabitants.

The searchers were hampered by rarely being able to find records of even fairly recent burials and those they did manage to track down with the occasional help of a gatekeeper, had inscriptions in Arabic or other Eastern languages. As one of these caretakers helpfully put it. "There are so many dead," he had told them in spectral tones, "So many dead. Everybody must go and try to find the graves they want to see for themselves."

Slowly and painfully, it became apparent their task was a completely hopeless one as in their hearts from the very beginning of their journey, the sisters had feared it would be. Cissie continued to provide unstinting support by being defiantly optimistic but after ten days of combating the heat and the flies, all three of them were doing little more than going through the motions.

Their thoughts, especially those of the twins, were beginning however reluctantly, to turn towards England and home although none of them could bring themselves to be the first to broach such a sensitive subject. It would be an admission that would mean the abject failure of their quest and render all the trials and tribulations of their epic adventure distressingly meaningless. The thought of such an outcome was beginning to make the sisters feel physically sick and even after their daylong exertions, they barely toyed with their suppers taken on the veranda in the blessed cool of the evening.

It was becoming a time for ever more desperate measures and Cissie in all seriousness, suggested they concentrate their minds deeply on their mother before going to sleep in the hope she might appear to them in a dream. Feeling that they simply had nothing to lose, the twins tried this for several nights but despite using the most feverish imagination they could summon up, the desired vision never materialised. It was then the indefatigable Cissie took another tack that seemed to be equally outlandish and left the twins fearing that, despite the wide brimmed hat she constantly wore on their forays, she was suffering from a touch of the sun.

"Let me look at the photograph again," she demanded holding out her hand as they sat late one afternoon in the lounge having curtailed their activities earlier in the day amid a growing mood of pessimism. "I want to stare into your mother's eyes. They often have something important to tell you about the person. Something you may have missed before." The sisters could only look at each other and exchange discreet if astonished glances. Their dear companion had often looked at the picture of their mother when she had displayed it to onlookers during their endless searches. Whatever she might glean from the expression of Mrs Harrison, it would be a clue that was over fifty years old and by any stretch of the imagination, considerably out of date.

Cissie, perching on the edge of the sofa, put the portrait on her knees and began staring at it with a tremendous intensity. The twins, anxious to aid her concentration, kept as quiet as mice and sat as still as possible. The amateur clairvoyant, her face a mask of intent with its taunt cheeks and unblinking eyes, resembled their last faint hope of ever making progress and it was one that died immediately. "Well, that was the most ghastly waste of time," she declared, picking up the unhelpful picture and placing it on the side table next to her. "I don't think she was thinking of anything when this was taken."

Miss Alice said nothing in reply but handed over the waterproof cover for Cissie to put back the offending photograph and who when sliding it in, gave a puzzled frown. "What's this? There's something else in here."

"Yes, that's the telegram mother sent us," replied Miss Mary as if having her memory jolted. "We haven't read it since the day it arrived. We couldn't bear to look at it again yet somehow could not bring ourselves to throw it away."

Inserting two long fingers, Cissie gingerly extracted the yellowing and tattered piece of paper folded in two whose ends had become stuck together. Gently and with great care, she prised these apart with an adroitly manoeuvred fingernail. Spreading out the creased and badly faded document on the side table she proceeded to run her eyes over it. She did this several times, her lips pursed and with an increasingly thoughtful expression. "That's not a spelling mistake," she finally exclaimed, remembering their description of its dramatic arrival at The Rectory. "Don't you see it's a name?" She looked at them wide eyed with excitement "Didn't you realise that? Your mother did not run off with a camel driver. No, what's she's saying is she ran off with Kamel Driver."

"How do you know it's a name?" asked Miss Mary who suddenly felt faint.

"Because I've heard of it, that's why." Cissie rose to her feet barely able to control herself. "But where? Oh God where did I hear it?"

"Think, think," cried Miss Alice equally caught up in the electric atmosphere and grasping Cissie by the shoulders.

"I have to keep moving to think clearly," she replied gently evading Miss Alice's hands as she began pacing the room while the sisters holding their breath, watched every move. Cissie walked resolutely in continuous circles with her head thrust forward. "Vague ideas start at the back of the brain and must come to the front," she explained. "A steady rhythmic tread helps to bring them alive." She lapsed into silence as the twins exchanging incredulous glances, wondered if their friend had gone out of her mind. Finally Miss Mary's already strained patience snapped. "Is it working?" she almost shouted. "Is it working?"

"It's a ghastly thing to say but I'm afraid it's not," came the response. "It often does work, but this time the idea seems to have hit a brick wall when on its way forward. It's frightfully annoying but of one thing I'm certain. I have heard of that name."

"Well, if you have heard of the name," responded Miss Alice, "then so will have other people."

"Then if that's the case," replied Cissie who had returned to sit on the sofa for a rest. "He must be someone who is quite well known. What we have to do is try to find him."

"Well if he's quite well known," added Miss Mary, "then he must be some sort of public figure."

"Yes, but what kind?" asked Miss Alice.

"That's what we've got to find out," Cissie replied decisively.

"But how?" came the question again.

"People like that usually get their activities reported.

So the first thing we've got to do is to look through the newspapers. I know there are at least two English language ones in Cairo. There is the Daily News and the Egyptian Gazette. One of these will surely produce something if we could get permission to search the archives."

Chapter 26

The sun had barely started its remorseless climb into the heavens when the three women set out for The Daily News the following morning. Such was their simmering impatience, they wanted to be there waiting when its doors were opened. They had no thought in the cool of the early hour of hailing a taxi. The sisters, despite the tiredness in their weary bones, discovered they had a real spring in their step. Neither had been able to sleep as their imaginations had run riot conjuring up all kinds of images of the mysterious person Cissie had apparently heard of.

Their dear companion, striding beside them, normally so positive and optimistic however desperate the situation, was meanwhile urging caution. It was not exactly that she was having second thoughts of having heard the name or not, but whom it might relate to. In her crowded life, many men had made fleeting appearances - and some not so fleeting - and it could have been a chance partner on the dance floor or a brief acquaintance at a cocktail party. And these meetings, if that was what they were, may not even have taken place in Egypt.

She had become uncharacteristically quiet by the time they entered the building to be directed down a long dusty corridor to the department where the archives were kept. They were greeted by a tall, thin woman, who surrounded by shelf after shelf of neatly stacked brown envelopes, wished her visitors 'Good morning' in clear English and asked how she could help them. Cissie, pulling herself together, resumed her normal role of being in charge, explaining they were looking for any references to a Mr Kamel Driver she might have in her files. To emphasise her request, she slowly and carefully spelt out the name letter by letter.

"K-A-M-E-L D-R-I-V-E-R."

The woman leaned her elbows on the counter. "You mean THE Kamel Driver?"

Cissie looked at the two sisters with raised eyebrows. "Yes, I suppose we do."

"You're English aren't you?"

"Yes we are."

"It's always nice to meet members of his international fan club."

"No you are mistaken," replied Miss Alice. "Our friend here Cissie St Claire has vaguely heard the name but we don't know what it refers to."

The woman produced an indulgent smile. "A lot of older women don't like to admit their fantasies for these show business heart throbs but whether you are or not, I can tell you he's got a lot to answer for." This brought a further exchange of bemused glances between the searchers. "My daughter has bought all his records. I'm sick to death of listening to them. I can't hear myself think."

"You mean he's a singer?" said Cissie.

"Singer, nightclub entertainer, showman. That's him if you mean THE Kamel Driver."

"Are there any others?"

"There may be because it's not than much of an uncommon name, but not in this reference library. I was hoping you were going to give me an exciting task but he's all over the place."

"Where can we find him?" asked Miss Mary who felt her heart beginning to pound.

"He's not far from here at all."

"Is it possible to visit him?" asked Miss Alice barely containing her excitement at the significant progress she sensed they were at last making.

"Yes, I'm sure he won't mind."

"Do you have the exact address?"

"Of course."

"Can we have it?"

"Certainly. He's in the cemetery next to the History Museum. His tomb is just inside the main gates on the left. He's been dead for eight years."

"Dead?" gasped Cisse. "My God, how absolutely frightful."

"Yes. A heart attack on stage. It could not have been more dramatic. There were thousands at his funeral and there are still constant pilgrimages by his admirers to his grave. My daughter goes at least once a month."

It was Miss Mary who voiced what all three at that very moment were thinking. "Was he married?"

This produced a short laugh. "Married? I'd say he was married. At least five wives according to gossip. He tried to keep his personal life private. Like most Egyptian men he left them at home so we have no names or photographs in the files."

"Could one of them have been English?" asked Miss Alice.

"Who can tell? As I said, he kept that kind of thing secret. But from what they say, he liked all sorts of women as long as they were pretty. However if you want to know about his shows and songs we have lots of cuttings."

"No thank you. You've been a wonderful help and we're awfully grateful," said Cissie, realising there was nothing more to be gained from prolonging a conversation that had suddenly taken a frustrating turn.

Outside, they at once decided to brave the increasing glare of the sun to visit Kamel Driver's last resting place while they were so close. They found it just where the woman had said, the top of the mausoleum being visible from the road. It consisted of a vast slab of pink marble in a rectangular shape which was surrounded by recently painted black railings. At the

277

base of the tomb bouquets of flowers in various stages of disintegration, lay in profusion. It was certainly a perfect example Cissie said, of being gone but not forgotten.

Stepping inside the little gate, they peered intently at the gold lettering etched in three neat lines on the pristine surface. Although none of the onlookers were able to decipher it, one thing was abundantly clear. There was no separate entry. No one, at least yet, had been buried with him.

With the heat of midday now beating down upon the searchers, they decided to take a taxi back to the flat to ponder their next move. Despite the evidence of the telegram, the sisters could not quite bring themselves to believe their mother, the well brought up and sensible character they remembered, could have become besotted with what appeared to be an oily middle eastern playboy. The mere thought of this made them wince and they firmly believed they had identified the wrong man and were embarked on a wild goose chase.

Cissie, so much more worldly wise than her companions who had led such sheltered lives, especially when it came to men, strongly disagreed. She could easily see it happening to Mrs Harrison, poor dear, because on more than one occasion she had nearly become a victim herself. Their mother, she declared, being a young and healthy tourist was unlikely to have spent her evenings locked up in her hotel. No, she would be enjoying the sights and sounds of Cairo after dark and this would include a visit to one of the many nightclubs. And the entertainers in these places were without any exception, absolute cads.

Cissie's voice shook with indignation. "The despicable thing is they know you are vulnerable. All women in night clubs are. On your night out, you try your very best to look incredibly attractive. That's human nature. And it puts you in the mood for romance. It's not your fault you're in danger. It's the clubs'. They surround you with low lights, glasses brimming with champagne and music that weakens your defences. And God help you if you're just a group of women or on your own. In your mother's case, she could have been with others from the hotel. That's when the cads pounce. As I said it nearly happened to me."

She appeared to shudder at the memory. "I was sitting there alone waiting for my escort when I felt his eyes on me. Not the escort's, the scoundrel that was singing. I was wearing the dress I only wear when I'm feeling really brave. I felt his gaze moving down from my neck and then it just hovered right here." She gave her bosom a sympathetic pat with a rather shaky hand. "It was pure cheek. I hadn't given him the slightest encouragement. I might have casually thrown a glance at the stage but certainly not exactly at him. Anyway, after that, I just couldn't escape his steady stare. It was then that he appeared to read my mind. He sang one of my favourite songs, Blue Moon."

She broke off and hummed the opening bars before pulling herself together. "Where was I? Oh yes, I had the uncanny feeling he was singing it only for me. It was the most ghastly trick to play but annoyingly it always seems to work. That's when you can't help being drawn towards them. Mine was exquisitely handsome and had sneakily undone the top buttons of his shirt." She gave a deep sigh. "Oh the divine hairs on his chest."

The sisters watched in fascination as their dear friend struggled to come to terms with what must have been a most nerve-racking experience. "Luckily that was when my escort arrived," she went on. "Of course I immediately regretted my weakness. It was really not like me at all. If you have half an ounce of breeding in you, you realise it has all gone too far and effect disinterest by looking anywhere but at the stage."

Her mood became more sombre. But even then, she explained, there can often be no escape. Her friend Pearl was highly accomplished at this, but all too often would find herself let down by the interval. "The singer appears at your table asking if he may join you," Cissie continued. "And of course you feel ill mannered or churlish if you refuse. Or a waiter hands you a discreet message from him inviting you to his table. Again it is fiendishly difficult to say no for apart from anything else, the cost of drinks are so horrifyingly high a free one is always welcome.

"And what happens next according to Pearl can be absolutely fraught. He leans towards you in a most charming manner and places his hand innocently in yours. And then after topping up your drink and whispering endearments in your ear, he moves it shall I say, to somewhere rather more intimate." Cissie closed her eyes as if such a picture was too painful to contemplate. "I am so sorry my dears to say this in front of you, but I do fear your mother has suffered just such a ghastly fate."

Miss Mary and Miss Alice were greatly shaken by this remark but their faith in the mother they had known remained steadfast. Yet Miss Mary, with a stab of guilt, wondered what she would have done if it had been Le Grand Bandit's liquid brown eyes turned upon her. She had not thought of him recently but he had a nasty habit of reappearing at unguarded moments.

So could something like that really have happened to her mother? Cissie had said earlier if they believed she had run off with a camel driver, they must agree it was more likely she had fallen for an urbane, civilised man however caddish. Yet Miss Mary felt, as she was sure her sister did, their mother would have preferred to be with a simple native and his animals living a pure but spartan existence in a desert which had attracted generations of Englishmen of her class.

Cissie brought her out of her reverie by announcing that they were wasting valuable time. Their next highly important step would be to discover the last known address of Kamel Driver. One of his wives or family members might still be in residence and able to shed some light on what was becoming an ever more intriguing search. And that, Miss Alice declared from painful experience, would be easier said than done, as it was with anything you tried to do in such a strange, hot, and dusty country.

The problem confronting the three women was the sheer size of Cairo. Yet as Cissie quickly pointed out, the vast majority of the districts need not concern them at all. There was no doubt Kamel Driver had been a rich man and so bound to have lived in one of the more affluent suburbs and probably in the most exclusive.

And it would be easy to discover where this was. The information would be provided by taxi drivers. Cissie admitted to feeling quite faint when somebody had once suggested that she travel by public transport. Shuddering at the memory, she said she could only possibly travel by taxi and she had learnt long ago their drivers knew everything and could not wait to air their knowledge, whether you wanted them to or not. Kamel Driver may have liked to keep his life private, but it would have been a social one involving a good number of visitors. And many of these for one reason or another, would have travelled by taxi. So, she declared, they must start by visiting the taxi ranks in the city centre to see if they could jog a few memories.

Bringing up the subject of Kamel Driver among the drivers sitting in their long line of well washed cars could not have been easier. Almost without exception they had heard of the singer and several could pinpoint the district where he had lived. But the house? That was a different matter. Eight years was a long time to be dead and they had taken many, many fares since then.

That had been the reaction at the first rank they had tried and it was the same with the second and the third. One driver who said he might have taken somebody to that address, offered to drive his questioners around the area to see if he could find it again. They accepted gratefully but the expedition turned out to be a fruitless and expensive one, and they arrived back at the rank with an uneasy feeling that they had literally been taken for a ride.

They realised unless they could get more accurate information they would have to resort to knocking on doors and this they were most reluctant to do. There might only be one or two streets involved, but all properties in affluent districts were surrounded by high walls with entry gained only through an intercom. And even if these were answered, it would probably be in a language they could not understand.

Their fruitless drive had been the last of the morning and they stopped to have a lunch of cold lamb and salad to revive their flagging spirits before making one more attempt in the afternoon. The next rank in an almost deserted square, had only one car in it and its owner's feet were sticking out from underneath. Hearing their approach, he emerged holding a spanner he had been using to tighten a loose exhaust. He was in his late twenties with short black hair and an honest, open face. Cissie who was never one to waste time where business was involved, asked. "Do you know where Kamel Driver used to live?"

The young man wiped his hands on a rag. "You mean the singer?"

"Yes," replied all three women in unison.

"He's been gone a long time but it's one address I'll never forget. I had just taken over the car from my father and it was my first ever fare. I think it was his agent or a record producer. He gave me a very large tip and I thought what a wonderful job I had but I have never had such a large one since." Although his English with a slight American accent jarred on their ears it was the sweetest music they had ever heard.

"Can you take us there now?" asked Cissie feeling her own rising tide of excitement that matched the sisters'. "This very minute?"

The young man who introduced himself as Omar replied with a smile. "I'm here to be hired. Get in." Opening the rear door, he ushered all three women into the back seat where they squeezed together with Miss Alice, who was sitting in the middle, grateful that it stopped her knees from shaking. Omar who had not asked the reason for their journey, pointed out passing landmarks in his best style for foreign visitors completely unaware of the tumult of emotions taking place behind him.

His passengers barely took in a word he was saying as they concentrated their thoughts on what was going to happen next. Like their visit to the newspaper office, they felt they were taking another big step forward but wondered if this would only result in them finding another intimidating hurdle standing in their way. It gradually became apparent that they were entering one of the more affluent parts of the city. The houses behind their high walls were becoming larger and their grounds more spacious while the streets were more thickly lined with trees. Finally, after twenty minutes, Omar swung left into a broad, leafy avenue and slowed to a crawl as he eyed the front of the properties standing well spaced out on both sides of the road. "I'm pretty certain it's round here somewhere, but I'm not remembering as clearly as I thought I would," he said doubtfully. "All the streets round here look the same."

Cissie closed her eyes as if wishing she wasn't there and the sisters instinctively sought each other's hand as they sensed the approach of another failed venture. Reaching the end of the road, Omar turned the car round and began creeping back along the other side. He began whistling to himself in a low melancholy tone as, eyes half closed in concentration, he continued to study the high walls creeping past. Finding nothing that looked familiar, he tried the next avenue with the same result. Yet he had barely started on the third and was resorting to sorrowfully shaking his head, when with a sudden exclamation, he brought the car to a halt. "That one there," he almost shouted. "I'm sure that's it."

His passengers craned their necks to peer through the window. A high stone wall of a faded pale pink colour stood either side of a pair of black wrought iron gates. Confronted with what could be their moment of truth, the sisters found themselves unable to move until Cissie said gently. "Don't you think you ought to get out? It's your family affair so I'll wait here. Good luck."

Miss Mary, nearest to the door, opened it and stepped uncertainly onto the pavement followed by Miss Alice whose legs again felt as if they might give way at any moment. Under the inquisitive gaze of Omar, they approached the gates and found the intercom set into the left hand side of the wall. They could not work out the lettering beneath the array of buttons but with a nervous intake of breath, Miss Mary started pressing. "Surely one will work," she said while her sister standing by her elbow, could only nod silently in agreement. Having tried them all, Miss Mary stepped back conscious of Omar's and Cissie's unseen eyes fixed intently upon her as she waited for a response.

Yet as the seconds ticked by the machine remained stubbornly silent and Miss Mary with a painful stab of doubt, wondered whether it was working. Despite standing in the welcoming shadow of the wall, she felt the beads of perspiration growing on her brow. Fumbling for her handkerchief, she dabbed at them haphazardly before once more pushing the buttons with an urgent finger. This time she stood where she was, her nose almost touching the grill as if wishing it to speak. Almost at once it came to life with a rather hoarse male voice uttering an unintelligible demand. Miss Mary leaned forward. "Do you speak English?"

There was a long nerve-racking pause before the reply came. "Yes."

"We are looking for a Mrs Kamel Driver. Does she live here?"

"Mrs Driver is fast asleep."

"Can you wake her?"

"No, it is impossible."

"It is really important."

"No, it is impossible. Come tomorrow morning at eleven o'clock and I will take her instructions." Before Miss Mary could respond further, there was a sharp click from the machine to signify their conversation was at an end. The twins wearing deeply thoughtful expressions, returned silently to the car and got in.

"Well?" said Cissie, raising her eyebrows as she shifted over to make more room.

"It seems to be the right house which is a great relief," replied Miss Mary. "There is a Mrs Kamel Driver but she is asleep and we have been told to come back in the morning."

"But you don't know her identity?"

"No. We didn't have time to find out."

"But the voice we listened to spoke English," chimed in Miss Alice. "That has to be a good sign."

"Not necessarily so," replied Cissie. "I don't want to dampen your expectations but we have to be realistic. If Kamel Driver entertained international audiences in his nightclubs he would have to be well versed in the language. And when he entertained such guests at home, it would be essential for some of his staff to be able to speak it as well. If, as it appears, there is one of his wives still in residence, the big question is which one is it? If the rumours are true that he had at least five, then there is a five to one chance that it is Mrs Harrison, your mother. The fact that whoever it is, cannot have her siesta disturbed indicates she is likely to be old. Your mother fits that category for she most certainly is, but then it is highly likely that so do the other four."

Cissie produced a sympathetic frown as she noticed the flickers of dismay on the faces of her companions. "I'm frightfully sorry about this but I have to play Devil's Advocate. It would be absolutely ghastly if you convinced yourselves it was your mother and this mystery woman turned out to be somebody else." The twins digested this salutary advice with heavy hearts and could think of nothing to say in reply.

Chapter 27

Omar dropped them at the flat, and hoping he would be their talisman, they asked him to be free to pick them up at ten thirty sharp the following morning. He arrived ten minutes early to find his impatient passengers already waiting for him on the pavement. To the sisters, every second of the previous evening had seemed like an hour. To help pass the time, Cissie had produced a pack of cards and cajoled them into playing a game of gin rummy. Yet neither could concentrate for more than a moment or two, such was their nervousness, that she soon gave up and resorted to playing patience.

This time Cissie sat in the front, deciding it would be more companionable to be next to the driver in case she had a long wait if the sisters managed to get inside. Omar was given a brief inkling of what was afloat and immediately adopted a more businesslike air. This was going to be much more exciting than showing passengers the sights of the city that he had seen thousands of times before. The twins, sitting pale and tight lipped in the back, were turning two big questions over in their minds. Would Mrs Kamel Driver's instructions be to invite them inside and if so, who would she turn out to be?

The taxi pulled up outside the wrought iron gates at exactly ten fifty but neither sister could bring herself to endure the agonising seconds that would have to tick away until the appointed hour. With Omar's heartfelt 'Good luck' echoing that of Cissie's, they got out and Miss Mary immediately began pressing the buttons. This time there was no delay. Whoever was on the other side had been waiting for their arrival. "Please identify yourselves," announced the same voice they had heard earlier.

"Alice and Mary Harrison," she replied trying to

keep her own voice calm as she battled a sudden and dizzying surge of emotion.

"Wait please." A buzzer sounded and the gates slowly creaked open. No sooner had the pair stepped through than they closed again behind them with a clang. They were confronted by a small elderly man with the inscrutable expression so well practiced by orientals and who produced the merest hint of a bow.

"Did you know our names, or who we are?" asked Miss Alice eagerly but their escort, showing no desire to communicate, had already turned his back and was leading the way towards the house. She and her sister exchanged despairing glances. They would not be able to learn who they were going to meet before coming face to face with whoever it was. So how could they possibly prepare themselves?

The twins had entered a large paved courtyard filled with an array of exotic shrubs in tubs of all shapes and sizes which created a blaze of colour and filled the air with a heady scent. But they were hardly aware of their surroundings as they followed the diminutive figure clad in a uniform of plain grey cloth that matched his undemonstrative demeanour. Mounting a series of broad steps, they entered a large hall with a stone flagged floor covered with several ancient looking rugs. The walls were adorned with vast paintings of hunting scenes depicting falcons and hawks who looked down with beady eyes upon the intruders. Two giant porcelain vases, almost as high as the twins, stood either side of a wide marble staircase which the old man had already started to climb.

As they made their way upwards behind him to the first floor, the pair slowly became aware of the deserted air that hung over everything. It was as if they were in a museum in which all vibrant signs of life had drained away. At the top, a long corridor thickly carpeted in a rich oriental pattern, stretched before them. The walls were again lined with pictures of desert scenes while beneath their gilt edged frames stood rows of stuffed birds of every kind in neatly labelled glass cases. At the far end a door of highly polished wood stood ajar. The old man gently pushed it open with an outstretched arm and announced "Mary and Alice Harrison to see you."

The reply was a simple "Thank you Gupta" but it thrilled the nerve-racked sisters to their very marrow. It was older and more quavering but they instantly recognised it across five decades as the voice of their mother. The room they entered was in semi darkness with a half drawn curtain allowing a single shaft of light to barely illuminate the surroundings. A four poster bed with a thick overhead canopy lay alongside the furthest wall. On it, propped up by a large pillow with enormous tassels at each corner, lay a fragile figure in what appeared in the gloom to be a black dress. As the twins approached, the apparition raised a thin languid hand and waved them onwards. "Is it really you my girls? Come closer, let me look at you."

Answering the summons with wildly thumping hearts, the twins found themselves advancing on tiptoe to be confronted by a pale, deeply lined face beneath a mass of pure white hair. Despite the poor light, they could see the sparkle of two magnificent diamond earrings. Miss Alice noticed on closer inspection that the gown of woven silk was a deep blue colour and must have cost a fortune.

"Did you know we were coming mummy?" asked Miss Mary reverting, despite her own advanced age, to the manner in which she had always addressed her.

"Yes. Gupta saw you getting into your car yesterday and I realised from his description it could only be you. I rarely have visitors these days and certainly not from what he calls foreigners. I'm afraid the years have sadly ravished me but I wanted to look my best when I knew you were coming." She turned her eyes which shone with a fevered brightness upon them. "And Henry your father? Is he still alive?"

It was Miss Alice who answered. "He died the very day we received the telegram. You did not know?"

"How could I child?"

It was the shock of you leaving," explained Miss Mary. "He suffered a heart attack and fell stone dead at our feet. We called an ambulance immediately and tried to save him but despite all our efforts we couldn't."

Her mother gave a grimace of horror and put a hand to her mouth. "Oh how awful. You see, I knew nothing. I had no option but to make a choice when I met Kamel. I knew I would not be able to live in two worlds. It would have been much too painful. That's why I decided not to keep in touch. It was the most difficult thing to do and I agonised over it many, many times. Yet I thought that would be best for all of us." She raised her head slightly to look more closely at them. "Don't imagine I didn't think of you. I did, oh my goodness how I did, every day for years but then England began to fade."

"But mummy," said Miss Alice. "I thought you really loved daddy. You always seemed to us to be so happy together. We had so many wonderful times and did so many wonderful things as a family."

"I did love him, or I thought I did until by sheer chance I met Kamel." She gave her daughters another glance. "But you two? Did you never get married?"

"No we did not," replied Miss Mary. "We lived quietly alone for all those years at The Rectory."

"Then you don't know anything about love. You don't know anything about men. Your father was kind and trustworthy and loyal, but oh so dull!"

"But from what they say, Kamel Driver was the sort

of person who mistreated women," cried Miss Alice, who despite herself, was becoming quite upset. "He betrayed all of you."

Her mother sighed. "Yes child but you don't understand. He was completely unpredictable and exciting. You never knew for a moment what he was going to do next. Many people's lives are grey and boring although they do their best to cover it up. They need something to brighten their existence. Kamel was like a searchlight beaming into mine. Your father, how can I put it, was by comparison at very best a sixty watt bulb."

"So how did it happen?" interrupted Miss Mary who had adored her father but felt she and her sister had to know the truth.

Her mother gave a short grimace. "It wasn't deliberate. I must stress that I wasn't looking for anybody. I just found myself suddenly being kissed."

Miss Mary's eyed widened. "By someone you didn't know?"

The recipient of this astounded response struggled into a more upright position and slowly began to tell her story. She was dining at a restaurant with another female friend from her hotel. An incredibly handsome man with a finely styled moustache and dark piercing eyes occupied the next table. When they got up to leave, he insisted on giving them a lift. Cairo, he said, was no place for two unescorted ladies at night. When they arrived back at the hotel, he suggested having a late drink at the bar. Her friend, who had a headache, went to bed but she found herself in the basement night club with this most attentive stranger. Everybody seemed to know him. He ordered a bottle of champagne and then stepping lightly onto the stage, sang a song to her.

The speaker's face lit up in a rapt smile at this

memory. It was 'If You Were The Only Girl In The World' and it had made her feel like it. He offered, like the gentleman he was, to escort her to her room. She seemed to be floating on air as they soared up in the lift. Outside in the corridor, he took her in his arms and kissed her. She at last knew the meaning of being swept off your feet. She could find no will to resist. Her knees gave way and he had to carry her over the threshold. She turned her head from her horrified listeners to face the wall. He had still been there in the morning.

"Didn't you think of father?" gasped Miss Mary.

"No, I can honestly say I didn't. And from that moment I was a different woman." She turned to face them again. "Don't you see, as I said he was so exciting and charismatic. You never knew where you where with him. He was elusive. He made life interesting." She lay back to regain her breath and then went on. That very day he had taken her back to his house. He said his wife at the time would understand. She always did.

Listening to her, the sisters were struck dumb and could only shake their heads in utter amazement. Each was thinking their own horrified thoughts but as usual they were entirely in tune with each other in the highly charged atmosphere. Their mother incredibly, had behaved like an irresponsible teenager. Or even, which was much more hurtful, a wanton woman.

"You have no idea what the house was like then," said the frail figure breaking into their reverie. "It was vibrant, so full of life. I felt as if I was walking on air."

"Yes," responded Miss Mary. "But what about his wife?"

"Lola? She was number four. We shared all our duties if you understand what I mean."

Miss Mary frowned. "Didn't she mind?"

"She came from the East. Such things are normal

there."

"But what about you? Didn't you mind?"

"Mind? How could I mind? I was madly in love. Lola and I got on quite well until that awful business."

"What awful business?" asked Miss Alice who was now sitting on the edge of the bed.

"This house has a long flat roof. Lola and I used to go up there in the cool of the evening. It was a wonderful place to be with the scent of the flowers rising from below and the changing sky at sunset all around us. If Kamel was away working, which he often was, we used to drink wine. And on that night Lola in particular had drunk quite a lot. This always put her in an exuberant mood and she would get up and dance about. Somehow the twirling hem of her skirt became caught up in her feet and she suddenly lost her balance and fell over the side. She landed head first on the stone paving of the courtyard and died three days later in hospital without regaining consciousness."

"What a dreadful accident," exclaimed Miss Mary.

"Yes it was, but not everybody thought so. No, it was a very difficult time. Being a white woman and, in their eyes, an interloper, the servants were against me although I was always very careful to be polite to them. Their gossip started rumours that I had pushed Lola and at one stage it seemed the police might become involved. But Kamel believed me explicitly and for that I shall always be grateful to him. He smoothed things over and the fuss eventually died down after he ordered some of the more antagonistic servants to leave. Anyway after a decent interval, I think it was around six months, he married me."

She screwed up her eyes again, dragging bits from her memory. "That was over forty years ago. But I didn't go meekly like a lamb to slaughter. I said I would only become his wife if he promised I would be

293

his last one. He didn't keep all his promises but that was one he did. I'm not saying he never had another woman. Sometimes he did not come home at night but I believe in his heart he was always faithful to me."

"But he is gone now," said Miss Mary. "Your life with him is finished. You must come home with us."

Her mother slowly shook her head. "No, no child. It is too late for that."

"But you could be buried with father, in our family plot." said Miss Alice.

"My strength is ebbing. I will not be here much longer. It is all arranged. I will be laid to rest next to Kamel. I will be the only one with him. It is a beautiful monument."

"Yes mummy," replied Miss Mary. "We have seen it. But your place of rest is in an English graveyard with daddy."

The old woman's voice had an unmistakeable air of finality. "You cannot take me back to a world that has long gone. Even you, my dear daughters, are complete strangers to me as I am to you. That is what time does. You cannot escape it." She lay back and closed her eyes. The sisters looked at each other in dismay, waiting for her to go on. There was only silence. Each remembered the last time they had seen her. She had looked so strong and so beautiful as they had waved goodbye, expecting to see her again in just a few weeks.

But what of the change in their own appearance? The fresh faced schoolgirls with their long, flowing dark hair and peach like complexions had long vanished into the mists of time. Miss Mary tentatively put out a hand and touched her mother on the shoulder. The figure stirred. "Yes child?"

"We will be spending some time in Cairo and could get to know each other once more. Could we come again tomorrow?"

A note of alarm crept into the quavering reply. "No, no it would be too painful. We cannot bring back the past."

Miss Alice's voice was barely above a whisper. "Do you mean we can never see you again?"

"It is for the best child. You will come to understand that." Her eyes flickered open. "You must go now. I will not be keeping Kamel waiting much longer." She pointed to a small bronze bell on the bedside table. "Ring that and my faithful Gupta will show you out."

"But mummy," cried Miss Alice almost beside herself with anger and frustration. "We've come hundreds of miles, encountering all sorts of horrible dangers, to find you."

"Not me child. You have found a mirage."

"How can you say that? You are here in front of us in flesh and blood."

"No. The mother you came to look for has not existed for fifty years. The one that waved farewell to you at the front gate exists only in your imagination."

"No, no," burst out Miss Mary. "You are real. You are our mummy."

"I have already told you," came an almost exasperated reply. "Nothing stays the same, nothing stands still. Time changes everything." With a great effort, she managed to sit upright. "Kiss me."

The sisters looked at the raised face as if unable to move. If they did, they felt they would irrevocably be saying goodbye. Yet it was obvious their mother had made an unshakeable decision and they could not being themselves to put her under further strain. At least not at this moment. Miss Mary found herself reluctantly leaning forward and brushing her lips against the parched cheek which were dry and lifeless. She watched her sister do the same and then with a sigh, summoned Gupta.

The door opened immediately as if he had been waiting outside. His expression remained inscrutable as he led the numbed visitors silently back down the stairs and out into the courtyard. Miss Mary felt she had to ask the question for much needed reassurance before it was too late. "Gupta, is Mrs Kamel really happy here? We want to take her home." The diminutive figure, shading his eyes from the sun with a bony hand, stopped to look at them. "This is her home. She is Egyptian now."

"But is she happy?" persisted Miss Alice.

"Who is happy? Nobody knows. I look after her. She has everything she wants." With that, he pressed the buzzer and the gates opened and the pair reluctantly stepped out into the street. They stood uncertainly on the pavement as these clanged shut behind them. The wonderful reunion they had dreamed of, the one that had driven them forward through all their incredible difficulties, had lasted barely an hour. By the time they reached the car with their heads bowed and shoulders hunched, tears were streaming down their faces. Cissie, her own thrust out of the window was full of anxiety. "So it wasn't your mother?"

"Yes it was," Miss Mary managed to reply. "But not the one we thought we knew."

"She doesn't want to see us again," added Miss Alice. "She is adamant. She has shut us out of her world." She stifled a sniff. "We just want to go home now. We will book a flight for tomorrow. We have just enough money left."

Cissie's mind, always good in a crisis, was working swiftly. "That could be your best idea. Your mother is of course in deep shock at meeting you. She will certainly want to see you again and if she knows she only has a few hours in which to do it, it will force her to take immediate action. And when she does, you can cancel your flight. If you were to stay on in Cairo she would not feel the need to hurry."

"But how will she know?" responded Miss Alice.

"When you have booked your tickets we will send Omar back to the house with your departure time and the address and phone number of our flat. I feel certain that Mrs Driver or Mrs Harrison as I prefer to call her, will contact you."

Partly reassured, the distraught twins dabbed away with their handkerchiefs as they related the traumatic events of their meeting while Omar, a discreet and sympathetic presence in the front, drove them home. That evening, after they had bought their tickets for the flight, he made a second journey to the house to deliver the information into Gupta's hands.

Cissie, meanwhile, insisted on taking the sisters out for a farewell dinner at one of the city's posher restaurants. It was one she had frequented with the last of her four husbands and she felt it would be better for the twins than sitting brooding in the flat.

And there, among the gleaming silver, bowls of orchids and spotless white tablecloths, she tried valiantly to lift their spirits which had sunk to their lowest ever ebb. Not in their darkest moments since leaving home had they felt such intense despair. "What had it all been for?" Miss Mary mused aloud as she toyed listlessly with her napkin. Their extraordinary achievement had come to nothing. They would have been better off staying at home and weeding the garden.

"Yes our mother has betrayed us," added Miss Alice nodding her head in sombre agreement. "Everything that we have done has been wasted."

"But it hasn't," interrupted Cissie in a voice tinged with indignation. "Can't you see that? No, you mother hasn't let you down. If she hadn't vanished you would never have set out to look for her. And if you hadn't set out, you would never have discovered what you are capable of. You have proved yourselves to be very courageous and resolute which is something to be proud of. Countless people are never fully tested in their whole lives. They have no idea of what they can really do."

Cissie earnestly encouraged the pair to relive some of their most dramatic experiences which would give them great satisfaction now these were over. She knew it was vital to keep their minds off the agonising question of whether, as the last hours ticked away, they would see their mother again.

Looking back, Miss Mary had to admit it was quite extraordinary what she and her sister had endured. And Cissie had been right. They had learnt a lot about their own characters, and at the same time, other people's. Their dear companion had made it plain her own surprise that they had actually reached Egypt because, there were, as she had put it, so many ghastly individuals in the world to deal with.

But from the sisters' experiences, every person like Le Grand Bandit or Augustus, had been countered by a host of Good Samaritans. She thought of Bert the lorry driver who had taken them out of Calais, and Marise who was going to go all the way with them but had only lasted a few kilometres. Of Bernard who had led them to the top of the Alps and then dropped dead. Of Dino who had escorted them down the terrifying tunnel to escape the Mafia and Paul who had rescued them from the Greek police.

The list seemed endless and she wondered if any of those helpers, apart from poor Bernard, had ever asked themselves if the two eccentric old English women had managed to reach their destination. It was such a pity that she and Alice would never be able to thank any of them.

Chapter 28

The sisters' last day in Cairo, or at least the one they expected it to be, began with a violent thunderstorm shortly after five o'clock. Woken by the peals of thunder, they watched the lightning zig zagging across the sky feeling it was a fitting scenario to the climax of their journey. Yet by the time the sun was starting its climb, the dark clouds had fled away across the roof tops leaving a glistening landscape in their wake which soon disappeared in the growing heat.

Omar was not due to take them to the airport until six o'clock in the evening, but they had packed the last of their few belongings well before midday. And so began their long vigil dominated by the hands of the clock on the wall above the mantelpiece which remorselessly recorded the passing of the hours. The telephone remained stubbornly silent, no matter how often they looked at it, when not otherwise watching the street in the hope of seeing their mother miraculously appear. But there was very little traffic and what there was, sailed on past without slowing.

Despite Cissie's assurances that blood was thicker than water and that Mrs Harrison would definitely arrive, their belief they would see her again was rapidly weakening. "We have to accept that we are total strangers to each other," said Miss Alice. "That is what she made clear to us. She disowned her daughters a long time ago."

"But the incredible effort you made to find her will have its effect," replied Cissie. "She is after all your own flesh and blood. She gave birth to you."

Yet the watchers remained undisturbed as the sun crossed the sky moving the ever lengthening shadows from one side of the flat to the other. Finally it was time for Omar to come and as usual he was ten minutes early. The sisters watched him emerge from the front of his cab with wildly fluttering hearts. Their last hope had been that when delivering the message to their mother, she had asked him to pick her up first so she could see them off. But he did not go to open the door at the rear, instead he headed for the side of the building to ring their bell. Full of deepening gloom, they collected their luggage and began disconsolately to descend the stairs. Cissie, leading the way, made yet another valiant attempt to keep their spirits up. "You don't know how much you've changed from the shrinking violets you were before you started your adventure," she exclaimed. "Your chap Archie won't believe his eyes when he sees you. I wish I could be a fly on the wall to watch." The twins fervently hoped he had received the wire they had sent earlier to meet them at Heathrow in his van, and had themselves wondered intriguingly what their reunion would be like. Their dear friend, who was going to see them off, helped to put their rucksacks in the boot. She had promised to come and stay at The Rectory in a week or two, knowing they would not find it easy to settle down to a quiet life again.

Yet even as she spoke, there was a movement at the end of the street. Busy with their last minute preparations, nobody noticed a large black saloon pulling up a little way down on the far side of the road, half hidden by the sprawling branches of an overhanging tree. As the engine came to a stop, a tinted window in the back slid noiselessly open. A pale, once beautiful woman, her eyes narrowed against the last rays of a fast sinking sun, peered at the scene taking place on the opposite pavement. Her pure white hair was neatly tied by a bow of light blue velvet and she wore a plain yellow dress held at the waist by a thin leather belt with a silver buckle.

As the three passengers began to climb into their seats, a white, almost emaciated hand, in the black saloon reached out and took hold of the rear door handle. The fingers gripped it with a brief intensity but made no move to push it open. As if the effort had been too much, it suddenly went limp and fell back by its owner's side. And there it remained as Omar brought his engine to life and gently slid away from the kerb. With the cab's tail lights disappearing into the growing dusk the waiting driver, barely visible above the steering wheel, looked over his shoulder with an unspoken question.

The voice that replied was lifeless and devoid of any emotion. "That will be all Gupta. You can take me home now."

THE END